9.99

6/24/13

Iron Jaw
AND
Hummingbird

BOOKS BY CHRIS ROBERSON

Iron Jaw
AND
Hummingbird

CHRIS ROBERSON

VIKING

VIKING
Published by Penguin Group
Penguin Group (USA) Inc., 345 Hudson Street, New York, New York 10014, U.S.A.
Penguin Group (Canada), 90 Eglinton Avenue East, Suite 700, Toronto, Ontario,
Canada M4P 2Y3 (a division of Pearson Penguin Canada Inc.)
Penguin Books Ltd, 80 Strand, London WC2R 0RL, England
Penguin Ireland, 25 St Stephen's Green, Dublin 2, Ireland (a division of Penguin Books Ltd)
Penguin Group (Australia), 250 Camberwell Road, Camberwell, Victoria 3124,
Australia (a division of Pearson Australia Group Pty Ltd)
Penguin Books India Pvt Ltd, 11 Community Centre, Panchsheel Park, New Delhi—110 017, India
Penguin Group (NZ), 67 Apollo Drive, Rosedale, North Shore 0632,
New Zealand (a division of Pearson New Zealand Ltd)
Penguin Books (South Africa) (Pty) Ltd, 24 Sturdee Avenue, Rosebank, Johannesburg 2196, South Africa

Penguin Books Ltd, Registered Offices: 80 Strand, London WC2R 0RL, England

First published in the United States of America by Viking, a member of Penguin Group (USA) Inc., 2008

1 3 5 7 9 10 8 6 4 2

Copyright © MonkeyBrain Inc., 2008
All rights reserved

LIBRARY OF CONGRESS CATALOGING-IN-PUBLICATION DATA IS AVAILABLE
ISBN 978-0-670-06236-2

Printed in U.S.A. • Set in Granjon

to Sharyn November, who asked for it

Contents

ABOUT THE CELESTIAL EMPIRE

HISTORY TEACHES THAT CHINA'S REACH ONCE SPANNED the globe, and the Dragon Throne came near to ruling the world.

In the fifteenth century AD—during the reign of Zhu Di, the Yongle Emperor—the Treasure Fleet of China was commanded by the Muslim eunuch Admiral Zheng He. It traveled as far as India and the east coast of Africa, possibly even reaching the west coast of South America. Had the Chinese continued to extend their reach, they might have eclipsed the great powers of Europe and given rise to a world dominated by the Dragon Throne. In 1424, though, the Yongle Emperor died and was succeeded by Zhu Gaozhi. Also known as the Hongxi Emperor, the man who now sat upon the Dragon Throne ordered the Treasure Fleet destroyed and all seagoing vessels outlawed, under the advice of Confucian officials who felt that the previous emperor's expansionist policies had robbed them of influence and power. From that point onward, China turned inward and lost contact with its newfound trading partners across the seas.

That is what history teaches, but ours is not the *only* history.

In the alternate history of the Celestial Empire, the Yongle Emperor was instead succeeded by Zhu Zhanji, the Xuande Emperor, who not only continued to employ the Treasure Fleet but expanded its scope and mission. Before Christopher Columbus set out to discover a new route to the east, dragon boats of the Treasure Fleet rounded the tip of Africa and arrived in Europe. In the centuries that followed, China grew to become the dominant cultural and political force on the planet, rivaled only by the Mexic Dominion, known in our history as the Aztecs. In time the Dragon Throne extended its reach into the heavens, sending manned missions into space, building bases on the moon, even sending missions to the red planet fourth from the sun.

It has been nearly five centuries since man first came to the red planet, which the Chinese call Fire Star. In those long centuries, the once-dead world has been gradually changed, slowly becoming another abode for life. But while the atmosphere is now breathable, and temperatures have risen to comfortable levels, there are still hardships on Fire Star. Life is possible on the red planet, but it is far from perfect.

PRELUDE

WOOD HARE YEAR, FIFTY-SECOND YEAR OF THE TIANBIAN EMPEROR

GAMINE LOOKED OUT THE COACH WINDOW AT THE streets rushing by. She arranged herself on the cushion, trying to keep her teeth from chattering. This early in the season the air was chilly, and her new *qipao* banner dress left her arms bare and cold. She was thankful that the current style called for ankle-length hems and a high collar, at least; she'd have frozen near solid otherwise. Her reflection could be seen dimly in the windowpane, ghostly, as in a half-silvered mirror, her faint likeness drifting past the shops and houses and temples of the darkened streets of Fanchuan. She almost couldn't recognize herself, so complete was the transformation from her typical appearance. Her hair was arranged in tight coils on the top of her head and lacquered in place, her face powdered, and her eyebrows painted high on her broad forehead. Gamine felt that this new appearance made her look so much older than thirteen; she could almost believe that one day she might be a grand lady like her mistress.

Gamine was alone in the coach with Madam Chauviteau-Zong—a rare occasion. Rare that Gamine would travel with the mistress at all, rarer still that they should do so alone. On those few occasions Gamine had gone about with the mistress before, it had been in the train of the household servants and advisors, with Gamine's tutors and instructors on hand to keep watch over her. This evening, however, the party consisted only of the coachman—a red-faced man of few words who operated the vehicle from his perch on the roof—and the two passengers, who sat side by side on the cushions in total silence.

Gamine had no notion where they were going, and burned to discover, but was well trained enough to know it would be importunate to ask so direct a question of her mistress. Besides, Madam Chauviteau-Zong would do nothing that wasn't in Gamine's best interest, so what had she to worry about?

It was sometime past sunset, the two moons racing toward one another across the sky, when they reached the Hall of Rare Treasures, the residence of the governor-general of Fangzhang province, Governor Ouyang. Gamine recognized it from lithographs she had studied of the city's notable architecture, as well as from the many tours of the city she had taken with her tutors. The hall rose several levels above the street, crowned by a multitiered roof of yellow tiles, corners curved up toward the heavens. The gold-embossed ideograms spelled out on the red walls shone in the light of the paper lanterns strung from poles in the forecourt. Lights glowed warmly from within, and through the high door came spilling the sound of music, zithers and lutes and drums. Gamine recognized the music as the overture to an opera she'd seen performed the season before, Song Huagu's *The Miner's Journey*.

Gamine waited as her mistress climbed from the coach, and then gracefully stepped down onto the cobblestones. Madam Chauviteau-Zong swept up the steps to the entrance, and Gamine followed along behind, entranced.

Huang Fei stood between his mother and father, at the side of the grand room of the Hall of Rare Treasures. Across the way, Huang could see the players of the Red Crawler Opera Company beginning their performance, but he didn't recognize the music. Hardly surprising, as he had never been one with much time for such pursuits, and music and the other arts left him cold. He preferred the more engaging distractions of fencing, or games of chance with his friends, or betting on pit fights between dogs, or whiling away the long hours of the night with a hot cup of wine in hand and the hotter-still body of a young lady at his side.

Tragic, then, that in less than a day's time, Huang would have to say good-bye to all such pleasant pastimes. His future promised only dust and sweat and impossible boredom. Already his uniform, which he wore tonight for the first time, felt heavy and clinging on his shoulders. He'd hoped that the clothing of an officer in the Army of the Green Standard might at least allow him to present a dashing profile, but the cut of the garments was lumpen and unflattering, and he'd not have worn them at all had his parents not strenuously insisted. The only faint light of hope glimmering on Huang's horizon was that his posting would put considerable distance between himself and the ministrations of his parents. Cold comfort, since some superior officer or other would be taking their place, regimenting his every waking hour, but Huang took his solace where he could find it.

Huang had just turned eighteen, the oldest of three sons. Having taken and failed the imperial examinations for the fourth time, he clearly would find no place in the imperial bureaucracy. His parents weren't overly worried about the family name, since their second son was a prodigy; he had passed his *juren*-level examinations by the age of sixteen and was well on his way to completing the *jinshin* examinations and becoming a "presented scholar," already guaranteed a place in the emperor's service. Huang's youngest brother, for his part, was of a somewhat spiritual bent, destined for one of the lamaseries in the Southern Fastness. For Huang, only one path remained. Calling in family connections, his father had arranged for Huang to be commissioned as an officer in the Army of the Green Standard and posted to a military fort in the western desert, in the shadow of Bao Shan, the tallest volcanic mountain in the solar system.

Huang's parents had insisted that he thank Governor Ouyang personally for approving the posting, and had dragged him to the reception for the governor-general's return from the outer provinces to Fanchuan, capital city of Fangzhang province. Huang's father was a younger son of a distant cousin of the governor's uncle by marriage, and had the governor not intervened, Huang would likely have been forced to stay at home, wasting his days in idle pursuits, living off his parents' savings. Yes, Huang had *so* much for which to thank the governor.

"Hummingbird," Huang's mother said, tugging at his sleeve. "Stand up straighter, and hold your chin high. Slouched like you are, you look more like a monkey we've dressed in the clothes of a man than a proud officer of the Green Standard."

Huang wanted to object that monkeys, whether in human clothing or in their natural state, had more control over their destinies than he felt at this moment, but his father interrupted before he could speak.

"Mei!" Huang's father said in a harsh whisper. "Do not address our son by his milk name, as though he were a child!"

"But husband, remember the fluttering of his kicks in the womb? He is our baby, still."

"*Mo*-ther," Huang said, rolling his eyes.

"No." Huang's father crossed his arms over his chest, glowering beneath his heavy brows. "Fei is a child no longer, and it is time to stop treating him like one." He shook his head, glancing across the room where Governor Ouyang stood on a dais, meeting dignitaries in turn. Others like Huang and his family lined the room—bureaucrats, wealthy merchants, and other district luminaries—waiting for their brief audience. "I am thankful only that you did not insult our son in the earshot of his Excellency, the governor."

Huang's father turned to him and placed a hand briefly on his shoulder.

"Do not dishonor our family, Fei. At least no more than you already may have done in your youth."

Huang rolled his eyes again and tried to lose himself in the sound of the opera's overture.

Gamine lingered in the entrance to the hall, her eyes wide; she'd scarcely seen anything like the festivities before. Along the right side of the hall, the players were just beginning to perform the opera, the singers in their costumes and masks, the musicians seated in a crescent behind them. Low tables were spaced at intervals through the hall, piled high with food and beverages of all varieties, each adorned with decorative centerpieces of intricately wrought bronze and crystal, topped with what appeared to be real peacock feathers. In the rear of the room rose a low platform, a dais upon which Governor Ouyang stood, with a servant at his side. Men and women milled around the hall, resplendent in their finery, and went before the governor singly or in small groups, speaking in low tones.

As the lead vocalist began his theme, Gamine recognized the players as belonging to the Red Crawler Opera Company, which she'd seen perform several times in recent seasons. It was one of the finest touring companies on Fire Star, boasting incredible acrobatics and juggling along with its standard musical repertoire. Gamine felt it was criminal that she seemed to be the only one paying attention. Only one other, a young man in the uniform of an officer in the Army of the Green Standard, standing between a middle-aged man and woman at the far side of the room, seemed even to notice the presence of the players.

Gamine didn't get to listen to the opera for more than a moment, to her sorrow. Just as the players began the first movement of *The Miner's Journey*, Madam Chauviteau-Zong directed her to a large antechamber that opened off the southern wall of the main room. While the lights of the hall had been warm and inviting, comfortable shadows lingering in the corners, the illumination in the antechamber was cold and hard, so bright that it seemed to chase all the shadows from the room, as though seeking out any hidden flaw or imperfection.

"Stand there, child," her mistress said, and motioned to the center of the antechamber, where gathered a half dozen boys and girls her age.

Gamine did as she was told. Her mistress went to stand beside a man in the dress of a wealthy merchant, with whom she exchanged a few quiet words. There were seven adults in the room, men and women, one or two of whom Gamine recognized as occasional visitors to the Chauviteau-Zong residence. All wore wealth and power in the same way that Gamine wore a red silk dress embroidered with golden dragons: as though they thought no more of their position than they would a bit of jewelry or an item of clothing.

Gamine wondered why she had been brought to this place, and what business she had with these other boys and girls, or with these adults who seemed to study them all so intently. She wondered but knew not to speak, as that would offend propriety. So she stood, as silent as the other six children, all of them waiting for instruction.

And then the questions began.

Huang Fei was so distracted by the performance of the players that his father had to nudge him twice, the second time with such force that he nearly lost his balance and fell to the floor.

"Now!" his father said, between clenched teeth, his face locked in an unconvincing smile. "It is your time."

Huang's father motioned with his chin to the dais, and Huang turned to see the governor's personal secretary looking back at him impatiently.

"Go," Huang's mother said, waving him forward. "Make us proud."

Huang swallowed hard.

"I'll try. . . ." he said, and then walked on reluctant legs to the dais. He became overly conscious of his movements, of the beating of his heart, of the position of his tongue in his mouth. He was unaccountably terrified, and his hands shook like leaves at his sides.

The governor's personal secretary, his eyes appraising Huang uninterestedly, motioned him to stop just before the governor, whose attention was momentarily on the opera players.

Huang stopped in front of the governor, his eyes on the floor.

"And who," Governor Ouyang boomed, turning his attention to Huang, "is this to approach with such solemn mien my own august personage?" He paused, smiled, and gave Huang a wink. "Or, put in the language of men, what troubles this boy?"

"Your Excellency," the personal secretary said, "this is your distant relation, Huang Fei of Fanchuan, who has been invested as a Guardsman of the Second Rank in the Army of the Green Standard, with your permission."

The governor folded his hands over his belly and nodded slowly, looking Huang up and down. He motioned for the secretary to step closer, and then whispered something that Huang could not make out.

The personal secretary's glance darted to Huang, his eyes narrowed, and it seemed to take a moment for the governor's words to make their way through his brain. But he regained his composure and, bowing slightly, hurried away from the dais.

"I am well pleased that a relation of mine would choose to serve the Dragon Throne with the strength of his arm and the mettle of his will, rather than hiding behind perfumed fans in the corridors of power, practicing calligraphy and the art of gossip." The governor's voice was loud and low, and Huang could feel the words almost as physical blows. "Too many children of privilege follow the easy path, the comfortable path, and never learn the true meaning of sacrifice. It makes my tired old heart soar to find in you such devotion, such selflessness."

The personal secretary returned, panting only slightly, holding in his hands a sheathed saber.

"Your Excellency." The secretary held the saber out to the governor in both hands, bowing slightly from the waist.

Governor Ouyang drew the saber from the sheath. The blade, its metal having a faint red tint, was of the willow-leaf design, curving slightly to the point, with a phoenix motif picked out in ivory on the hilt and carried through in etchings along the blade length and on the fittings. He held the saber point up, admiring it for a moment.

"This is the blade I carried during my recent tour of the northern province, which spilled not a little bit of insurrectionist blood. There are many raiders who learned to fear its red gleam on the sands, and many more for whom the firebird of its blade was their last living sight."

The governor slid the sword back into its sheath with a *snick* and held it out to Huang.

"I am pleased to present you with my own saber, that it might serve you half as well. And if you should die for the Dragon Throne, remember that you die for a purpose greater than yourself, to preserve and protect the rule of the emperor."

Huang took the saber from the governor's hands, feeling numb. He tried to stammer some response, but no words would come. Finally the personal secretary was forced to take Huang's elbow and steer him back toward his parents. Huang shuffled across the floor, the eager expressions on his parents' faces awaiting him, and felt the heavy weight of the sword in his hands.

Gamine answered every question correctly, danced the quadrille flawlessly, and devised correct solutions to any number of ethical and logical problems put to her. The seven adults asked questions or posed riddles or otherwise gave instructions, each in turn, addressing the children individually. It seemed that each adult could question any child, as often as he or she liked. If ever a child failed to answer a question or perform a task correctly, guards were summoned who escorted the child out of the antechamber, through a doorway, and out of sight.

As the evening wore on, one by one the other children faltered, taking a misstep in their dancing, or incorrectly parsing a grammatical fragment, or misremembering trivial bits of historical data, until only Gamine was left standing at the center of the room.

Then each of the adults questioned her once more, one examination from each, and again Gamine answered them all without error.

She beamed with pride, her chest thrust forward, eyes seeking her mistress's approval. Whatever Madam Chauviteau-Zong's purpose in bringing her to this gathering, Gamine had performed admirably. Her mistress's features were, as always, calm and unreadable, sapphire blue eyes in a face of flawless porcelain, but her posture and the slight movements of her hands suggested deep satisfaction.

A chime sounded somewhere in the hall, and the other six adults all turned their attention to Gamine's mistress.

Madam Chauviteau-Zong swept forward, stopping just short of where Gamine stood, and regarded her, blue sapphires briefly meeting Gamine's own jade green eyes. Gamine stiffened. Might the mistress be preparing to embrace her? Had Gamine performed well enough to be so regarded? Gamine had never come into physical contact with Madam Chauviteau-Zong, and she readied herself for the jolt and the joy. But the embrace never came.

The guards who had escorted the other children away returned, as though awaiting instruction.

Madam Chauviteau-Zong regarded Gamine for a long moment, and then turned aside momentarily, directing her attention to the merchant with whom she'd spoken on their arrival.

"I told you, Fong, that mine was the likely contender."

"Yes, Cerise, and you'll have your winnings in the morning," the merchant said. He paused, and said with a smirk, "But don't expect to be so lucky next time."

Madam Chauviteau-Zong nodded regally and then turned and glided toward the door.

Gamine's throat constricted, and she found it difficult to breathe.

"Mistress?" Gamine said, in a tentative voice, the first time in living memory that she'd addressed her mistress without being spoken to first.

Gamine's mistress, not pausing, glanced back at her, and then motioned to the two guards with a languid movement of her hand.

"Do see to the child," Gamine's mistress said distractedly, and then left the antechamber behind.

Gamine did not understand what was happening. Her mind raced. The two guards stepped to her side, and each took an arm.

"What do we do with this one?" one asked the other in a loud whisper.

"The same thing we've done with the rest," the other answered. "Remove any articles of value she might have squirreled away, and toss her out the nearest door."

The men searched her quickly, with rough hands, and came away with a tortoiseshell comb her tutor had put in her hair and a jade pendant at her throat.

"Wh-what have I done wrong?" Gamine managed to say as the guards pocketed her valuables and dragged her from the room. "What is happening?"

The guards refused to make eye contact, their expressions hard.

"Pl-please! What have I done?"

The guards took her through servants' corridors, far away from the light and warmth of the main hall, coming at last to a back entrance. The night air outside was cold, and the streets were empty and dark.

"Sorry, kid," one of the guards said, picking Gamine up off her feet. "Tough break."

The guards threw her bodily out of the doorway like a sack of rice, then closed the door behind her, shutting off the last faint light from inside. Gamine was left in the dirt, cold and alone.

Huang's parents had scarcely had time to question him about his audience with the governor, and about the sword in his hands, when they spied a merchant across the room with whom his father had recently opened negotiations.

"You'll excuse us, Fei," his father said distractedly, already hurrying to the other side of the room. "We have business to conclude."

"Yes," his mother said, following along, "we'll see you before you leave in the morning, to speed you on your way." Her eyes flicked to the saber in his hands, seeming not to notice the confused, horrified expression on his face. "We're so very proud of you, Hummingbird."

Huang did not pause, but tucked the saber into his belt, grabbed a jar of wine off a nearby table, and slipped out the hall's back entrance.

The night air was cold, but Huang had gotten half the jar in him before he even felt the chill. If he hurried, he could meet his friends at a nearby tavern for one last night of leisure before leaving for the ends of the world. And for the end of Huang, for all he knew.

Somewhere in the darkness he could hear the sound of a girl crying softly, but he paid it no mind.

ACT I

•

GAMINE'S THEME

WOOD HARE YEAR, FIFTY-SECOND YEAR OF THE TIANBIAN EMPEROR

GAMINE OPENED HER STINGING EYES, GRIT GATHERED IN their corners, as the city began to wake up around her, fishmongers making their morning deliveries, shopkeepers rolling up their shutters to begin a day of trade, the priests in the temple ringing the morning bells. She was in the Sun-Facing District, not far from the Hall of Rare Treasures, and wasn't sure whether she had slept at all, feeling more tired now than she'd been when she'd stretched out on the cold cobblestones in the lees of a temple, its high walls serving to block most of the wind but doing nothing to keep her warm. Gamine's clothes were damp from the light dew that clung to the ground, and she shivered in the chill.

Gamine had never thought that she'd end up back on the street. In the long, cold, sleepless hours of the night, she had begun to wonder if the last eight years had been a dream, and if she was now merely waking up to horrible reality.

• • •

Madam Chauviteau-Zong had always called her Gamine, though whether that had been her name, surname, or a term of endearment, she had never known. Even so, for most of her life she had been Gamine, and Gamine she would remain. In her more optimistic moments, she liked to think that her mistress had said *Gao Ming*—meaning "clever," or "a good strategist"—but considering what came later, the old woman had likely been drawing upon her own Gallic heritage and meant exactly what she said. Gamine was a gamine: a child of the streets, alone and unloved, with no family, clan, or station.

Gamine was of mixed descent, her hair the straight black of the Han race, but her narrow nose and jade-colored eyes suggesting a strain of Briton, Francais, or Deutsch. The line of her jaw was a touch too strong—at least that's what her mistress had often said, too masculine a frame for an otherwise appropriately feminine face.

Until the age of five years old, Gamine had been a nameless child of the streets. She remembered nothing of her parents, or any relations, her earliest memories those of surviving hand-to-mouth in the back alleys of the city. Then everything changed. Men in the fine livery of household servants plucked her off the streets, bathed and clothed her, and presented her to a fine lady in a well-appointed room. The woman, dressed expensively, had alabaster skin, eyes the color of sapphires, and a Francais surname. She was a high-born lady, with family ties to the imperial court and an inherited fortune from a merchant forbearer.

The lady had looked over the little, well-scrubbed urchin girl, and said, "Gamine. She'll do." In the eight years that followed, Gamine had lived in the grand lady's house, trained by the finest tutors money could buy. She learned to read, write, and speak a half dozen languages, how to paint calligraphy with perfect brushstrokes, how to dress and present herself, how to ride, shoot a bow, and fight barehanded. She learned the history of the Imperial Throne all the way back to the Yellow Emperor and the Three Sovereigns of legend, and she learned the science that had brought man to the red planet they called Fire Star, turned its deserts into arable lands, and built cities in its low, warm places. And then, at the end of the eighth year, she was taken to a grand ballroom in the capital, to a formal reception honoring the governor-general. And her world came crashing to an end.

Gamine's first thought was to return to the only place of warmth and comfort that she knew. It was the work of hours to walk across the breadth of Fanchuan, from the Sun-Facing District in the east to the Green Stone District in the west. Her feet were crimped into formal slippers of elegant silk, with soles so thin that she could feel every stone and pebble in the street; by the time she reached the Chauviteau-Zong estate, her toes were swollen and her heels were bruised and numb with pain.

At the front gate, the grounds of the estate visible behind the bars, she was stopped by the house guards, who barred her way with crossed staves, refusing to let her pass. Gamine thought she could see something like sympathy flickering behind their cold eyes, but their expressions were set and hard. Plead as she might, they refused to budge, and she was forced away.

Her stomach grumbled audibly as she slunk away from the gate, hugging herself against the chill.

Gamine came to a restaurant, where she had once eaten with her tutors and the other household servants while the mistress was abroad in the city conducting business. Madam Chauviteau-Zong had dined in a private room, conferring with a high-ranking city official behind closed screens, and when the company returned home that afternoon, Gamine found that many of her personal possessions had been moved from one corner of her little room to another. Later she would overhear some of the staff talking behind their hands, complaining about their things being misplaced in their absence, and whispering their theories that the mistress had taken them all out of the house that day to give some mysterious party an opportunity to break into the estate and search the rooms. Who would want to search the household, and what they might be looking for, no one knew for certain, but many on the mistress's retainer were happy to voice their opinions, though never when the mistress was within earshot.

Episodes like that had been common throughout Gamine's years living at the Chauviteau-Zong estate, and many times dramas were acted out in shadows, of which Gamine only saw fleeting glimpses, and the meaning of which she could never hope to understand. It was a place of secrets and hidden mysteries, and none but the mistress herself knew the depths of all of them.

All of which, though, bore no interest for Gamine at the moment. She could think now only of that day when the whole household had gathered in this restaurant, and of the fish-head stew she had eaten. It was the best she'd ever tasted, though her tutors had scolded her for the noise she made in slurping from the bowl, lashing her knuckles with a metal rod that left them bleeding. The bruises on her fingers had faded, while the memory of the fish-head stew had stayed with her to this day.

Gamine, with dust all in her clothes, and her hair matted and dirty, walked in the front door of the restaurant. Her mouth would have already been watering, had her throat not been so parched and dry.

"What do you want?" came a shout from within the darkened interior, and a man in a plain white vest and gown came rushing from the rear of the restaurant, drying his hands on a cloth. "You cannot come in here! You must go back outside; this place is for paying customers only!"

Gamine forced a smile, and gave a gracious little bow.

"O honored sir, I am sorry to say that I cannot pay, but if I could have just a bowl of your delicious fish-head stew, I would be most grateful." Her manner was courteous and courtly, her elocution and diction precise and perfect enough to dazzle the courtiers at the Imperial Palace on faraway Earth.

The waiter seemed not to be impressed.

"Ha!" His laughter was a hard, grating sound. "We are not a charity, and serve no one without the coin to pay for the meal. If you have no money, you get no food." He leaned forward, towering over her. "Do you have money?"

Gamine shook her head, eyes wide.

"Then get out!" The waiter shooed her out and closed the ornately-carved door behind her.

Gamine stood in the street, as foot traffic and coaches passed hurriedly around her. She realized with a faint shock that she had not held a single coin in her hands since she'd been five years old and had begged a single disc of copper stamped with a square hole in the middle from a passerby to pay for a few grains of rice and a lump of near-rancid meat from a street vendor's stall.

She needed money. Perhaps she could find a job or turn her hand to begging again. The grumbling in her belly told her that however she managed it, she would need to eat, and soon.

Gamine gnawed on a discarded rib bone, trying to get the last bits of meat off it, and thought about how best to break it open to suck out the marrow. In the two days since she'd been thrown out in the streets by the guards, she had eaten only a handful of stale rice and the bits of rotten meat and moldy pastries she could find in trash bins behind the city's restaurants. She had to fight the rats for the few scraps she could lay hands on, and she'd narrowly avoided nasty bites that might have been deadly, considering the diseases the rats no doubt carried. It was an unwelcome irony that her education had covered information on a full gamut of infectious diseases and plagues but had not touched at all on emergency medicine or first aid. Were she bitten, she'd know precisely the progressive stages of the disease that would no doubt kill her, but would have no notion how to stop it.

She'd tried to find work, but it was the same wherever she went: what she could do, no one was hiring for, and what people were hiring for, she could not do. Though she was a child prodigy in the pleasant pursuits of the ruling class, she was completely unaware of how to make her way in the world. Able to speak a half dozen languages and explicate the intricacies of nuclear fusion, she didn't have a single practical skill with which to earn a crumb to eat. She could not clean, could not build, could not wash, could not sew.

She had tried several times to return to her mistress's home—hungry, tired, and exhausted—but each time the guards had turned her away, and on the last attempt they threatened her bodily harm if she tried again.

Gamine finished her exertions with the bone and decided to beg.

She'd done so every free moment of the last two days, when not busy going through trash bins or pleading with restaurateurs and waiters for scraps of food. But whatever skill she had at begging as a child of five years old she'd lost as a girl of thirteen. Perhaps as a little orphaned waif she brought out feelings of sympathy in passersby that a girl of teenage years did not engender.

She stood in the street, calling to drivers of coaches and vans as they sped past, shouting out that she just needed only a little help to make her way in the world.

"Ha ha ha!"

For the second time in as many days, Gamine was brought up short by the sound of cruel, mocking laughter. She looked from side to side, searching for the source of the noise. Finally she spied him, leaning against the side of a nearby building. His laughing eyes were fixed on her, a cruel smile on his thin lips.

"L-leave me alone!" Gamine shouted, and turned back to the passing vehicles. She tried to call out to the drivers again, begging for any spare coins.

"You're doing it all wrong," the man said, calling over the sound of the traffic, a bemused tone in his voice.

Gamine turned and glared at the interloper.

He looked like he was in his sixth decade of life, with teeth missing in his smile and wisps of hair around the sides and back of his balding head. He had a scraggly mustache that drooped down past his chin on either side of his mouth. He was wearing rough-made and well-traveled clothing, looking like a merchant who had seen better days, and the soles of his sandals were worn as thin as parchment. He had a walking staff in one hand, a bundle wrapped in leather straps in the other.

"What do you mean?" Gamine asked defensively.

The man moved forward, quicker than Gamine would have thought possible, and took hold of her elbow.

"Come with me and I'll show you," he said in a low voice, and dragged her off the street.

He took Gamine to the rear of a nearby manse, palatial home of some local notable. There was a cistern near the back wall, where the owner's servants would water his animals. From beyond the wall, Gamine could hear the strange calls of exotic creatures brought in from Earth. Through the wrought iron bars of the gate, she could see a zebra, giraffe, and horse, even a pygmy elephant.

The old man dipped a cloth in the water and used it to clean the grime from Gamine's face. His movements were rough, but not mean-spirited. He just didn't regard her any more than he would an object that he'd found in the streets. Which, really, was what she was.

"That's a little better," he said, tucking the cloth back into his robes.

With her face and hands more or less clean, he did what he could about arranging her hair and clothes.

"Stand up straighter," the man said, taking a step back and giving her an appraising look. "Now, look haughty but afraid. Like you're scared but think yourself above everything you see."

Gamine did her best to follow his instructions, contorting her expression as he described.

"Eyes open a little more," the man said, "but bring your brows down in the middle. Mouth straight, but purse your lips together a little more, to suggest controlled anger. Perfect. Now, come with me."

The man turned and walked away, trusting that Gamine would follow along. Numbly, her stomach roaring, she followed behind.

"Where are we going?" Gamine asked, when they had gone several blocks in silence.

"None of your prittle-prattle," the man called back over his shoulder, his pace not slacking. "There's work to do and an important lesson for you to learn."

They came at last to a street in the Southern Gate District, at a busy commercial intersection, with shops and businesses crammed close together.

"There!" The man pointed to a bureaucrat hurrying down the street. "See that old puff guts? He's an easy mark, or my old eyes betray me."

Gamine glanced without interest at the heavyset man walking toward them.

"But what are we doing here?" she asked, a whine creeping into her voice. "I was doing just fine where I was, and . . ."

"You were doing nothing, hop-o'-my-thumb, but wearing out your larynx!" the man snapped. "Now, shut your bone box and listen to me, or you'll be hungry and stay hungry, for all I care."

Gamine wasn't sure what her bone box was but shut her mouth and nodded silently.

"Now," the man said, "let's hope you've a memory on you. What I want you to do is go to that pompous toad and say exactly what I'm about to tell you. Tell him that you are the daughter of an imperial bureaucrat in Penglai province, a child of privilege, desperate for airship fare back home. Point to me, and say that I am a family retainer who has gambled away the money your parents gave you for a journey to visit the holy shrines of Fanchuan, in honor of your maternal grandfather, who was born in this city. If he will only provide airship fare, you can return home and report on the generosity of the kind people of Fanchuan, and not have to admit how your family retainer brought you so near to ruin."

Gamine listened intently, falling back on the habits of many years of concentrated study.

"Do you think you can remember all that, my little sprite?"

"Yes," she said with a nod.

"So go to, little one, go to." The man waved her on, and went to stand in the shade of a nearby shop building.

Gamine walked on sore feet to the thoroughfare and angled directly toward the heavyset man. In his haste, he nearly collided with her, and was brought up short by the near miss, annoyance spread across his ruddy face.

"Watch yourself, guttersnipe!" the heavyset man barked.

"Your pardon, but I . . ." Gamine paused, swallowing hard, trying to remember what to say next. "O honored sir," she went on, with increasing confidence, "I come from Penglai province, where my father is an official in the emperor's service. My . . . family retainer"—she pointed to the man standing in the shop's shadow, a short distance away—"accompanied me to your . . . to your fine city . . . so that I might visit the holy shrines of Fanchuan. To honor the memory of my departed maternal grandfather, who was born here. Sadly, though, um, that is, my chaperone has gambled away all of the money my parents provided for my journey, and I am left without a means of returning home. If you could see your way clear to loaning me a small sum . . . to cover airship fare . . . I can return home and report on the generosity of your fair city, and not be forced to admit how near I was brought to ruin by my family retainer."

The well-fed bureaucrat, who at the beginning of Gamine's speech had looked ready to take to his heels, seemed genuinely moved by her deception, and pulling a purse from his belt, filled her palm with coins.

"You should report the man to your parents on your return home," he said officiously, "and have him severely flogged."

With that, he reached out, patted Gamine on the top of her head, and then puffed on down the street, glaring at Gamine's newfound friend as he passed by.

Gamine returned to where her new tutor stood, who took her arm and led her down a side street. When they were safely out of sight, the man took the coins from her hand, and it didn't once occur to Gamine to object.

"Well, now," he said, counting out the coins, "it's not enough for airship fare, damn his cheap hide, but it's easily the price of a meal and a night's lodging for both of us at an inn I know. It's in the shadows of the city wall, not far from here, and they do marvelous things with a chicken."

Whistling through the gaps in his smile, the man started off down the street, the coins rattling in his fist. Gamine, licking dry lips at the thought of anything done with a chicken, followed close behind.

They were on their second course, her belly full of rice and chicken broth and with dumplings in each hand, before Gamine paused to collect her thoughts. She washed down her last bite with green tea and sat back, a feeling of warm contentment washing over her.

"What's your name, my little sprite?" the man asked, dropping a gnawed chicken bone into his bowl.

"Gamine."

"Well now, that's an unusual name, and one I've not heard before." He smiled, took a sip of hot wine. "And what does it mean, this Gamine?"

She diverted her eyes, uncomfortable.

"I—I don't know."

"Fair enough," the man said, dabbing at the corners of his mouth with a cloth. "Well, if we've moved on to the stage of the evening where we make formal introductions, allow me to present myself. I am Temujin, master of fakements, grifts, dodges, and cons."

When, after a long silence, Gamine didn't answer, the man went on.

"That means, in short, that I am a confidence man, a trickster, one who plies his trade by parting other men from their hard-won coins. I was born poor, to a mother who never had two coins to string together. She worked as a cook in a roadside inn and, from the travelers who stopped by there, I picked up enough of the patter of merchants and bureaucrats that as an adult I could pass myself off as belonging to one of the wealthier classes. When I was a young man, I used to pull a con where I'd claim to be the only surviving child of a horrible accident, the last son of a merchant family, and work the Grand Trunk from one end of the Tianfei Valley to the other with that dodge. As I got older, though, I couldn't pull off the gaff, and had to fall to other, meaner pursuits. Now I pull short cons on merchants on the road, posing as a trader in exotic goods who needs just a few coins to get my goods out of hock, promising that I'll share the haul with the hapless mark. Things like that. Carrying greater risk than the more charitable 'donations' I got as a younger man, since I'm now forced to promise goods and riches I can't deliver, but I do what I must to survive." He paused and took a sip of wine. "Which is not to say that I'd be forced to fall so low as to be a cutpurse, foyst, cracksman, or footpad. I'll not earn my day's wages by violence or destruction of property, no sir. What I take from my fellow man, I get by the power of my own voice. I *talk* their wealth out of their purse and into mine. And I know of no nobler pursuit."

Gamine could only nod, trying to take it all in.

"And you, my dear?" Temujin said. "What profession do you call your own?"

Gamine chewed on a bite of chicken and swallowed it before answering.

"I was once a beggar, and then was a student, and now it would seem that I am a beggar once more."

"Not a very good one, mind you. Meaning no disrespect, of course." Temujin smiled and refilled his cup of wine. "Well, bung your eye!" He drained the cup in one swallow and poured himself another.

• • •

Gamine and Temujin shared a room that night, bought with the coins she'd gotten from the bureaucrat. She was happy to be well fed and out of the elements, with a blanket across her and a roof over her head, but it seemed that Temujin was after something more, besides.

Once the lights were dimmed, Gamine lay on her sleeping mat, staring up at the darkness, listening to the sounds of Temujin settling on the other side of the floor. Her blanket was threadbare and thin, but the inn was warm and dry, at least compared with the cold cobblestones of the city streets.

Gamine heard Temujin rustling on the far side of the room. He coughed, an unpleasant rattling noise at the back of his throat, and then spat his mucus onto the floorboards.

"Excuse you," Gamine said absently, and closed her eyes, drifting gradually off to sleep.

She was awoken suddenly by the feel of rough hands on her arms and shoulders, and a weight across her legs and stomach.

"What are you doing?" Gamine sputtered.

"Don't fight it, little one. It'll be over soon." Temujin's breath was hot in her ear and smelled heavily of wine.

Gamine fell back on years of self-defense instructions. She reached out and grabbed Temujin's hand, bending his pinky finger back at a vicious ninety-degree angle. Then, as Temujin started to howl, she slid to one side, and keeping hold of his hand, she wrenched his arm up behind his back until the tips of his fingers nearly touched his head, and heard a satisfying popping noise from his shoulder joint.

Temujin rolled off across the floor, his arm flopping painfully at his side, sobbing. In the dim light, Gamine could see tears flowing down his hollow cheeks, his face twisted into a mask of agony. He crab-walked across the floor to his own sleeping mat and collapsed in a heap.

"Excuse you," Gamine said, only slightly annoyed, and promptly went back to sleep.

The next morning, they breakfasted down in the main room, Temujin eating in stony silence. Gamine thought nothing of his attempt at intimacy of the night before; while she found it in poor taste, it didn't bother her any more than his belching, or farting, or any of the other antisocial things he'd done since they met. She simply didn't understand his actions. What she knew of human sexuality was relegated only to biology and courtly dance steps, and she had no concept of the dealings of men and women.

Temujin, still without full range of motion in his left arm, set down his bowl and looked at Gamine across the table.

"Well, my little sprite, you must think me a right nickninny for my crude antics of the night, but you must understand it was all a lark. It was just . . . tickling, like. And I certainly won't do anything of that sort again, no sir." With his right hand, he drew his robe aside slightly and prodded at his left shoulder, which was swollen and discolored. "You can take care of yourself, and no question. But that engenders in me a concern, I must admit. If you stay here in the city, on your own, you'll as likely as not be starving again in days. You're a dab hand at the martial arts, but your skills at the maunding arts are lackluster at best."

Gamine blinked at him, solemnly, making it clear she'd no idea what Temujin was saying.

"Maunding, as in 'to beg,' my dear," Temujin explained. "You're no beggar, I say, but you've got the makings of a great trickster within you. If you come with me on the open road, I could teach you a trick or two, and we'd be able to turn a tidy profit in a short amount of time. You told me yesternight about all your schooling and tutoring and such. Well, with your ability to speak in a half dozen languages, quote scientific fact and formula, and discourse at a high level on matters of politics and economics, you'd make a gem of a confidence man . . . er, um, confidence *woman*."

Gamine set down her teacup. "Do you really think so?"

"Why, undoubtedly. We could even retool the con I used as a young man, making you the lost daughter of a bureaucrat's family, perhaps even one with blood ties to the Dragon Throne, and me in the role of the faithful family retainer. With you as part of the spiel, we can cadge rides and handouts from bureaucrats and noble families on the road, and from poorer merchants of sufficient means and greed, reeling them in with the hope for a grand reward in exchange."

Gamine had no real reason to stay in the city. She couldn't get back into the household of her mistress, and she had nowhere to live and no means by which to support herself. The only sort of kindness she'd had since she was tossed out of the governor's hall into the dirt had come from Temujin, and apart from his horrible manners and his untoward advances of the night before, he seemed a decent enough sort.

"Very well," Gamine said, bowing from the waist. "I will go with you."

Gamine and Temujin left the city, heading east on the Grand Trunk, the road that traveled from the northwest to the southeast along the bottom of the Tianfei Valley, through the provinces of Fangzhang, Penglai, and Yingzhou. As the story went, when man first came to Fire Star, his initial residence had been down in the Tianfei Valley, sheltered by the high cliff walls, down in the deepest reaches of a canyon larger than any found on Earth. The first settlements had been little more than collections of pressurized huts, but infinite patience and near unlimited manpower carved the foundations of the first great cities on the valley floor—Fanchuan, Shachuan, and Fuchuan. The higher atmospheric pressure at that depth meant that the valley was the first spot to enjoy the benefits of the atmosphere mines of the northern plains, the first place where men were able to go abroad without breathing masks and constrictive suits. Some said that one day, when Fire Star had been transformed completely into a world like distant Earth, when the northern plains became a great ocean, that the whole valley would be flooded with water, the cities lost forever beneath the waves of an immense system of rivers; but that day was dozens of generations away, if it was to come at all.

The Grand Trunk had been carved at the floor of the valley when the first cities were still being built, straight and level and true, to ensure that imperial shipments from one city to another would never go astray. In those days, the war with the Mexica Aztecs was still a recent memory, not the dimly recalled bit of folklore—a legend almost become myth—that it was now. The builders of the great valley cities, architects of the Grand Trunk, designed the massive road with an eye toward protecting shipments at all costs, with no convenient hiding places along the road for raiding parties to wait in ambush; the road was miles from the valley walls on either side and ran straight northwest and southeast to the horizon in either direction. Any approaching force would be seen for hours, even days, as the dust cloud of its movements came closer and closer. On the Grand Trunk there could be no surprises.

In their first days on the Grand Trunk, Temujin worked out their patter, and Gamine learned the art of the trickster.

Gamine and Temujin sat in the dim light of a fire, a short distance from the road. Had they traveled by coach, van, crawler, or wagon like most other travelers on the Grand Trunk, they'd have already reached the first way station, but traveling as they did by foot, their first two days' journey had brought them only a fraction of the way. Gamine had complained at first, but Temujin had insisted that the slower path was the proper speed for a trickster, and that even if they could travel more quickly and with more ease, they needed the extra time so that she could learn the basic skills.

Gamine was only glad that Temujin had purchased new clothing and walking shoes for her when he spent the last of their coins on provisions for the road. Liters of water, compacted foodstuffs, and a fire kit for each of them depleted the rest of their meager savings.

She had never seen a fire kit before or, she realized, even seen a fire except those penned safely in a hearth or fire pit. With so few trees on Fire Star—outside of city parks and private arbors like those of the Chauviteau-Zong estate—and those few held so dear, early settlers had been forced to find other ways to stoke fires for warmth and cooking. Fortunately for them, during the early days of the atmosphere mines, an unexpected answer was found.

The mines were established by the Dragon Throne to help turn Fire Star into a livable world like Earth. From them were dug carbonate and nitrate deposits that, with the introduction of microorganisms brought from Earth, released carbon dioxide and nitrogen, which terrestrial plants in greenhouses and arbors then converted into a breathable oxygen atmosphere. In the clinker and slag left over once the nitrates and carbonates had been extracted, the miners found an unusual chemical compound. Inflammable in the presence of sufficient oxygen levels, it produced a low light and a weak greenish flame that, while hardly as satisfying as the flickering yellow and orange glow of burning wood, was sufficient to heat food and drive away the cold on a desert night. Fire kits, which held a small but almost inexhaustible supply of this compound, were standard issue for anyone traveling along the Grand Trunk, with so many hundreds of miles of road between civilized areas.

"Always carry your fire kit, my little sprite," Temujin said, stoking up the greenish flames, "whether in the city or out on the wide plains. A trickster never knows when he might have to travel fast and light, and it wouldn't do to find yourself out beneath the cold night sky without any source of warmth."

After heating a small metal jug of water over the fire, he produced two cups from his pack, and once both cups were filled and steaming, he poured into each the contents of a package of seasonings and dried noodles.

"This won't win any culinary awards, but you'll not starve with it in your belly, neither. And one cup's all the food and drink a body needs for the day, barring unexpected exercise."

Gamine sipped at the broth and forked a few of the noodles into her mouth.

"What kind of unexpected exercise?" she asked after swallowing. The broth's flavor was only one step up from water, and the noodles were undercooked and too cold, but Temujin was right—it was better than starving.

"Well, usually in our line of work, that equates to running away." Temujin regarded her with a thoughtful smile. "A professional tries to avoid the need to scamper, but in a pinch, we all do it."

"If the victim of your con catches on, you mean?"

Temujin's face darkened, and he narrowed his eyes.

"Not victims! Never victims. They're marks, and always will be." He shook his head, as though to clear the thought from his mind. "Don't get yourself thinking that way, or you'll get all twisted out of true. Those as we take coin from, part with it willingly. Usually because they're too blasted greedy *not* to give us the coin."

Gamine blinked slowly, not understanding.

"See," Temujin went on, "the main trick in any successful grift is to work out what it is that the mark most wants, and figure a way to offer it to him. See in him what is his greatest weakness, and exploit it. We're not taking advantage so much as we're creating a situation whereby the mark's own worst instincts can act against him."

"So the . . . mark . . . defeats himself?"

Temujin smiled. "Exactly."

• • •

The fire had been extinguished, and Gamine lay watching the moons coursing toward each other overhead, as the distant stars twinkled coldly in the night sky. Temujin lay curled up on the ground a short way off, his cacophony of snores occasionally punctuated by trumpeting flatulence.

Gamine thought about what Temujin had said, that she should never view those duped by their cons as "victims," only as "marks." And she couldn't help but be reminded of her former mistress. Gamine wondered how Madam Chauviteau-Zong had thought of *her*.

Whatever the purpose that Gamine had been brought up out of the gutter only to be tossed back again, whatever the strange game Madam Chauviteau-Zong had been playing, Gamine was undoubtedly its victim. Is that how her mistress thought of her? In order to conscience what she had done to a blameless, nameless child of the streets, did Madam Chauviteau-Zong use some colorful euphemism in the place of "victim," when thinking of Gamine? Or did she think of Gamine at all?

And if Gamine learned to assuage her guilt in taking advantage of others by thinking of them as anything other than "victims," which was clearly what they were, was she really much different than Madam Chauviteau-Zong? Was she any better?

At the moment, it seemed that she had little choice, with Temujin's life of grifting being the only alternative to starving in the alleyways of Fanchuan. But she couldn't help but wonder where her current road might lead her, if she succeeded in fooling her own conscience while learning to deceive others.

At the caravanserai, where travelers on the Grand Trunk rested for the night, Gamine and Temujin tried their grift for the first time. Itinerant vendors set up portable stalls in the shadow of the way station, selling foods, drinks, and other comestibles. Parked alongside the wide road were coaches and vans and carriages of all shapes and sizes, their motors cold and resting. Dozens of men and women of all ages, and not a few children, gathered around fires in the shelter of the way station, or gave silent prayers at shrines set back in low-lit alcoves, or just slumbered on pallets laid out on the ground.

Gamine and Temujin approached the circle of light given off by the caravanserai, coming in from the darkness of the road by foot.

"You are certain you know what to do?" Temujin asked in a low voice, for the tenth time. "Repeat again for me the cover story, and I'll know you have it true."

"I've repeated it already a dozen times! I was already nervous, but you're just making things worse by hounding me."

Temujin glowered but didn't speak. They were now almost within earshot of the nearest crowd of travelers and already on the lookout.

"There," he said in a whisper, pointing to a merchant sitting off to one side by himself. "That cove is our mark, no question. Go to, little one, and I'll follow close behind."

Gamine took a deep breath and arranged her expression as Temujin had taught her. When she felt focused and calm, she stepped out of the darkness and stopped just before the merchant. He sat near a small fire, a jar of wine in his hands, lost in thought. His right eye seemed to droop, giving him a slightly comical look. He was dressed in finery, though, and on his fingers were gold rings set with precious gems.

"Excuse me, honored sir," Gamine said with her head bowed, stepping into the circle of firelight. "Might we borrow a moment of your time?"

The merchant looked up, his eyes bleary, taking a moment to focus on Gamine. He set the wine jar down, the contents sloshing liberally over the sides, and it was clear that this was not his first jar of the night.

"Erm, certainly, child," he said, his tongue thickened with drink. "What might the matter be?"

"I am Mei Li, your grace, a lowly orphan, sole survivor of an airship tragedy that claimed the rest of my family. My father, while living, was a successful merchant in far-off Fuchuan, and amassed a considerable fortune. If I could claim my inheritance, I would be lifted out of my current state. However, I am unable to convince the holding company of my bona fide status by tachygraph, and I must journey to Fuchuan to plead my case in person. I, along with my companion, loyal family retainer and the only other survivor of the catastrophe"— Temujin stepped forward and opened his mouth as though to speak—"himself, sadly, struck mute by the trauma and the injuries he sustained"—Temujin glowered at Gamine but closed his mouth with a snap and backed away silently—"must reach Fuchuan by the end of the season, or my father's estate will go into receivership, and my family's wealth will be lost."

Gamine fancied she could see a tear glistening in the corner of the man's drooping eye.

"That is a sad, sad tale," the man said, his voice laced with genuine emotion.

"It is indeed, honored sir," Gamine said, concealing a smile. "But if a kind gentleman such as yourself could only see fit to loan us a few coins, to help us on our way, I would be in a position happily to repay the loan fivefold once my wealth is restored to me. If you would simply give me your name and home address, I will direct the money to be sent to you as soon as my mute servant and I reach Fuchuan."

The man picked up his jar again and drained it to the dregs.

"Fivefold, you say?"

Gamine nodded.

"Well," the man said magnanimously, patting his ample belly for several moments before finding his purse, tucked in his belt. "How much did you say you would need?"

Temujin stepped forward, his mouth opening, but Gamine silenced him with a glance.

"A dozen bronze coins should help us on our way," she said.

"And if a dozen bronze coins would help," the man said through a sloppy smile, shaking his purse out into the palm of his hand, "then no doubt *two* dozen would help even more, yes?"

Gamine's eyes widened, involuntarily, and she bit her lip.

"Yes," she managed to reply. "Most helpful."

The man held out his hand but pulled it back before Gamine could reach for the coins.

"And you confirm that you will be paying me back five times as much?"

Gamine pulled a small slip of paper from her sleeve and an ink-filled pen. "I'll be happy to write you out a receipt."

After drawing the characters representing the money owed, Gamine added notation that it would be paid back at 500 percent interest. The man scribbled his own name and address on the back of a wine-jar label and greedily swapped it for her receipt.

Gamine carefully dropped the coins into her own purse, and bowed low before the man.

"You have my most humble thanks, O honored sir," she said. "You may well have saved my life and that of my loyal *mute* servant." Gamine couldn't help but emphasize the word *mute* again, and she turned and hurried away from the man's fire before she burst out laughing.

They left the mark behind, greedily rubbing his hands, thinking of the riches that would await him at home. When they were out of earshot, Temujin snatched the purse from Gamine's hands, scowling.

"What's all that folderol about me being mute?" he snarled. "I was a prize lickspittle after that, forced to roll my eyes like a spastic and make foolish miming gestures and all. If you do something like that again, you're out on your backside, and that's a promise."

"I'm sorry," Gamine said, her tone suggesting otherwise. She composed a response about her feelings about his persistent nagging, and how nice it was for him to keep silent for a change, but she opted not to voice the thought.

"Well," Temujin said, "that said, I am impressed. Your delivery was a little shoddy, and there were a few holes in your story that a less trusting mark—or a more sober one—would have seen through immediately, but luckily for us, our first target was blinded by greed and addled by drink. He swallowed the story without even chewing it over."

That night, Gamine felt the briefest pangs of guilt. The man with the drooping eye hadn't seemed a terribly bad sort, and if his act of generosity was motivated by greed, did that make it any the less generous?

She closed her eyes, and the face of her former mistress appeared unbidden in her thoughts, looking down at her dispassionately, as though Gamine were a pet, or even an article of furniture. Looking down at her as anything but a victim.

Gamine shook her head, as though to knock loose those thoughts, and reminded herself not to think of people as *victims* but as *marks*.

When she ate, her dinner tasted of ashes, but she ate it, all the same.

They would revise the con in the weeks and months to follow, but the essentials were worked out in those first days, and they stuck to the basic play throughout their travels on the Grand Trunk.

In time, what had begun as a plausible but somewhat thin story of a poor orphaned girl and her loyal retainer, who needed only a moment's kindness and a few coins to make their weary way in a wicked world, became an airtight epic of a backstory that no one could gainsay.

The grift worked a treat, and they amassed a heavy purse between them. Traveling on foot as they did, they moved much slower than the convoys of merchants, bureaucrats, and pilgrims who stopped by night at the caravanserai along the roadside, so they could linger by the way stations and hit several groups in a row, one night after another, before picking up stakes and moving on to the next stop.

Moving slowly like that, days at a time at any location, then walking from one way station to another, they worked their way southeast gradually. Of all the time she would travel at Temujin's side, Gamine would later come to look upon these as some of the happiest days.

Weeks passed, then months, before they reached Shachuan, the capital city of Penglai province.

Gamine had never been to Shachuan before, of course, but had read about it in her studies and seen lithographs of the skyline and notable neighborhoods. Smaller than her home city of Fanchuan, and not nearly as cosmopolitan as Fuchuan in the east, Shachuan was a city of industry. Ringed with mills and foundries and manufactories, the city was nearly obscured by the low cloud of black soot that seemed to pour ceaselessly from the industrial chimneys, and a smell like rotten eggs and offal could be detected on the air in even the best parts of the city. But the locals seemed not to mind the soot or to notice the rotten-egg smell. Gamine, even after a few days in the city, could scarcely bring herself to breathe deeply.

"I was in Shachuan once, years ago," Temujin said as they first entered the city. "Ah, Shachuan. Not an easy sight for weary eyes, but there are pleasures here to soothe a weary breast. The best dumplings I've ever tasted are to be had at a hostelry in the city's rougher district, and there is a wine produced by an old family in the northern part of the city that is beyond compare. Our purse has grown so comfortably heavy these last weeks, my sprite, that I think we could do with something of a vacation from our labors. Have you any objection?"

Gamine could only smile and think fondly about the possibility of sleeping under a roof once again, after so many long weeks on the Grand Trunk with only the dim stars and the twin moons above for a blanket.

Gamine and Temujin spent a few days and nights enjoying what the city had to offer, spending enough of their coin to purchase rooms in a decent inn and to eat in the finest restaurants.

But the vacation was short-lived. After only a few days of rest, Temujin was already hatching a new scheme.

"Do you play an instrument, little one?" Temujin asked, the question arriving unheralded, like an unexpected flash of light from a clear blue sky.

They were in a pawnshop, looking over the wares. There were cases of jewelry (most of the gems either cut glass or paste), rows of tools and gardening implements, and, hanging from hooks in the wall, all manner of musical instruments.

"Why do you ask, old man?" Gamine answered, lingering over a patently fake sapphire that sparkled in the harsh light.

"Never you mind the wherefore, just answer the question. Do you play an instrument?"

Gamine sighed.

"My tutors included musical theory and application in their instructions, and I was trained to play the *erhu* fiddle, the *dizi* flute, the *guqin* zither, and the *pipa* lute, though I find that my talents might leave me best suited to be a vocalist."

"Fine, fine," Temujin said, waving her quiet. He reached up and took an *erhu* fiddle and its bow down from the pegs overhead. He walked to where the pawnbroker sat on a stool, and paid the man a couple of copper coins.

"Here," he said, handing Gamine the instrument as they stepped back out into the street. The sun overhead looked distant and dim through the habitual haze. "We have to eat our dinners separately for the next few days, I'm afraid."

Gamine shrugged. "Fair enough, but what am I to do with this?" She held the fiddle out before her, the bow in the other hand, as though they were snakes that might bite her at any moment.

Temujin hurried up the street, and Gamine had to rush to keep up.

"While you slept late this morning, I went exploring this fair city, and I found a restaurant near the financial district that is a plum ripe for the picking. Though the place is fairly modest, they serve their humble fare with a certain workman-like charm, and their breakfast and lunch traffic is brisk. By the end of the day, no doubt, their cashbox is full to bursting. It falls to me to ingratiate myself to the owner and staff over the coming days, becoming a familiar face to them before we put our plan into motion."

"*Our* plan? I don't even know what the plan *is*!"

"Never you mind, my little sprite. I know the whys and wherefores of it, and that's all that matters."

"And where am I to be while you're busy making friends at this eatery?" Gamine stopped short, her expression set.

"Why, you'll be busy practicing your fiddle playing in our rooms at the inn, naturally," Temujin said, not bothering to slow down. "Now, that's enough of your jaw. We've work to do."

On the third day, Gamine went to the restaurant in the morning as planned, hours before Temujin typically arrived. She sat on the pavement across the street, arranged the fiddle in her lap, and played a mournful tune. She set a knotted kerchief on the ground in front of her, and as the day went on, passersby dropped a few small coins into it, to her muttered thanks. She watched the restaurant fill with patrons for lunch as the streets of the district swelled with bureaucrats, merchants, and couriers. As the day waned, and the workers returned to their homes, the district emptied out, and the streets were left almost empty.

When there were only a few people in the restaurant, and the skies overhead had turned a ruddy shade of gray, Gamine gathered up her day's earnings and her fiddle and walked across the street. She studied the menu tacked up outside and made a show of counting out the coins in her pocket. Then she sat down at a table just inside the door and ordered a simple bowl of stew and rice. Her fiddle she laid across the table, the bow at its side.

Gamine was already halfway through her meal when Temujin arrived, carrying under his arm a cloth-wrapped bundle. As they had planned, they pretended to take no notice of each other. Temujin was all smiles when he greeted the owner by name, and he took his accustomed seat at a back table. He was friendly and generous with the waitstaff, all of whom recognized him from the last few days.

The restaurant emptied as Gamine and Temujin ate their solitary meals. Aside from a large man with only one hand—his other arm ending at his stump of a wrist—who entered after Temujin, ordered a meal, and ate in silence at the rear of the restaurant, they were alone with the owner and the few members of his staff.

Gamine finished her meal and waited patiently while the owner tabulated her bill. When it arrived, she read over it carefully, made a show of counting her coins once again, and then called the owner back over, almost on the verge of tears.

"Oh, kind sir," she said, her voice quavering, "it shames me to say, but I now realize I do not have enough coin to cover the cost of my meal. I had miscalculated the price, and find myself several coppers short."

The owner's brow furrowed. His instinct clearly was to raise his voice in anger, but the expression of shame and sorrow on Gamine's face drew him up short.

"That's highly irregular, er, that is, custom demands . . ." His voice trailed off, and he rubbed at his wide forehead with a hand the size of a ham. "I suppose . . . We *could* take what you have and just call it even. . . ."

"Oh, no!" Gamine objected, shaking her head. "I absolutely will not take charity. I want to pay my way." She wrung her hands, deep in thought. "There *is* one way I can raise the money quickly. A vendor not too many blocks from here owes me a day's wages, as I swept out his shop last night. I could run and collect from him what I'm owed, which would be more than enough to cover the difference."

"Well, I suppose that—"

"But don't worry!" Gamine interrupted, grabbing her fiddle off the table and proffering it to the owner. "I leave with you my *erhu* fiddle as security. It is a fine instrument, well crafted." She leaned closer, her voice lowered. "It cost me fifty copper pieces when I bought it used, and its value cannot have diminished by much."

The owner took the fiddle, wearing a befuddled expression.

"If you insist . . ."

"Let me go and collect my debt," Gamine said, hurrying to the door, "and I will be back in moments to pay what I owe."

With that, she slipped out the door into the darkened streets and was out of sight.

The owner was left holding the fiddle, looking at it quizzically.

Temujin had just finished his meal and was himself walking out, his cloth-wrapped bundle under his arm. Passing by the owner and calling his good-byes, he caught sight of the fiddle.

"Oh, by the Eternal Blue Sky," Temujin said, feigning awed surprise. He approached the owner cautiously, his eyes wide. "Where . . . where did you get *that*?" He pointed at the fiddle.

The owner shrugged and pointed with his chin toward the open door.

"Some girl, short on her tab, left it as security while she runs to get the rest."

Temujin blinked slowly, and licked his lips. He reached out tentative hands but stopped just short of touching the fiddle with his fingertips. "M-may I?" he asked, his voice tremulous.

The owner nodded, somewhat bewildered, and handed the fiddle over.

"Oh my," Temujin breathed, turning the fiddle over in his hands. "I cannot believe my old eyes. The fiddle is surely the work of the master craftsman Fong Li, who crafted the zither used by Pan Xo, and whose *erhu* fiddles were played in the court of the emperor himself." He paused, and met the owner's eyes. "The fiddle is worth a *fortune*."

The owner's eyes widened, and he looked down at the fiddle. Before he'd taken another breath, he reached out and snatched the fiddle from Temujin's hands. "On second thought, I better hold on to it," the owner said, "seeing that it was left in my care, after all."

Temujin was breathless. "You must introduce me to the owner. I am late for an appointment as it is, but I will happily wait for the opportunity, for the slim chance, to purchase such a fine instrument."

The owner nodded dully, unable to take his eyes off the fiddle.

Long minutes passed, and Temujin paced the floor, acting more and more desperate by the second.

"I can delay my appointment no longer!" he finally said. "Please, dear friend," he said, bowing slightly to the owner. He wrote out his name and address on a slip of paper with quick strokes, and pressed it into the owner's hand. "Swear to me on our friendship that you will pass this along to the owner. I am prepared to pay three hundred gold coins for this fiddle, on the spot."

The owner's eyes would have opened even wider if such a thing had been possible.

"Oh, yes, erm, certainly," he stammered, looking from the slip of paper to the fiddle and back again, doing sums in his head.

"You have my eternal thanks, my friend," Temujin said, and rushed from the restaurant, out into the darkened streets, clutching his bundle to his chest.

As soon as Temujin was out of sight, the owner rushed to the cashbox and began to count out the day's receipts, working out how much he would be able to offer Gamine for the fiddle on her return. One hundred gold coins would no doubt dazzle the little street urchin but would mean a threefold profit for the owner when he resold the fiddle to Temujin himself.

Or so he thought.

Gamine and Temujin met in a back alley, a short walk from the restaurant.

"Hurry, my little sprite," Temujin said, out of breath but smiling broadly. "There's the risk the owner might seek a second opinion, and then the game is ruined. When he makes his offer, though, play up the fiddle's sentimental value to you, worth so much more than gold, and then haggle him up to no less than two hundred coins before you agree to part with your 'beloved treasure.'"

"I know my part," Gamine said with a grin. She turned to hurry back to the restaurant, but a giant shape blocked her way.

"Um, excuse me?" Gamine said.

"No," rumbled a deep voice. The giant shape resolved itself into a man, stepping out of the shadows, with one arm ending in a stump instead of a hand. "You two are going nowhere."

Gamine dropped back into a ready stance, calling on years

of martial training, but she had never faced so big an opponent, one handed or not.

"You," the man said, pointing at Temujin with his stump. "Zhang, or Fu, or Temujin, or whatever your name is. We have an account to settle, by my reckoning."

"Oh dear," Temujin said as the enormous man drew nearer.

"Temujin?" Gamine asked, glancing over her shoulder at her companion, turning his name into a question. The one-handed man came ever closer, and Gamine was ready to attempt to repel him, fruitless as the attempt might be.

"Everyone remain calm," Temujin pleaded, holding his hands in front of him, palms forward, forcing an uneasy smile. "I'm sure that we can work this out, whatever it is, Mr. . . . ?" He trailed off, raising an eyebrow.

"You don't remember me, do you, pig dung?" the one-handed man said. "Or perhaps you don't recognize me. I'm not surprised; the years have been long and hard, and when last we met, I had both hands."

Temujin shook his head nervously.

"You have my most humble apologies, noble sir, but I'm afraid I don't recollect . . ."

"The Far Sight Outpost, Green Standard garrison, five summers past."

Temujin's eyes widened, but to his credit his smile faltered only a moment.

"Oh, oh, oh," he said, searching for the words. "Of *course*, I remember. Dear . . ."

"Xian," the man said, looming over Temujin.

"Dear Xian, of course. I, um, I was forced to leave the area unexpectedly and wasn't able to find you before my departure, but I assure you . . ."

"You left as soon as you had bled me of my last coin. My life turned to manure after that day, and I have you to thank for it. I'd given up any hope of properly . . . repaying you, so imagine my surprise at seeing you yesterday at that inn. I've followed you since then, making sure you were the man I remembered, but now that I am, we can begin."

"Um, Temujin?" Gamine said, still in her martial stance.

"Not now, little sprite."

"Either you don't know your friend as well as you think, girl, or you're cut from the same cloth as he. Which is it? Would it surprise you to hear that your 'Temujin' had conned an honest soldier out of his life's savings, over the span of weeks, and left him penniless?" Xian laughed, mirthlessly. "After your friend and I parted company, I had considerable gambling debts to cover and no access to ready coin. I ended up cashiered from the service after I was caught stealing from the company quartermaster, but not before my left hand was cut off as punishment, a reminder of my crime." He held up the stump, his expression dark.

Gamine looked from one man to the other, unsure what to do. From the street beyond the mouth of the alley, she could hear raucous voices raised in laughter, coming closer.

"Look," Temujin said, nervously, "I'm sure there's just been some misunderstanding. . . ."

"No," Xian barked, and his right hand produced a wicked-looking knife. "I understand perfectly. And you will, too, once I've had time to properly . . . explain it to you." Xian smiled and stepped closer. "I won't kill you right away, don't worry. But in the end, you'll beg for death."

At that moment, Gamine caught sight of a group of young men, on wavering legs, their voices raised in drunken laughter as they staggered past the mouth of the alley.

"Help!" Gamine cried out, falling to the ground dramatically. "Rape! Help!"

"What?" Xian said, glancing down at Gamine cowering on the ground. "I've no interest in you, dung brain."

From the mouth of the alley, came shouting voices.

"Look!" "It's just a young girl!" "That guy is a *monster*!"

The group of young men had stopped short, crowding into one another, and peered down the alleyway.

Xian half turned and waved his knife at the group of men. "Pass on by, sprouts, this has nothing to do with you."

The men glanced at one another and smiled drunken smiles.

"Get him!" one shouted, and they rushed forward, screaming battle cries as best they could.

Xian took a step back, bewildered, and the first of the men in the charge had the unlikely good fortune to knock the knife from Xian's hand. The one-handed man didn't seem to mind, but readied himself for a brawl. The men tackled Xian's arms and legs, or let fly with punches and kicks in what they appeared to hope was an impressive display of martial prowess, but which really looked like nothing more than the stumbling antics of drunken boys.

Gamine grabbed Temujin's sleeve and dragged him farther down the alley.

"Come away!" she said in a harsh whisper, but she didn't have to tell him twice. While Xian was buried momentarily under a pile of drunken men, she and Temujin made their escape.

They couldn't return to their rooms. There wasn't time, not with Xian knowing where they were staying. They had no choice but to flee as quickly as possible. That meant leaving the city, taking with them only the clothes on their backs, their purses, and whatever they carried. Temujin still clutched his cloth-wrapped bundle tucked under his arm.

Exchanging as few words as possible, Gamine and Temujin made their way to the eastern extremity of the city—where the Grand Trunk continued to the southeast—and, under cover of darkness, left the city of Shachuan behind.

Later, as the lights of the city were far enough behind them that they twinkled only dimly on the horizon, they left the safety of the road and took shelter behind a cluster of rocks more than a mile from the Grand Trunk. Obscured from view, Gamine started a fire, glad that she always carried her fire kit tucked inside her robes as Temujin had taught her.

For a brief instant, it was almost like the many nights they had spent together after first leaving Fanchuan, when Gamine first learned the art of the trickster—the stars arching overhead, the twin moons in their stately course across the sky, the heat and crackle of the fire at their feet.

Then Temujin began to unwrap the cloth bundle he'd carried from the city, and out rolled a clay jar of wine, ideograms engraved on the side.

"Beyond compare," he said, breaking off the wax seal. He raised the jar to his mouth and gave Gamine a weary look. "Bung your eye," he said, and lifted the jar to his lips, wine pouring into his mouth and coursing down his cheeks and chin.

Gamine had tried wine only once and not liked it in the least, but she was thirsty and had no choice. She reached out for the jar, shrugging.

"No!" Temujin snapped, pulling the jar away from her reach. "This is mine."

"But I am hungry and thirsty, and we don't have anything else."

"At first light we'll make for the first caravanserai along the road. We should reach it by midday, or thereabouts, and will doubtless find there vendors selling comestibles. Now leave me be."

Gamine thought to object, but Temujin raised the jar again to his lips and drank so greedily that she conceded that he needed it more than she.

The moons were higher in the sky, and the jar lay empty on the sands beside the fire, when Temujin spoke again. When he did, though his voice was thick with drink, his words were as clear and lucid as any Gamine had ever heard him say. It was almost as though her companion of these months past had been an act, a sham put on by the man now before her; or else the man she knew was a better actor than she'd supposed, and the man she saw now was the act. Either way, he spoke with a passion and intensity Gamine found surprising, with none of the habitual colloquialisms and crudities peppering his speech.

"My people are the Mongols," he said. "And I, springing from the clan Borjigin, am a direct descendant of the great khan, Jenghiz. My people, if we revere anything, worship only the Eternal Blue Sky, which stretches above us and sees all that men do.

"Jenghiz Khan, genius warrior and king, rose from nothing and brought all the wandering tribes of the Mongols together under a single banner, creating a dynasty from nothing. He then conquered all the lands from the eastern ocean to the western sea and created a great empire. I myself was named after the great khan, whose natal name was also Temujin.

"The Han, the Hind, the Tatar, and Muscovite—all soon fell under the iron grip of the khanate. But the empire was divided as it passed from generation to generation, and later khans were not as apt as Jenghiz at maintaining their hold. So the empire shattered like glass, each nation to itself, and the Mongols were once more a nomadic people.

"Just like me. I am a nomad, and always have been, since I first got out from under my mother's skirts. I've had a chance or two to settle down, over the long, weary years of my life, but I've always chosen instead to continue moving, to continue forward. It is the warrior spirit in me, I suppose, that refuses to let me rest."

He paused, staring into the firelight.

Gamine considered asking Temujin if his warrior spirit was also what drove him to bilk innocent people of their life's savings but, seeing the fire in his eyes, thought better of it.

"Warrior spirit," he repeated, his voice low, and then fell silent.

Long moments passed, and soon Gamine could hear the rumbling of Temujin's drunken snores.

She sat looking at the dim light of the chemical fire, deep in thought, until morning came.

Weeks passed, then months, as Temujin and Gamine worked their way from the west, pulling their familiar cons at caravanserai, way stations, and villages along the way. Almost a year after leaving Fanchuan and first embarking on their journey, they neared the great city of Fuchuan, capital of

Yingzhou Province and the eastern terminus of the Grand Trunk. There, they planned to rest awhile, divide their money between them, and enjoy the comforts of city life for a time. This time they would be careful, though. Temujin hadn't been back in Fuchuan in more than a decade, and he was not now the man he'd been then, but he would be particularly careful anyway. Neither of them had spoken about their narrow escape from one-handed Xian in Shachuan, or about the possibility that more former marks—Gamine thought of them as victims, though Temujin had forbidden her to use the word—might be waiting for them in the next town along the line.

Gamine and Temujin entered Fuchuan, leaving the Grand Trunk behind.

Temujin had explained that Fuchuan was one of the most progressive and welcoming cities on the planet—with temperate weather, cheap hotels, and fine restaurants—and that as a result it was a refuge for con artists and road tramps, who tended to find the liberal denizens of the city to be easy marks for the simplest of cons.

The memory of their last experience in a big city still fresh, Gamine and Temujin reached an unspoken accord. Neither suggested any new cons or angles, instead approaching the city as just what they appeared to be—two travelers weary from a long journey, ready to spend the coins in their full purses. In the months past, Gamine had come to think of games of confidence, the art of the trickster, as something best practiced out in the shadows of civilization, if at all—in dark places away from the bright lights of cities; amidst such a crush of people, it seemed out of place, even dangerous. Better to act the part of the tourist to the hilt and avoid any difficulty. Or better yet, perhaps give up the game of the trickster altogether, if some alternative could be found.

Their second day in the city, though, the temptation proved too great for Temujin.

They were in the restaurant of a resident inn situated in the shadow of the Lower Temple, opposite the square from the Imperial Fuchuan Opera House. Gamine and Temujin each sat before a steaming bowl of bird's nest soup in the late afternoon, alone in the dining room. The owner sat at a table on the far side of the room, going over the day's receipts.

"Where do you think you might like to visit today, little sprite?" Temujin asked. "We've taken in the opera house and the Lower Temple. Would you like to tour the provincial governor's palace, see how the nabobs live when they're at home?"

Gamine blew across the top of her soup and tried to suppress a shudder. "I'd prefer not to visit a governor's home, actually."

Temujin arched an eyebrow. "Why?"

"Poor associations," Gamine said simply, and sipped from her bowl.

A woman entered the room, dressed outlandishly in a strangely cut suit of gray wool, her blond hair cut short. She clutched a leather handbag in both hands, and angled toward the owner.

"I suppose we could go . . ." Gamine began, but Temujin cut her off with a slight wave of his hand. He leaned to one side, cocking his ear to hear.

Gamine listened closely, trying to see what had caught his attention.

The woman was talking to the owner, conversing in low tones. From her accent and pale skin and hair, she seemed to be of Briton extraction. And, to all appearances, she was in trouble. Gamine watched her reach into her handbag and bring out a long string of gold coins, and saw the owner's eyes widen at the sight of them. Once she had finished her story, though, of which Gamine caught only isolated words and phrases, the owner shook his head uninterestedly.

"No," the owner said in a louder voice, gathering up his receipts and pushing away from the table. "I'm afraid I can't help you. Good day."

The owner walked away, leaving the Briton woman sitting at the table alone.

Temujin dabbed at the corners of his mouth and pushed his bowl away from him.

"I believe that poor woman looks lonely over there, don't you?" he said, glancing over his shoulder. "And I'm a right hobberdehoy if I don't go over there and give her some company."

"Oh no," Gamine said, shaking her head. "Really? I thought we were just tourists in this city."

"We are," Temujin said, standing up. "But tourists can fit in a bit of business now and again, in amongst all their merry larking, can't they?"

Gamine crossed her arms over her chest, glowering.

She considered getting up and leaving. She had no desire to stay and watch Temujin try to con this poor woman. However, she had two courses of her meal still to come, and the bird's nest soup had hardly been filling, as tasty as it'd been.

"Damn," Gamine said under her breath, and slumped back in her chair.

Gamine's noodle dish arrived by the time Temujin had insinuated himself into the woman's company. He'd introduced himself with some alias or other and struck up conversation. Small talk at first, no pressure at all, what Temujin had always called "baiting the hook." One needed to first capture the marks' attention before beginning to reel them in.

Gamine decided, in that moment, that she'd had enough of the trickster art. That was it; no more. No grifts, no cons, no ruses. When she'd first set out on the Grand Trunk at

Temujin's side, it had seemed fun, a kind of game, but now she couldn't help but be bored by it all. It was too easy in most instances but too dangerous in too many others. No, she'd have to find some other means of support, and if Temujin wanted to stick to the trickster trade, he'd be on his own.

While Gamine ate, the woman had warmed to Temujin by inches. Despite herself, Gamine couldn't help overhearing their conversation, taking careful note as Temujin had always taught her.

"My name," the woman said, her speech laced with a slight Briton accent, "is Marlowe Constance. Mistress Marlowe Constance." As she spoke, she wrung her handbag in her fingers nervously. "I am originally from Earth, and have journeyed to your world only to come to the aid of my countryman and kinsman the Duke of London, who is currently incarcerated in the prisons of the hegemon of the Southern Fastness."

Gamine knew the Southern Fastness only from her studies and from the stories of travelers on the Grand Trunk. It was a sovereign state, a strange mélange of cultures that arose from those who came to Fire Star in the early centuries of colonization. The Southern Fastness was in effect a satellite of the Dragon Throne, though it did not have formal relations with any of the latter's vassals, among them the island of Britain.

"I am worried," Mistress Marlowe went on, "that if the hegemon's men should learn who the duke truly is, they will not release him for the relatively paltry bond they have initially set; or worse yet, they will not release him at all."

Temujin reached out and patted the woman's hand tenderly. The gesture was carefully calculated to increase feelings of trust between the two, diminishing the physical space separating them and subtly leading the woman to draw nearer to him emotionally. Gamine had seen the maneuver countless times and had performed it herself almost as often.

"I have some money," Mistress Marlowe said, smiling slightly, "but not enough to post bail. I'm looking for assistance, and I fear I've come to the end of my rope. Once the duke is out of jail and free from the hegemon's grasp, I know he will handsomely reward anyone who comes to his assistance."

Gamine could see that Temujin had adopted the pose of a wealthy merchant, slack jawed and simple. She also knew that from the brief glimpse he'd had of her string of coins, he knew exactly how much Mistress Marlowe was worth.

"I would be happy to help," Temujin said sweetly, "and I have sufficient funds to do so. However, it will take me a little time to put together the money. I'd planned on leaving the city—I came to visit my granddaughter, whom you see seated across the way—and return home to Penglai right away, and if I am to stay, I'll need a few more coins to cover expenses."

The woman was overjoyed. She pulled her string of coins out of her handbag and handed it to Temujin without question.

"Will this be enough?"

Temujin smiled and held the coins briefly aloft, his gaze flicking to where Gamine sat. From her vantage point, Gamine could count easily fifty gold coins. "Yes," he said, "I think this should be sufficient for my needs. I'll send word by tachygraph to my family that they should send the money right away."

"Oh, thank you ever so much," Mistress Marlowe said. "If you will meet me at this precise spot in two days' time, at noon, we shall straightaway work to free my friend the duke, and secure your reward!"

"Two days' time, at noon," Temujin repeated with a grin. "And I'll have with me enough to repay your generous loan and secure the duke's release."

Mistress Marlowe nodded and rose from the table, clutching her handbag. Flashing Gamine a slight smile, she hurried from the restaurant into the bright sunshine.

Temujin paused a moment, in character, and when the woman had gone, danced over to Gamine's table, the coins jingling in his fist.

"Don't you wish you had this to share?" Temujin rattled the string of coins, tilting his head to one side as though to better hear the sound. "And all I had to do for it was listen to a bit of prittle-prattle."

"You are a tiresome old man," Gamine said, and turned her attention back to her noodles. Temujin just grinned, showing the gaps in his smile.

• • •

Three days passed, in which Gamine saw the sights the city of Fuchuan had to offer and wondered about her future. Temujin rested in their rooms at the inn, so Gamine wandered the city streets alone, visiting vendors' stalls, galleries, and museums, reveling in the newfound feeling of freedom that came with her decision to leave behind the art of the trickster. She was a regular person again, like all those around her. They were marks no longer, nor victims, just people going about their business. She liked not having to worry about how much that one might have in his purse, or how easily she might get another to buy into a flimsy tale. She was strictly a tourist, enjoying the city of lights.

In Red Flower District, on a crowded street, Gamine felt a rough hand grab her arm. Annoyed, she looked up into a pair of eyes, one of which drooped comically. It was a man dressed in finery, gold rings on his fingers.

"I *thought* it was you!" the man snarled.

It took Gamine a moment to place the face, as distinctive as it was.

"Oh no," she breathed. It was the man from whom she'd conned two dozen bronze coins, nearly a full year ago, when she and Temujin had first set out on the Grand Trunk.

"Oh, yes, damn your hide," the man said, his tone vicious. "You promised me a fivefold return on your loan, but imagine my surprise when I found that the name you wrote on your

'receipt' proved as false as your promises. Clever, clever girl."
His face was twisted in a hateful sneer. "Well, we'll see how
clever you are now."

A city guardsman was crossing the street a hundred yards
away, his hand on the pommel of his saber.

"Guardsman!" the droop-eyed man yelled. "Help!
Quickly!"

The city guardsman turned at the cry, and walked over, in
that officious, stately manner that Gamine was sure only police
could carry off. From a nearby corner, another two guardsmen
turned to see what was happening.

"What seems to be at issue?" the first guardsman said, his
eyes narrowed.

"This girl is a thief," the droop-eyed man said, pointing to
Gamine with his free hand, his other still holding tight to her
arm.

While the droop-eyed man's attention was momentarily on
the guardsman, Gamine saw a slender thread of opportunity
and seized it.

Grabbing the pinky finger of the hand that gripped her
arm, she bent it nearly all the way back. The droop-eyed man
howled in pain and released his hold on Gamine, tears welling
in his eyes.

Gamine turned and ran away into the crowd. The first
guardsman and the two lingering at the corner didn't delay,

but took to their heels, chasing after her, hands on their sabers and ready for action. The droop-eyed man followed just a moment behind, shouting obscenities.

Gamine reached the inn, unsure whether she'd lost her pursuers or not. She'd last seen them a few blocks back but had ducked down a side alley and doubled back. The trick might have worked, but if it hadn't, they wouldn't be too far behind.

"Old man, we've got to go!" she shouted, bursting into Temujin's room.

The room was a chaotic, crowded mess. Temujin was pinned against the wall by a pair of enormous men with pale skin and light brown hair, while two other pale-skinned men stood just a few feet away. Standing in the middle of the room, a wicked stiletto knife in one hand and Temujin's money purse in the other, was the Briton woman they had encountered in the restaurant three days before, Mistress Marlowe Constance. But gone was the wide-eyed expression of the foreign traveler. Her eyes were hard and narrowed, and when she spoke, it was without a trace of an accent.

"Ah, I was waiting for you to show," she said with a sneer. "No sudden moves, kid. I wouldn't want my friends here to hurt you unnecessarily."

Gamine looked from the woman to Temujin. She could tell that he was mostly unharmed, though a reddening on his left cheek, already shading into a bruise, suggested some recent violence.

"Gamine, you remember our friend Constance?" Temujin said, trying for a convivial tone and failing.

"Quiet, *Temujin*," the woman barked. That she used his real name, and not the alias that he'd provided at the restaurant, suggested these people knew more about who he and Gamine were than she'd have liked.

"Who are you?" Gamine asked, trying to act casual while working out the best possible route out of the room and away from the woman and her four large friends. She didn't want to run out on Temujin, but it was his fault he was in this mess, whatever it was. And Gamine didn't want to linger too long, for fear that the guardsmen might be following close behind.

"We're with the Diggers, kid, if you must know," the woman said venomously, "but more importantly, we're the people your pal here owes a fair pile of coin."

Gamine had heard of the Diggers, even back in Fanchuan. They were one of the most notorious of the Parley gangs. Named after an ancient Briton form of governance, the Parleys were originally instituted by Britons who'd been brought to work on the atmosphere mines centuries before. Surrounded by Han who were not always as kind to foreign subjects as they might have been, the Parley gangs had banded together for self-protection. In later generations, though, imperial reforms meant better living and working conditions for non-Han on Fire Star and back on Earth; the gangs found themselves with less to protect themselves against and eventually turned their attention to more illicit goals. A significant percentage of all crime and vice in the city of Fuchuan involved the Parley gangs, and much of that was due to the Diggers.

"Now," the woman said, "we wasted a full day tracking you two down, when the 'wealthy merchant' here missed our appointed meeting yesterday. When he didn't show, it didn't take long to figure that we'd been had. And, considering that the coins we'd given him were just seeds for a long con, we were more than a little annoyed by the discovery."

"The Iberian Prisoner con," Temujin said, unable to keep the hint of admiration from his voice. "You played your part perfectly, my dear, the damsel looking only to help her powerful friend."

"Wasted on you," the woman snapped. "Now look, we're not unreasonable people"—Gamine couldn't help but doubt *that*—"but we wasted three days because of you two, days in which we might have rolled that seed money into some serious coin, if we'd found an honest sucker to catch on the hook. But now I've got to report this to my boss as a loss of profit, and he *hates* to hear the words *loss* and *profit* in the same sentence. So you two need to come up with some serious coin in the next few minutes here, or we're going to be taking it out of your hide. If I can't bring my boss the money, I can at least bring him the scalps of the two jokers who loused it up for us."

Gamine didn't see that she had any choice. If she was to escape, she might have to run off and leave Temujin behind. She had a clear path to the doorway, with the woman and her four pale-skinned friends all farther inside the room. The only other way out was a wide window on the far side of the room, but to reach it Gamine would have to make it past the woman and her friends, which didn't seem likely. So she'd have to run for it and hope for the best.

As the woman finished her lengthy and colorful threat against their lives, Gamine slowly inched backward. Everyone was so intent on listening that they didn't notice that Gamine was now almost all of the way out of the room. She was about to turn and run for her very life, when she heard a shout coming from farther down the hall.

"There she is!"

Gamine looked over and froze.

Six guardsmen, tall and broad shouldered, were barreling toward her, hands on the sheathed sabers at their sides.

"Stop!" one of them yelled.

Gamine saw her chance and took it.

"Temujin!" she shouted, rushing back into the room and heading straight for the window. "Follow me!"

The woman and her four friends looked at Gamine as though she were insane. Any one of them was only a few steps away from reaching her, and she couldn't possibly hope to reach the window without being stopped.

"What's this?" came an officious voice from the doorway, followed by the rattling of sabers.

Gamine didn't pause to look back but raced for the window.

"It's Thompson Mary and her boys!" one of the guardsmen shouted.

"Guys, whip the dung out of these pigs," the woman ordered.

Gamine reached the window and threw back the sash. Temujin was at her side by the time she'd climbed up on the windowsill.

"Our friends appear to be a bit distracted by the hurly-burly," Temujin said by way of explanation as he followed Gamine out onto the ledge. The room behind him had exploded into a violent melee as gang members and guardsmen plowed into one another, all shouts and fists, sabers and knives. Everyone had, for the moment, forgotten about them.

"Let's go." Gamine dropped to the street below. Without waiting for Temujin, she pounded away down the back street as quickly as her feet would carry her.

That night, the lights of Fuchuan only a dim glow on the western horizon, Gamine and Temujin sat huddled together in the darkness. They had nothing with them: no coin, no provisions, no fire kit. They could not return to the city, not with both the authorities and a Parley gang out for their blood. To the south and east was nothing but sand and rock, interrupted on rare occasion by military outposts and refueling stations.

The Grand Trunk lay far to the west. To the north, beyond the steep walls of the Tianfei Valley, stretched the northern plains, wide prairies dotted with little hamlets and agrarian villages, rice plantations, and atmosphere mines.

"It occurs to me," Temujin said, his few teeth chattering in the cold, "that it might be time to take a little vacation from the trickster life. Maybe see what life is like for the masses who sweat and toil for a living . . . not that I plan to sweat and toil, mind, but I'm sure we can come to some sort of accommodation."

"You are a tiresome old man," Gamine said, shivering. She huddled closer to Temujin to conserve their warmth, and looked at the dark sky overhead, the twin moons moving gradually across the backdrop of stars. Then she sighed. "North? Well, I don't see that it could be any worse."

They had been walking for days on end, and Gamine was hungry, thirsty, and tired.

There was nothing as far as the eye could see in any direction but rocks and hardscrabble dirt, rising and falling endlessly, like frozen waves, with the unbroken sky stretching above. They subsisted off what they could catch with their meager skills, and drank from shallow pools after the all-too-infrequent rains.

They didn't talk. There wasn't much to say.

Most of Gamine's thoughts were concerned with putting

one foot before the other, making slow progress toward the north, where Temujin insisted that somewhere, just beyond the next ridge, or the one after that, they would find sanctuary and salvation.

So far they had found only rock, and dirt, and sky.

Gamine didn't think she'd ever been so hungry or so tired.

Late the night before, as they had tried to catch a few moments' rest beneath the stars—curled up shivering on the cold, hard ground—Gamine had realized something. She'd never put it into words before, but at that moment—her hands and feet numb with cold, her teeth chattering in her head, her stomach knotted with hunger—Gamine realized that she wanted to live.

She had no desire to die, and she wasn't about to lie down and stop trying. She was going to survive. And more than that, she was willing to do whatever was necessary to make sure that she did.

She remembered all those who might have stood in her way, or not cared if she lived or died. She thought about her mistress, Madam Chauviteau-Zong, who had cast her aside like rotten fruit. Gamine wouldn't die. No. She would live. She would survive in the hopes that one day she might see her former mistress again. First, Gamine would ask why she had been taken off the street and educated only to be thrown back again. Then, her questions answered, Gamine would take her revenge.

Now, in the cold light of day, Gamine wondered whether she'd be able to go through with it. Would she be able to kill? If her life depended on it, even?

Perhaps. She wasn't sure. Perhaps not.

But one thing was certain. She had no intention of giving up. Would she con again, and cheat, and steal? Most definitely, if that was the only way. She would feel guilty about it, more than likely, and would try to make it right later on, but she would still do it, all the same.

Gamine put one foot in front of the other, trudging over the unforgiving landscape.

Survive. No matter what.

It was some weeks before they reached the first settlements of the north plains. Both had lost a considerable portion of their body weight, and as they walked down the hard-packed dirt road that was the main thoroughfare of the little farming community, their hollow cheeks, gaunt faces, and vacant eyes drew worried stares from the villagers as they approached.

Lips cracked, throats nearly too dry to swallow, Gamine and Temujin stumbled into the village, desperate for a drop of water and a crumb of bread.

"Please," Gamine croaked, approaching a woman carrying a small child, her voice almost too faint to hear. "W-water."

The woman drew her child tighter to her breast and hurried away without sparing Gamine a word.

"Noble . . . sir . . ." Temujin managed, painfully making his way toward a heavy man slopping pigs. The man dumped a bucket into the low, narrow trough—animal bones, old vegetables, dinner scraps, and trimmings all mixed in a murky, brackish water. "My . . . friend and I . . . have traveled . . . great distance, and if you could . . ." Temujin paused, wavering slightly. "Water . . . and food . . ." he finally finished simply.

The man shook out the rest of the bucket and tossed it to the corner of the pen.

"We don't take very kindly to beggars around here, stranger," the man said, his eyes narrowed suspiciously. "But I've had good fortune this season, and it'd be an ill deed not to pass on at least a little of it." The man rubbed the whiskers on his chin. "Tell you what, if there's anything left once they're through"—he indicated the two pigs greedily eating at the trough—"you can have what's left. That's all I can do for you."

Temujin scowled momentarily but forced a weak smile.

"Thank . . . you . . ." he said, his eyes on the pigs.

Gamine drew near.

"H-heart attack, pig," she said, her eyes on the trough, wishing as hard as she could. The foul mess in the brackish water was, at that moment, more appetizing than the finest meal in Fuchuan.

In the end, they didn't wait for the pigs to finish. Squeezing through the bars of the pen, they waited until the man's back was turned and worked their way to the far end of the trough, as far from the two monstrous pigs as possible. Luckily for them, the animals were too busy eating to pay them any mind, and Gamine and Temujin were able to scoop out handful after handful of the stuff and cram it into their waiting mouths. It smelled foul, and tasted even worse, but it was edible and had water in it, both of which were all that mattered at the moment.

They ate as much of the stuff as their shrunken stomachs would allow, the first food they'd had in nearly three days, and if the pigs hadn't started toward them ominously, beady eyes regarding them almost as though they were dessert, Gamine and Temujin would have fallen asleep right in the muck. As it was, they scrambled back through the bars as quickly as their diminished strength would allow.

Smelling now worse than the pigs—slop dripping down their chins and fronts, and muck and manure all over their clothes and hair—Gamine and Temujin nevertheless breathed contented sighs of relief. Having crossed the unpeopled stretches of the plains, they had reached civilization again at last, though the journey had proved much longer and more difficult than Temujin had originally suggested, as Gamine was always quick to remind him.

"'Just a couple of days,'" Gamine said, trying ineffectually to wipe some of the muck from her clothing. "'We'll reach the farms of the northern plains in no time.' Isn't that what you said?"

"Well..." Temujin replied, dabbing daintily at the corners of his mouth with his sleeve, as though he'd just dined at a grand restaurant and not stolen scraps from a couple of pigs. "We're here now, aren't we, my little sprite?" He laughed slightly and glanced down at his ragged, soiled robes. "Perhaps a little more worse for wear, but still here, nevertheless."

"For all the good it does us," Gamine said, looking around. "Our first real meal since leaving the city is at a pig's trough, and it doesn't look as though our welcome is going to get much warmer."

Men, women, and children walked past, carrying bundles and farm implements down the dirt road, all of them giving Gamine and Temujin a wide berth.

"We'll work something out, I feel certain." Temujin pointed at the road, which wound deeper into the little village. "Perhaps it's just the folks on the outskirts here with such a dim view of tourists? Mayhap if we moved a bit inward..."

Gamine shrugged and followed Temujin. Their feet had become little more than one large blister days before, and Gamine had surrendered the notion of ever getting to sit down for more than a few moments; it seemed an impossible dream, like bathing or hot food.

In the middle of the village, in a wide square, they found a little market where the farmers sold one another their wares, and other goods and services were bartered and sold. This seemed as close to mercantile as this little community came. Gamine wondered whether she and Temujin might have skills that they could call upon, perhaps to get themselves hired on by a local. She wasn't sure what they had to offer a farming community, but at this point she was willing to work for nothing but room and board, and she wasn't particular about what kind of work it was.

Gamine thought about the promise she had made to herself on her way north: that she would survive, no matter what it took. What kind of work wouldn't she be willing to do, if the alternative was death?

"Look over there." Temujin pointed across the square, where a man with the shaved head, robe, and begging bowl of a mendicant preacher addressed a small collection of villagers. Temujin started across the square to listen more closely, and Gamine followed.

It was appropriate after-dinner entertainment, considering the meal they'd just had. Gamine and Temujin listened to the mendicant's unfocused ranting for several long minutes. Rambling and disjointed as it was, it had still captured the attention of at least a few of the villagers, who listened on with rapt expressions. The mendicant, who seemed not to be entirely sane, drew his religious lessons as much from works of popular entertainment as he did from the holy words of any established religion, mixing fictional characters, historical figures, and religious icons indiscriminately. He called them all "powers." Someone who was pure of heart could invite these powers to possess their form, leaving their bodies impervious to damage while their soul lifted temporarily to a higher plane.

"This cove is barmy," Temujin whispered behind his hand. "But look how these dirt lovers are just eating it up."

After a moment, Gamine nodded. "I think I have an idea. Watch for my cue."

"What?" Temujin looked over at her, a quizzical look on his face, but Gamine didn't pause to explain.

"O holy master," she said, stepping forward through the crowd, folding her hands in an attitude of prayer and bowing deeply from the waist. "Your words touch some spirit which resides within me. May I approach?"

The mendicant, his eyes wild and hair flying, looked down the length of his nose at Gamine, appraising her.

"Approach, daughter," he said dramatically.

"Thank you, master," Gamine said. She took to the impromptu stage, a little circle of dirt ringed by seated and standing villagers, all watching her intently. "I was passing by," Gamine declaimed, "and your words about the powers caught my ear. I could not help but feel that you were speaking directly to me. It was like something within me was eager to respond to your words, but—"

Gamine stopped short and bulged her eyes. She stuck her tongue out of the side of her mouth, and shook slightly, as though an electrical charge had just run through her body.

"My child?" the mendicant said, uneasily.

Gamine's mouth snapped open and a loud howl issued forth, for a brief instant. In the audience, the villagers drew back, startled.

In the days of my father, this land was all ours,
Before the coming of the worshippers of another sun,
With their sacrifices of blood, and pyramids to the stars,
Now we toil deep within the red soil for their pleasure,
And our children weep with their hunger in the night.

Gamine kept on, reciting lines of dialogue from *The Miner's Journey*, written two centuries before by the playwright Song Huagu; Gamine had seen it performed several times and she memorized it completely. The play was popular in the northern plains and would likely be one her audience would recognize. From the surprised glances that rippled through the gathered villagers, and the susurration of whispers that followed, Gamine was sure that they had.

Once she was sure she had the audience's full attention, Gamine stopped for a moment, closed her eyes, and rocked her head back and forth.

"But now," she went on, eyes still closed, voice raised, "another darkness covers our fair land. Strangers walk, their bellies full of nothing but hunger, their souls of nothing but fear. Who will take these poor children of man into their homes, and feed and clothe them? Who will extend to their fellow man the courtesy that villains never do?" She opened her eyes and pointed out to the audience. "Whoever does will find themselves rewarded tenfold by the powers, for they will truly be worthy."

Gamine stopped and scanned the crowd.

"The powers wish to provide a concrete demonstration for those who might still doubt. One of you now listening, come forward and be tested."

The villagers all looked at one another uneasily. In the brief silence that followed, Temujin took the cue.

"I am a stranger here," Temujin said, stepping to Gamine's side, "but I am eager to see what the powers can do."

The villagers, all relieved that they wouldn't be put to the powers' test, leaned forward in eager anticipation.

"You!" Gamine said in the voice of the powers. "Draw near this vessel and strike her across the face, as hard as you can." She pointed at her chin. "She will feel no pain, nor suffer any injury."

Temujin stepped back. He held up his hands, taking on a fearful expression.

"No, no!" he said, shaking his head. "I couldn't. She is but a child!"

Gamine shook her head. "Strike now, and strike true!"

Temujin took a tentative step forward. "Must I?"

"Yes!" Gamine answered in the booming voice of the powers. "Strike her!"

Temujin swung his fist toward Gamine's face. They had practiced falls and false punches many times on the Grand Trunk, in the event a con ever called for physical action, but this was the first time they'd put the routine into play.

With everyone's attention on Temujin's fist and her face, Gamine smacked the side of her leg; at the same instant Temujin pulled his punch, so that his fist stopped only a hairsbreadth from Gamine's cheek.

The villagers gasped as Temujin drew back his hand, his face contorted and his hand twisted, as though he had struck a solid wall.

"You see?" Gamine said, raising her arms. "The powers, invested in this frail frame, have given a mere slip of a girl a jaw of iron. She can withstand any blow, suffer any torment without complaint. What more could they do for you, if you prove your worth?"

Gamine paused a moment, reveling in the dropped jaws and wide eyes of the audience, to say nothing of the amused look on Temujin's face and the suspicious expression the mendicant wore. Then she closed her eyes again, opened her mouth wide, and let out another short yell.

Then, without warning, she collapsed to the ground like a marionette whose strings have been cut.

"Help her!" a woman in the crowd cried, and several men rushed forward to Gamine's aid.

"Ohhh," Gamine moaned, as though she were coming out

of a deep sleep. "What . . . what happened?" She opened her eyes, a confused look on her face.

"Don't you remember?" one of the villagers said, helping her to her feet.

"R-remember?" Gamine said. "N-no. I don't remember anything, just walking up here to talk to the holy master. I . . . I must have fainted." She paused dramatically. "I'm just so hungry."

The villagers erupted in excited whispers, and Gamine had to work hard to suppress a smile.

Gamine and Temujin sat on either side of the mendicant, a sumptuous feast spread on the table before them. All three had been washed and clothed, and were already on their third course.

"Um, daughter," the mendicant said uneasily. "Have you ever found yourself touched by the powers before?" The poor priest had barely touched any of his food and had fixed all his attention on Gamine.

"What?" Gamine said, swallowing a dumpling whole.

"He means your holy possession," Temujin said from the mendicant's other side. "Isn't that right, Master . . . ?" He trailed off, framing a question.

"Wei," the mendicant said, bowing from the waist. "This humble servant of the powers is known as Wei."

"Master Wei." Gamine took a sip of green tea and regarded

him thoughtfully. "I suppose you travel from town to town delivering your sermons, correct?"

The mendicant nodded.

"And does your sermon draw so many listeners in every village you visit?"

"Oh, no!" the mendicant said, shaking his head fiercely. Gamine's shoulders slumped visibly. "In most hamlets, my parishioners number *many* more than here."

Gamine looked past Master Wei at Temujin, who met her eyes and smiled.

"Master Wei," Temujin said. "My companion and I would very much like to accompany you on your travels."

The mendicant's eyes were wide. "You would?"

"Oh, yes," Gamine said, taking a bite of chicken, not minding that she spoke with her mouth full. "And perhaps we can help you with your sermons in other villages, as well."

Master Wei nodded, unsure. "I suppose . . ."

"Good!" Temujin said, slapping him on the back. "Then it's settled. Once we've gotten all we can out of the locals—"

"Once we've brought the word to all who will hear," Gamine interrupted.

"Yes, of course," Temujin demurred. "Once we've done that, then we'll move on to the next town."

"To bring them the good news about the powers!" Master Wei clapped his hands with delight. "Oh, this is splendid, to have fellow travelers and coreligionists join me in my mission."

"Oh, yes." Gamine smiled. "Splendid."

Master Wei wished them a good night and left to begin his evening prayers.

When he had gone, Temujin said in an undertone, "I thought you wanted to quit the trickster game, my little sprite."

"Well," Gamine said with a smile, "that was before I was hungry for a few weeks straight. Besides, I'm just using the power of my own voice. Could there be a nobler pursuit?"

"And only offering the mark what he most wants? In this life or the next?"

Gamine grinned. "Something like that."

ACT II

•

HUANG'S THEME

WOOD HARE YEAR, FIFTY-SECOND YEAR OF THE TIANBIAN EMPEROR

THE BODY OF THE CRAWLER WAS PAINTED A SICKLY yellowish green, standard military coloration, so that it stood out like an aging bruise against the red sands that lined both sides of the Grand Trunk and blew in gritty flurries across the roadway. Red dust clung to the knobby tires of the crawler and gritted the edges of the already grimy glass of the windscreen. Segmented like a centipede so that it could accommodate almost any terrain, the crawler still seemed to jostle and vibrate with every tiny bump and rut in the road, the sections of metal squealing against one another as they rode up and down and up again.

Huang Fei struggled in vain to find a comfortable position on the hard, warm metal of the bench, his uniform jacket wadded up and pillowed under his head. He lay in red-lidded darkness, eyes squeezed shut tightly but unable to block out the harsh light of day, and tried to sleep. It had been more than a day since he'd stumbled, bleary eyed and fuzzy headed, to the transport depot, clutching an empty jar in one hand and the governor-general's red saber in the other. He'd not slept all through the night, carousing until the rising sun turned the eastern sky a lighter shade of violet, and gone off in his newly purchased uniform to meet his fate. He thought he might sleep on the crawler during the long journey to the west; he was wrong.

Now, long hours later, he'd still not slept, kept awake through day and night by the constant movement of the creaky, rusting crawler, and by the unforgiving metal benches. The three drivers, who took their turns in the cab by shifts, seemed not to share this difficulty, nor did the pair of infantrymen who served as guards for the shipment in the crawler's hold. Their snores sometimes threatened to drown out the grinding howl of the crawler's engines. Huang wondered if there wasn't some trick to it, some secret approach that allowed them to snuggle down on the hard benches and drop off into restful slumber. He'd have asked, but the others seemed to have taken Huang's measure when first meeting him in the depot. Drivers and guards alike were of the common classes, and it wasn't hard to see what they made of Huang's aristocratic accent and bearing. They regarded him, when they deigned to notice him at all, with naked sneers and undisguised contempt. He was effete, he was a snob, and, even worse, he was an *officer*.

Huang suffered in silence on the hard bench and cursed

the fate that had brought him to this pass. What could possibly be worse than this?

The crawler was one of a half dozen vehicles in the supply convoy, heading west along the Grand Trunk. Their journey had begun in the transport depot of Fanchuan and carried them through the western extremity of Tianfei Valley, where the Grand Trunk ended at the labyrinthine complex of valleys and canyons called the Forking Paths. They would follow the maps with care through the twisting corridors of the maze until they trundled out the other side. Once on the highlands, they would continue on to the northwest through Fuxi and Nuwa, which along with Mount Shennong made up the Three Sovereigns range, bound ultimately for Far Sight Outpost, garrison of the Green Standard Army, in the shadow of Bao Shan, tallest mountain in the solar system.

They had climbed out of the Forking Paths, and were just passing the equator, but Bao Shan was still days away, or more. Ever since leaving the well-paved Grand Trunk, they had been traveling on increasingly rough roads, and once they were out on the highlands, the roadway was scarcely deserving of the name. More a rough track through the red sands, pitted and pocked, punctuated here and there by massive rocks. The convoy, able to travel only as fast as the slowest vehicle, made only a fraction of the speeds it had reached on the Grand Trunk, its progress slowed to a literal crawl.

They stopped for a few hours each night to let the crawlers' engines cool while mechanics scurried like ticks on a dog, tightening lug nuts and checking gaskets and oiling junctions and performing all manner of frenetic activity, none of which made any sense to Huang. The drivers and guards, thankful for the chance to stretch their legs on solid ground, huddled around chemical fires, passing flasks from hand to hand, laughing at well-worn anecdotes and filthy jokes. There were one or two women in the company, but they seemed as rough-hewn and ill-mannered as their masculine counterparts, as likely to tell a bawdy joke or recite an obscene limerick themselves as they were to join in the laughter when one of the men did the same.

Huang kept to himself in these evening stopovers, though it wasn't as if he had much choice in the matter. The closest he came to any interaction with others, beyond perfunctory brief exchanges that couldn't be avoided on either side, was sidelong glances thrown Huang's way, or the raucous laughter in response to whispered witticisms, doubtless at his expense.

"Dinner, sir?"

Huang started, surprised at the sound. He turned to see one of the guards from the crawler standing a few feet off. Dressed in the uniform of an infantryman in the Army of the Green Standard, the embroidery at his breast indicated the guard was not far at all advanced in rank, despite his obvious age. Though the guard was old enough to be Huang's father, protocol and custom still demanded he address the younger man as *sir*. Huang was an officer, after all, a Guardsman of the Second Rank, and however little the others might respect him, they were each of them soldier enough to observe the proper rituals.

"Hmm?" Huang hummed, eyebrow raised, not having comprehended the question.

"I said, dinner, sir?" The guard, with a weary sigh, pointed toward the nearest chemical fire. Men and women sat on their haunches around the greenish flames, their skin cast in sickly hues by the weak light, scooping rice and fish heads from bowls into their waiting mouths with chopsticks. The guard held a bowl in either hand and raised one to Huang, unceremoniously.

Huang was ravenous, but the smell of the meager dinner made him curl his lip in disgust, nostrils quivering. His first instinct was to refuse, reasoning that as bad as the stuff smelled, it doubtless tasted even worse. But he'd not eaten more than a mouthful since they left the transport depot in Fanchuan, and his hunger was getting the better of his tastes.

"Oh, all right," Huang said with a labored sigh, snatching the bowl from the guard's hand. He raised the bowl to his nose, sniffed experimentally, and then reared back, throwing his head to one side. "Aargh." He shook his head, as though to knock loose the scent from his nostrils. "And you're *quite* sure there's nothing else on hand? Nothing *edible*?"

The guard's sneer slid into a smile, and he shook his head. "No, sir," he said, chuckling. "And that's the best of it, too.

Real delicacy, that is." He glanced to the chemical fire, where the audience had lapsed into silence, listening to the exchange intently. "And you'll excuse my saying it's only downhill from here, sir."

Huang looked at the noxious stuff in the bowl in mounting disgust. "It gets *worse* than this?"

The guard stifled a laugh and nodded. "Oh, yes, sir. We won't get nothing as nice as this once we reach Far Sight Outpost, sir, mark my words."

Huang shuddered at the thought of any list of comestibles with undercooked rice and rancid fish heads ranked at the top. The guard gave an abbreviated bow and went to join the others. There were indistinct whispers as the guard related the full exchange to the others, who had caught only snippets at the distance, followed by loud peals of laughter.

Far from the green light and thin warmth of the chemical fires, Huang crouched down on the red sands and dispiritedly shoveled bits of rice and fish head into his mouth. It was better than starvation, but not by much.

Huang had never been much of a reader. He had always left that to his younger brothers. Now, one of them had already passed his *juren*-level examinations and secured a livelihood in the imperial bureaucracy, and the other was bound for a monastic life in one of the lamaseries of the Southern Fastness, while Huang was cramped in a sickly yellow-green crawler and sent off to the western wilderness, to the edge of civilization, to spend the next decades of his life at a military garrison to which, to all appearances, only the dregs of the Green Standard Army were sent. He had begun to suspect that those family connections of his father's that had resulted in his officer's commission might have borne some grudge against the elder Huang. Governor Ouyang had not seemed to consider the posting any form of punishment, but then the governor-general had thought Huang a worthy recipient of his own prized saber, so clearly the old man's judgment could be called into question. In approving the posting, for all Huang knew, Ouyang might have thought he was doing Huang a *favor*.

Huang wished that he'd picked up the habit of reading. Or at least had picked up a few books before boarding the crawler. Then he'd have something to *do* to pass the time. He'd even take his younger brother's popular novels, each of them the stirring tale of a man or woman who overcomes adversity through dogged adherence to the teachings of Master Kong, exhibiting proper ritual, filial piety, and loyalty to the Dragon Throne, to rise in the bureaucracy and attain some exalted position in the emperor's service; some of the novels even went further and detailed the sorts of positions these noble workers achieved in the afterlife, serving the celestial government in the afterworld as they had served the Celestial Emperor in life. For that matter, he'd even take his youngest brother's spiritual tracts, endless meditations on virtues and the nature of truth.

Anything would be better that this endless *nothing*.

But no, Huang had never read a book for pleasure—and seldom ever for his studies, either—and so now paid the price. In his younger days, he'd amused himself with sport, when he wasn't indulging his appetites for spirits and women. He tried horseback riding a time or two, in the course in Fanchuan's Green Stone District, having seen images of the sport sent from Earth, reportedly the emperor's favorite pastime; but even 250 years after man first came to Fire Star it was not yet a fully terrestrial world. Like most animals horses were still ill adapted to the thin air and low gravity. In another few hundred years, the atmosphere mines in the north might produce enough oxygen and nitrogen to blanket Fire Star in a breathable atmosphere like Earth's, and the last of the red dust would at last be carpeted in green grasses and forests. The world that Huang knew was habitable but, it often seemed to him, not much more than that.

Denied the pleasures of the horse track, and lacking the stomach for flying above the city in kites or balloons as so many young men and women of his class did, Huang was forced to find distraction nearer the ground.

His parents, of course, hoped that he would lose himself to his studies, as his brothers had lost themselves to theirs. But the only subject that interested him in the slightest was military strategy, and only because it seemed more a game than an intellectual pursuit. More often than not Huang would beg and plead with his tutor to devote an entire session to a round of elephant chess instead of the dry texts on the subject, moving the pieces marked as officers and scholars, elephants and ministers, horses, chariots, and cannons back and forth across the board, to see whether general or marshal would prevail. After a few years Huang bested his tutor more often than not, but even his parents were quick to admit that being adept at games of strategy scarcely made him a scholar.

With studies failing to hold his interest, Huang turned his attention to sport. He tried a bit of archery and riflery. In the low gravity of Fire Star, firing a rifle without properly bracing yourself could send you flying backward. The first time Huang fired a rifle at the range, he'd paid scant attention to the instructor, and the kick of the recoil knocked him off his feet. His backside had been bruised for weeks afterward, and it hadn't been a difficult decision to put the rifle aside forever. He'd had marginally better luck with the bow and arrow, but pulling the string back time and again just seemed too much like *work;* the bow went the way of the rifle.

It wasn't until Huang picked up a sword for the first time that he discovered his true calling.

Fencing wasn't work. Fencing wasn't even really sport. Fencing was a *pursuit.* Better yet, it was an *art.*

Huang was a little boy when he first saw a pair of martial artists giving a demonstration in the plaza in Sun-Facing District, near the Hall of Rare Treasures. Looking back on it later, Huang realized that the performers had been little more than beggars who'd picked up some small amount of skill. But at the time, he'd never seen anything like them. They seemed to glide back and forth effortlessly across their hastily erected platform, their blades dancing in their hands, long tassels dangling from the pommels, the sunlight glinting off jewels in the hilt that, while no doubt nothing more than paste or glass, had looked to his young eyes like treasures fit for the emperor himself. And the sounds of the swords meeting each other, ringing like bells, sending sparks flying, resounded in his ears for days and weeks to follow.

Later, Huang discovered the popular entertainments: the *wuxia* dramas of swordsmen and brigands, legends from Earth's history and folktales of the last two hundred years of Fire Star's colonization. Wandering heroes and knights-errant who faced evil and adversity only with the strength of their arms and their skill with the blade. The river-lake and the world of the outlaw. Brothers of the greenwood—bandits, burglars, and pirates—who maintained order when the authorities became corrupted by vice and decay. Stories like *The Water Margin* and *The Romance of the Three Kingdoms*. Huang lived in them when he was a boy, returning day after day to the cheaper theaters, oblivious to the world around him. Any nearby stick became a swordsman's saber, and woe betide any flowering plant that happened to grow in his path; each petal and leaf slashed to the ground was a fallen enemy, a vanquished foe.

One day, he'd chanced to see a group of children and young adults in a courtyard doing what appeared to be a strange kind of dance, and when he asked his parents, he was told that they were practicing fencing movements.

Fencing? Huang's mind had raced. Did they mean with *swords*?

Huang had insisted on the spot that his parents enroll him in the class. In the years that followed, while his brothers read their books and his friends soared high over the city with their breather masks and kites, Huang haunted that courtyard, listening closely to everything the instructors had to say, practicing the movements until his muscles ached, fighting bouts in his dreams. In time, he became one of the star pupils, always finishing first or second in the meets, always trading the top spot with his friend Kenniston An, the son of a prominent Fanchuan bureaucrat of Briton extraction.

Huang's room in his parents' house was filled with his fencing medallions, trophies, and prizes. There was a portrait of him and Kenniston in their fencing uniforms, sabers drawn. Crossed swords hung on the wall, surrounded by framed advertising posters for the *wuxia* dramas he'd spent so many hours watching. The small shelf of books beside his bed was filled almost entirely with fencing manuals.

He had left all of it behind, the morning that he came to the transport depot. None of it would do any good now. When Kenniston had finished his studies the year before, his parents had sent him off to the military, having determined that their son had no marketable skills to serve the family's interests. Huang had been horrified at the thought of leaving behind the culture and sophistication of the city for the harsh environs of the outer provinces, but Kenniston seemed not to mind. He'd opted to enlist in the Bannermen, the elite fighting forces trained to fight in any terrain, in any environment, desert or sea, planetside or vacuum. Huang had joked that Kenniston had taken one too many blows to the head in their practice bouts and ended up addled, but his friend had just laughed. Huang would understand when he was older, Kenniston said. One couldn't play at games forever.

Huang was only a year Kenniston's junior and had always gotten his back up when his friend tried to pull rank. Well, now Huang *was* older, and he wished he knew how to get hold of Kenniston, because he could prove conclusively that his friend had been wrong. So far as Huang was concerned, then and now, he could quite *happily* go on playing at games forever if the alternative was a lifetime of hard metal benches and the rude laughter of common soldiers.

But even that would be somewhat bearable if he had something to pass the time. Which led Huang to wonder whether he might not have an easier time of it now had he spent a little more time reading as a child and less time with a sword in hand. And, of course, if he'd brought a book or two to read. As it was, Huang had brought along only the red saber with the firebird etched upon its blade that the governor-general had presented him, which was proving poor distraction aboard the crawler. If only something would *happen*, he wished, anything to relieve the boredom.

They were still more than a day away from Bao Shan and Far Sight Outpost when the airship was sighted, high over the horizon. They were just boarding the crawlers after the night's stopover, the eastern sky violet with the sunrise, when a new star seemed to appear in the south. It was a few moments before it was discovered that the new flickering light in the southern sky was the glint of sunlight on metal, a few dozen miles away, and not from some more distant celestial source.

There was some little discussion about the airship as the drivers and guards arranged themselves in the crawlers, and the convoy set off to the west. Most presumed that it was one of the airships used for reconnaissance by the Army of the Green Standard, or one of those used by the elite corps of the Bannermen on maneuvers. It might even have been the pleasure craft of some wealthy aristocrat.

Near midday, though, as the airship drew nearer, it became clear that it didn't fly any of the eight banners of the elite fighting forces, nor the emerald signet of the Green Standard. And though the sunlight glinted off the bare metal of its engine struts and stabilizers, the fittings and fixtures were hardly those of an aristocrat's pleasure ship.

This craft appeared to have been salvaged and rebuilt repeatedly, the fabric of the envelope a patchwork of different colors and materials. The gondola, which hung down in front of the two hulking engines that propelled the craft forward, was constructed of bare steel and unpainted aluminum. Even the small balloons Huang's friends had used to sail high over the streets of Fanchuan had been more elaborate and baroque than this.

The guards shifted uneasily on their benches as the drivers debated whether to put on more speed or stop and circle the crawlers in a defensive ring.

"What is the matter?" Huang asked, his voice croaking as he spoke, so long had it gone unused. "It's just an airship." He looked from one worried face to another. "Isn't it?"

The oldest of the guards shook his head in a dismissive manner, but the youngest leaned over and studied Huang's face closely.

"Really?" the young guard asked, asking if Huang's question was sincere. "You don't know about the . . ." And here the guard paused for a moment as though concerned that someone might be eavesdropping. "About the *bandits*?"

Huang's eyes widened.

Everyone had heard the stories about the bandits who were said to prowl the unpeopled wastes, preying on travelers and then returning to their hiding places in the high mountain regions, where the air was too thin to breathe and so cold that a man's hairs became needles of ice on his head. But these bandits were not the noble brothers of the *wuxia* dramas. They were men who had turned their backs on civilized society.

"Bandits?" Huang repeated. He leaned forward to peer out the small, dirty window set in the crawler's sidewall. "Do you really think it could be?"

Huang turned back around to see the guard's answering sneer. "What *else*?"

Mouth hanging open, Huang looked back through the grimed window and watched the airship drawing ever nearer. It was hard to tell at this distance, but the long black objects slung underneath the gondola appeared to be some form of armament. Firing them would kick the airship back in the opposite direction, unsteadying it, but that would come as little comfort to the crawler hit by the blast. The crawlers were designed for mobility, not heavily armed for combat, and it wouldn't take a very large caliber cannon to do considerable damage.

Huang tightened his grip on the red saber. So much for boredom.

Huang stood at the center of the ring of crawlers, fighting the urge to run and hide.

"You all right, sir?"

Startled, Huang turned. Beside him stood the older guardsman who brought him his meals. The man had a pistol in his hand, cocked and ready, and was studying Huang with a worried expression.

"Y-yes, of course," Huang answered, perhaps too quickly. He tried to look calm and composed and knew he was failing miserably.

The guardsman nodded to the saber hanging at Huang's hip. "You know how to use that, sir?"

It was then that Huang realized that he was the only one of the two dozen or so drivers and guards assembled within the circle of the crawlers not to have a gun, sword, or knife in his hands. With an awkward motion, he reached over and grabbed hold of the saber's hilt, drawing it from the scabbard.

"Oh, yes," Huang said, with some measure of confidence. "I know how to use a blade."

The guardsman shrugged and turned away.

From overhead, one of the sentries posted atop the crawlers shouted down to the massed defenders that the airship was drawing nearer. It seemed to Huang as though it had been hours since the crawlers had pulled off the dirt track of the roadway onto a relatively level clearing, and the six vehicles laboriously maneuvered into position, forming a near-perfect circle, with the tail of one crawler abutting the nose of the next and so on. Now that he stopped to think about it, though, he realized it could not have been more than a matter of minutes altogether. Still, the waiting seemed interminable, standing with the others in the protection of the defensive ring, counting the moments until the bandits attacked.

"Here it comes!" shouted one of the sentries, and Huang

looked up to see the ragged airship hovering into view over-head. A hatch was open on one side of the gondola, and men in breather masks and insulated suits with rifles and long knives in hand began to pour out, rapelling down on cables. Huang could hear a faint noise, like the howling of distant wind, and realized he was hearing the bandits' howls and war cries even through the thin air.

As the bandits slid down on their cables and lines, directly into the defensive ring of crawlers, it occurred to Huang to doubt the wisdom of gathering all of the convoy's defenders *inside* an enclosed space. A circle of crawlers might have been an effective defense against attackers approaching overland, but it was suddenly clear to Huang that the tactics only served to hinder defenders facing attack from the air.

It was too late to do anything about it now, though. The first of the bandits hit the red sands, long knives flashing in the sun, and rushed toward the defenders.

Huang tightened his grip on his saber's hilt and tried to resist the urge to run and hide.

As Huang watched the defenders close with the bandits, it felt more like he was back in his parents' house in Fanchuan sitting over a game of elephant chess than being in a battle himself. He charted the ebb and flow of the battle with an almost unreal sense of detachment, as though it were something happening to someone else.

Huang noted that there were maybe a dozen of the bandits, so numerically at least the odds favored the defenders.

A body thumped to the ground at Huang's feet. It was one of the sentries from atop the crawlers, sputtering his last breath as blood foamed from the gunshot wound in his neck. Huang looked up and saw another of the sentries spasm in agony as sniper fire from the airship above lanced into him. In his detached fugue Huang fancied he could almost see the airship wobble with the recoil of the rifle's fire, but he was rational enough to know that the force of the rifle firing wouldn't be enough to move the airship more than fractionally. Still, the force of the bullets striking the sentries was clearly more than sufficient to remove *them* from the board.

Another sentry fell from his perch into the center of the ringed crawlers and managed to rise up on his knees, leaning heavily on the rifle he still held clutched in one hand. One of the breather-masked bandits rushing by paused just long enough to drive the point of his long knife down into the fallen sentry's shoulder, and as he kicked the rifle out from under the sentry and whipped free the gored blade of his knife, the sentry collapsed forward like a puppet whose strings had been cut.

Huang watched the sentry's blood spill out onto the red sand, eyes wide and mouth hanging open. He had seen blood, of course. It was a rare fencing tournament that did not see some scratch or cut, with blood welling up to the surface. But never before had he seen so *much*.

The sound of rifle fire boomed in Huang's ears, and he started, spinning around. One of the drivers had fired a shot at the oncoming bandits. But the driver had failed to properly brace himself against the ground before pulling the trigger and found himself hurled backward by the recoil, blundering into one of the other guards and sending them both sprawling onto the red sand.

"Come and get us!" another guard yelled with unconvincing bravado, brandishing a sword. Huang could not help but note the poor quality of the man's grip on the sword's handle. Then another shot rang out, this one from a bit farther off, and the sword-wielding guard crumpled lifeless to the ground as a cruel red flower erupted on his forehead. Huang glanced back to see one of the bandits braced against a low rise, a rifle cradled in his arms.

On Huang's other side, one of the drivers threw his knife to the ground and fell to his knees, raising his hands in supplication and begging for mercy. A few of the others apparently thought this a worthwhile tactic, for in short order they threw their own weapons down and were kneeling right alongside him, hands up and pleading for mercy.

One of the bandits unhooked the breather mask that covered the bottom half of his face and regarded the pleading drivers through the dark glass of his goggles. With the mask hanging down over one shoulder, his face was revealed to be surprisingly kind looking, his mouth spread in an easy smile, a neatly trimmed beard shading the curve of his jaw.

"Now *that* is simply embarrassing," the bandit said, chuckling, pointing with his long knife at the drivers on their knees before him.

Another bandit came to stand beside him, a tall, skeletal figure with a sword in hand. He removed his own breather mask to reveal a gaunt face, sunken cheeks, and high cheekbones. "I say kill them now, Chief, and be done with it."

The smiling bandit shook his head, laughing. "Where's the fun in *that*, Ruan?" He looked back and forth among the pleading drivers. "All right, I'll make you a deal. You'll get no clemency from the likes of us, but if you get back on your feet and pick up your arms, you can at least die with a bit of dignity, no?"

The drivers began sobbing, wringing their hands, screaming for mercy.

"*Now* can I kill them, Zhao?" the gaunt man named Ruan asked, stepping forward and raising his sword for a killing stroke.

The bandit chief shook his head, wearing an expression of distaste. "Stay your hand, Ruan. I can't stomach killing such low creatures." He spat in the dust at his feet. "Have them hog-tied and left by the side of the track. With any luck, they'll survive long enough to be picked up by the next vehicle to pass. When they tell others about our prowess and cruel efficiency, perhaps the next convoy will be even less tempted to put up a fight."

As the gaunt Ruan relayed the orders to another pair of

bandits, the man named Zhao turned to the rest of the defenders, still standing with their weapons at the ready.

"How about the rest of you, eh? Ready to wait by the wayside with your friends here, to tell the next convoy they oughtn't tangle with us? Or would you prefer to meet your end on your feet, like men?"

The defenders exchanged uneasy glances, and more than a few of them went to join the pleading supplicants on their knees, casting their arms aside.

Huang, who still stood motionless, with his red saber in his hand, watched it all unfold around him as though it were a game, or a drama acted out by players, his mind still filled with the image of the blood pouring out onto the sands.

"And you, boy?" the man called Zhao said, pointing to Huang with his chin. "Are you a man to stand and fight, or a squealing hog fit only to be tied?"

Huang looked at the drivers and guards on their knees. The fallen sentry had been on his knees when the bandit had driven his knife point-first into his shoulder, hadn't he? And this Ruan seemed ready to dispatch the rest of them just as quickly, and Zhao's mercy be damned. Could Huang trust that, if he surrendered and begged for mercy, he'd be left alive and not slaughtered like the fallen defenders had been? And even if they *were* left alive, there wasn't another convoy bound this way for another week. Could he last a week without food or water, unable to move? He wasn't in any hurry to find out.

"Well?" Zhao demanded. "Which is it?"

Huang had fought with a blade so often that he dreamed of duels, and yet he had never been forced to fight for his life. Could he do it? The sword was a tool used for sport, for *art*, not the kind of rank butchery he'd seen the bandits practice. Was Huang willing—was he *able*—to use the sword to hurt, even to kill?

To Huang's surprise, he watched the point of his red saber rise as though another man held it. His body fell into a defensive posture almost as if it were another man's body. The movements were instinctual, unexamined, years of fencing training taking over without any conscious thought on his part.

A handful of the guards were at his side, swords drawn and rifles ready. So were a couple of the drivers, with long knives and pistols in hand, and even a mechanic who carried only a heavy lug wrench in her hand.

"Well, there's *some* men among you, at least, even if some of them are women."

"Now?" Ruan asked impatiently.

The bandit chief Zhao laughed louder, and nodded. "Now!"

The bandits closed with the defenders, and the air rang with the clash of steel on steel.

Huang was only just beginning to tire when he realized that only he and one of the guards still remained on their feet. When the guard fell to a bandit's sword—a red rill cut through his tunic from shoulder to hip—Huang was the last left standing. Last left of the defenders, at least, facing almost a dozen bandits. He found himself standing at the center of a ring of sword points.

In all his years of fencing, Huang had never faced more than six opponents at one time, and then only with wooden practice swords. If he'd had the opportunity to slow down for a moment and consider his situation, he'd have been terrified. As it was, he was so occupied with the parry and thrust of turning aside blades and seeking for weakness in his opponent's form that it didn't occur to him to be afraid.

He fought on, knocking aside a sword as a bandit lunged forward, then spinning on his heel and parrying another blow from behind, then sidestepping and riposting, darting forward and scoring a hit against one of the bandits. It was a small cut on the bandit's shoulder, which in tournament play would have been a scoring hit.

When the bandit, his shoulder bloodied, bellowed in rage and rushed toward Huang, he was reminded that this *wasn't* tournament play, and that a scoring hit was meaningless in a contest of life and death.

Now, at long last, Huang began to feel the icy touch of fear.

In the end, though it took as long as it had taken the bandits to subdue all the other defenders combined, the sheer numbers overwhelmed Huang. His muscles ached; his arms and legs were covered in nicks, cuts, and bruises; and his weary fingers were numb. He had turned aside a final thrust when another bandit clubbed at his blade from the side, knocking the red saber from his hands.

A kick knocked Huang's legs out from under him, and he collapsed in a heap.

Sprawled exhausted on hands and knees, head throbbing, Huang lifted his eyes, mouth hanging slack, expecting the killing blow to fall at any moment.

But the blow didn't fall. Not yet, at any rate.

A bandit stood over him. His face was round and genial, though a wicked scar crawled up one side of his face from the corner of his mouth, making his face look frozen in a lopsided grin.

Another bandit rushed forward, holding his long knife in a two-handed grip, murder in his eyes.

"No!" The scar-faced bandit whipped out his hand and grabbed the knife wielder by the elbow, stopping the blow.

"What is it, Jue?" the other bandit said with an actual sneer curling his lip.

"Didn't you hear the chief?" the scar-faced Jue said, pointing with his chin to the other side of the circle.

The knife-wielding bandit hadn't, clearly, and neither had Huang. He turned his head, to see the bandit chief approaching, mouth open and yelling.

"Hold, I say!" Zhao had his sword sheathed at his side, a pistol in his hand.

Huang stopped breathing, his heart in his throat, expecting the bandit chief to raise the pistol and fire. To his surprise, Zhao instead stood over him, the pistol's barrel pointed to the ground, and regarded him with an approving look.

"Too admirable an opponent to kill in cold blood, wouldn't you say, Jue?"

The scar-faced bandit nodded to the bandit chief. "If you say so."

"And I do." Zhao chuckled. "And it seems ill fitting to leave such a prize hog-tied by the roadside, for all of that."

The scar-faced Jue shrugged, checking the action of his own pistol, a long-bladed knife tucked into his belt.

"What shall we do with him, then?" Zhao asked.

The gaunt bandit named Ruan joined the small circle standing over Huang, who now quivered with the terror it had taken him so long to feel. "If you've no taste for the killing, Zhao, let *me* do it." Ruan tightened his grip on his sword's hilt and eyed Huang hungrily.

Zhao seemed to consider the suggestion seriously for a moment, and Huang heard his own pulse thundering in his ears. Having held his breath so long, he now began to pant with fear, running the risk of hyperventilating.

The bandit chief finally shook his head. "No, there's been enough killing for one job, I should think." He scratched his chin through his well-trimmed beard. Then he turned and snapped his fingers at one of the bandits checking the bodies of the fallen for valuables. "Bring a length of strong cord," he commanded.

"I thought you weren't going to leave him hog-tied," said the scarred Jue.

"I'm not," Zhao answered, tucking his pistol in his belt. "I've decided we'll keep this one as a pet—and we can't take him with us without a leash, can we?"

Huang's eyes widened even farther. He wasn't sure whether the bandit chief was joking or not, and wasn't sure which was worse.

Huang found himself longing for the relative comforts of the crawler's metal benches and the comparative camaraderie of the drivers and guards who'd regarded him with naked contempt. He hadn't known how good he had it, just hours before.

Now he found himself trussed up like a chicken ready for the pot and deposited unceremoniously in a corner of the bandit airship's gondola. The dozen or so bandits—none of their number had been lost in the raid, though more than a few of them had bandages over wounds received at the end of Huang's red blade—went about stowing the booty prized from the holds of the crawlers. And though they passed flasks from hand to hand in rough good humor, they did not boast of their exploits or brag to one another about their martial prowess in defeating the defenders. These were men doing a job, nothing more.

After the bandit chief had Huang tied hand and foot and carried to the waiting airship, the bandits seemed essentially to have forgotten their new "pet." Or if he was not forgotten, they seemed to think so little of him that they scarcely deigned to notice his presence.

Huang's wrists and ankles chafed against the rough cords that bound them, but while his extremities grew numb from the awkward position and lack of movement, it seemed that the bandits had not tied the bonds so tightly that the blood was cut off. So he wouldn't be losing fingers or toes to poor circulation, at least. Small comfort, especially considering that the bandits might just decide to toss him out the hatch once the craft was airborne, at which point the fact that his hands and feet were still amply supplied with blood would hardly be much consolation.

Eventually, the bandits all returned to the airship, evidently having picked the convoy clean of the most valuable or useful items. They seemed to Huang to have concentrated on foodstuffs, fuel, and armament, leaving behind dry goods like clothing and textiles. They had, however, retrieved from the crawlers' engines various grease-covered mechanical components. Huang wouldn't have been surprised to discover that the whole airship had been constructed from such salvage, after seeing its interior up close. The whole affair had a jury-rigged look to it, bits and pieces of other vehicles and devices repurposed to the bandits' needs. The control mechanisms at the helm, for example, appeared to incorporate a velocipede wheel and the steering column of a ground car, while the knobs from a household oven appeared to control the airship's lift and forward motion.

The bandits stepped over and around Huang as they boarded the airship. Even through the sturdy fabric of his Green Standard Army officer's tunic and trousers, the metal of the deck was cold beneath him. The deckplates began to vibrate, subtly at first and more noticeably as moments wore on, and Huang could only assume that the engines at the rear of the airship had begun to thrum to life. The hatch was closed, and the bandits began to take their places around the cabin, securing themselves for flight.

Huang watched as the bandits fastened the stays of their insulated suits tighter around them and secured their breather masks around their faces. Most wore goggles, so that with the masks in place over their mouths and noses, their faces were almost completely obscured. He looked from the nearest of the bandits to the hatch, a thin and flimsy door of metal with small bars of daylight visible around the edges.

With a shock of horror Huang realized that the gondola was not pressurized.

Even as rugged and sturdy as it was, the fabric of his uniform was scarcely suited for the kind of temperatures that the bandits' insulated suits were evidently designed to withstand. And Huang knew from experience how thin the air got in the upper altitudes, from his one attempt at flying a kite over Fanchuan. Without a breather mask, the thin air would do little more than freeze his lungs; it would be insufficient to sustain him. His death would be slow but exceedingly painful.

Huang overcame his fears and tried calling out to the bandits. But he found his words swallowed by the mounting drone of the engines.

"Hey!" he tried again, rocking back and forth on the deckplates, trying unsuccessfully to rise up on his knees. He was on his side, his hands tied behind his back and his legs lashed together. *"Hey!"*

He could scarcely hear his own voice in his ears, so loud was the sound of the engines.

Now he was thrashing back and forth in earnest but succeeding only in rising up far enough that he bruised his shoulder when he fell back on the deck again.

"Hey! Help me! *I don't have a mask!*"

If he could not feel his throat made raw by the force of his shouts, Huang would not have been able to guess that he was even making a sound.

Through the grimy windows of the airship, each of them a different size and shape from the last, Huang saw the ground begin to drop away as the airship rose.

"HEY!"

Huang wasn't sure whether his shouts had been heard or whether the bandit chief just happened to finally remember he was there, but Zhao at last turned his way. Then he leaned close to one of the other bandits, pointing in Huang's direction, and made a few quick motions with his hands. The bandit nodded and then clomped across the deckplates toward Huang.

As the bandit approached, Huang tried to rise up. It occurred to him that it was just as likely that the bandit had come to toss him out the hatch as it was that he'd come to help. Zhao might have changed his mind about keeping his new "pet," after all. He tensed, unable to resist, teeth gritted.

The bandit tugged a spare breather mask from a pocket of his suit, and then crouched down to fit it over Huang's mouth and nose. Then, distractedly, he tugged what looked like a horse blanket from atop a crate and draped this over Huang's supine form. Then the bandit went back off to join his fellows.

Huang was taking short and shallow breaths, but he could begin to feel the warm, thick air of the mask fill his lungs with every inhalation. And while the horse blanket did nothing to prevent his body heat from bleeding into the cold metal of the deckplates, it at least shielded him from the worst effects of the cold air in the cabin as the thin wind whistled through the visible gaps in the gondola's hull.

When the airship reached its destination, Huang was near frozen, teeth chattering and lips blue. But at least he was alive.

• • •

Finally, the airship began to descend. Looking up through the portholes from his vantage point on the floor, his eyes bloodshot and stinging from the cold air, Huang could see the peak of a mountain heaving into view. At first, Huang thought that the pilot meant to land the craft on the mountain's slopes, but then the light dimmed on all sides as the airship continued to drop *through* the mountain.

It took Huang a moment to realize what had happened. There was a kind of cave or fissure near the top of the mountain, wide enough for the airship to drop down into it without touching either side.

How long the airship continued to descend Huang couldn't say, but the airship was moving slower all the time, so that even if it was for several moments, the distance might not have been very far. All he could say for certain was that the space beyond the grimy windows grew black as pitch, and then after a time began to grow lighter again. He could see rough stone walls dimly through the windows, and as the light grew brighter the walls receded farther away on all sides. It was as though they were descending through a chimney into the larger oven below.

Finally, with a jolt, the airship came to a stop, and the pitch of the howling engines began to descend as the rotors slowed and stopped. Having become so used to the vibration of the deck and the howl of the engines, Huang found it strange to be surrounded by sudden silence, as though he had been struck deaf. Then Zhao began shouting orders, and the illusion was shattered.

The bandits kept their masks in place, their thermal suits still fastened, and began to unload their plundered cargo. When a large section of the airship had been cleared, a pair of bandits hauled Huang indecorously from the airship, one grabbing his ankles and the other his shoulders, and stacked him outside on the cold stone floor with the rest of the booty.

Now Huang had a better view of their new surroundings. His image of a chimney and oven was not far off. They were in a roughly spherical chamber, large enough to dwarf the airship behind him, which was surmounted by a tapering passage that rose up through the living rock. High overhead was a bright patch of daylight.

The airship had come to rest on the roughly level floor of the chamber, near the exact center. The walls of the chamber were pocked here and there with holes of various shapes and sizes, some too small for a grown man to climb through, and some large enough to admit a dozen bandits walking abreast. The holes reminded Huang of something, and it took a moment before he could work out just what. They were like the bubbles that formed and popped in a vat of boiling tar, or cake batter, or any other viscous liquid that air passed through. Was the chamber the result of volcanic activity, the passages and holes—even the chamber itself—the product of hot gases passing through molten rock?

Huang hadn't paid enough attention to his studies to

know much about geology, nor remember whether the Three Sovereigns mountains were volcanic or not. But it seemed a reasonable assumption. However, unless the mountain were suddenly to become an *active* volcano, Huang was hard pressed to think of a reason why that was important to his present circumstances. He had far more immediate concerns than the geological origins of the cave.

An arrangement of steel, aluminum, and *wood* had been constructed in the mouth of one of the largest of the holes, right at ground level. It looked to Huang like a metal cork in a jar's neck, but when part of the assembly swung open, and light poured out from within, Huang realized it was instead some sort of door.

The air in the chamber was thin, but not as cold as the upper reaches had been, and sound was muffled at a distance. With the door open, the bandits began to shift the plunder from the piles outside the airship through the open door and beyond. They seemed to move almost in silence, since the sounds of boxes and barrels and such hitting the ground did not carry as far as the place where Huang lay.

Finally, it was Huang's turn, and once more a pair of bandits lifted him roughly in the air, one at his head and one at his feet. He swayed between them like a rolled-up carpet as they hauled him across the chamber floor to the open doorway. Only a small handful of bandits remained in the chamber now, tending to the airship's engines and hull, repairing small damages incurred in transit.

When Huang and his bearers passed through the door, the metal assemblage swung shut once more with a muffled clang. Dropped once more on the floor, Huang found himself in a narrow corridor crowded with bandits and their booty. At the far end of the corridor was another door, which was likewise shut.

Suddenly Huang's eyes stung and his ears rang. Sounds grew even more muffled for a moment, and Huang panicked, not sure what was going on. Then his ears popped, and the volume of the sundry noises around him jumped higher, roaring in his ears. He realized it was a change in air pressure that he'd been feeling. It was difficult to tell with the breather mask still strapped over his face, but it seemed to him as though the air within the corridor was growing thicker, and warmer, too.

The door at the far end of the corridor began to swing open, and as it did the bandits pulled their goggles from their eyes and tugged off their masks. They began unhooking the fasteners of their thermal suits, in unhurried, economical motions.

One of the bandits absently reached down and snatched the breather mask from off Huang's face, and Huang held his breath for a long moment before taking deep lungfuls of the thick, warm air. It smelled somewhat moldy and stale, like a locker room that had been shut up for a season, but it was better than the crisp thin air of the upper reaches, which was more like a forest of icy knives.

The corridor was an airlock, Huang realized. And the

space beyond, whatever it might be, was heated and pressurized.

The bandit chief Zhao strode over to where Huang lay, as the other bandits began to transfer the plunder. Huang did not fail to notice that Zhao now wore Huang's red saber slung from his hip.

"What do they call you, eh?"

Huang only blinked, feeling sensation return slowly to his cold-numbed face, feet, and hands.

"What's your name, pet?" Zhao barked, his tone growing more severe, and nudged Huang in the side with his toe.

"H-Huang," he managed tremulously. "Huang Fei."

Zhao shook his head angrily. "No, no, that won't do. I once labored under a foreman, name of Huang, who cheated me out of my wages. Rat bastard." He paused and spat in the dust at his feet. "And Fei? Even worse. A man called Fei once stole from me the woman I loved. I'd sooner kill any man named Fei as look at him."

Huang shifted uneasily on the cold floor, looking up at the glowering bandit chief. The good humor he wore when Huang had been taken captive seemed to have abated, leaving a more prickly demeanor.

"What other names do you have, eh?" Zhao poked the toe of his boot again into Huang's side. "What's your mother call you, what milk name?"

Huang lowered his eyes to the ground, and muttered, "Hummingbird."

"What's that?" Zhao leaned over, cupping a hand by his ear. "Didn't quite hear that."

"Hummingbird," Huang said louder, the color rising in his cheeks.

Zhao nodded appreciatively. He snatched a knife from his belt, crouched down, and sliced through the bonds on Huang's feet. Then he hauled Huang to a standing position, though Huang wavered unsteadily on his feet as the blood began slowly to move freely again.

"Much better." Zhao clapped Huang on the back, nearly sending him toppling over once more. "Hummingbird is a fine name. That's it, then." He turned and shouted to the bandits hauling the plunder. "Our pet's name is Hummingbird, men."

The bandits glanced uninterestedly at Huang and went back to their labors.

Zhao flipped the knife up in the air before him, end over end, and then snatched it out of midair. He wheeled Huang around, and for a moment Huang thought the bandit chief might stab him in the back. But instead he felt the bonds on his wrists falling away as well, and his arms fell to his sides.

"Come along, then, Hummingbird," Zhao said, as Huang tried to rub feeling back into his chafed, bruised wrists. "Get to work."

The bandit chief shoved Huang toward a tower of barrels near the wall of the corridor.

"Even pets work around here, Hummingbird." Zhao slid

his knife back into its sheath, reached down, and picked up a large wooden crate, which he balanced on his shoulder. "If you want to eat, then shift." Zhao stamped his foot. "Shift!"

Huang turned dispiritedly toward the barrels, shoulders slumped. Behind him the bandit chief laughed again.

Perhaps freezing to death in the airship wouldn't have been so bad, after all.

The bandits' mountain home was for Huang in those early hours a confusion of tunnels and chambers and corridors. He went where he was told, lugging heavy crates and barrels and boxes, shuttling from one end of the complex to the other. The bandits all addressed him only as "Hummingbird," and even then only to bark orders at him or to shout at him to clear out of their way.

Zhao was usually there in the thick of it, directing traffic, telling the bandits which barrels and crates went where. And when Zhao was away, the authority seemed to fall to the scar-faced Jue, or to the gaunt and skeletal Ruan, who appeared to be the ranking lieutenants in the operation. There were between two and three dozen people in the complex of caves, as near as Huang could work out—men and women, the oldest of them perhaps the age of Huang's grandparents, the youngest no more than a few years older than Huang himself. When they stripped out of their heavy insulated thermal suits, it turned out that a number of the bandits that Huang had taken for men were in fact women, though they were as rough around the edges as the women Huang had encountered in the convoy. But Huang also noted that Zhao and his lieutenants treated the women in the company as the equals of the men, both in terms of the tasks given them and in the effort expected of them.

The mountain, Huang learned, was Mount Shennong, the southernmost in the Three Sovereigns range. The cave complex, which the bandits called the Aerie, had originally been constructed by miners boring into the mountain searching for precious ores. The comparatively meager tunnels cut by the miners had eventually intersected with the extensive and naturally occurring passages and caves deeper in the mountain. The original mining tunnels were evidently still to be found near the base of the mountain, though they had been long before sealed off, the only remaining entrance the chimneylike passage the airship had entered, which the bandits called the skylight.

Many of the bandits, Huang noticed, were missing fingers. Some had only one ear, and a few had none at all. Many were scarred, most were missing teeth, and a few wore patches over one eye. More than a few of the bandits walked with pronounced limps, and one or two had arms that were twisted and gnarled like a crab's claw, though no less useful for all of that.

Who were these rough creatures, these men and women who had turned their backs on civilization? It was almost as if they *had* surrendered their humanity, as the rumors suggested, and as a result their bodies came less and less to resemble those of decent men and women.

What would become of him, Huang wondered, held prisoner by such creatures?

It was difficult to judge the passage of time deep within the cave complex of the Aerie, but Huang thought it must have been near nightfall when the last of the plunder was finally squared away and stored, and the bandits gathered together for their evening meal.

Huang was brought along as well, though with his labors finished the bandits had tied a length of cord securely around his neck and led him like a dog on a leash. His feet were unfettered, but his hands were tied wrist to wrist in front of him. It could have been worse, Huang knew. At least with his hands in front of him, he was able to lift a cup to his lips or feed himself if the opportunity arose.

The bandits came together in a wide chamber with a high ceiling, lit brightly by lanterns strung up on lines secured to the walls. There were three low tables arranged in a horseshoe shape in the middle of the room, with thin cushions ringing the perimeter of the shape on the ground. The bandits seated themselves around these tables, all facing inward, with the bandit chief Zhao and his two lieutenants at the head table.

Two of the youngest bandits went to work ferrying to the

table steaming bowls of rice and soup, trays piled high with salted fish, plates of dumplings, and what looked like bits of chicken and pork on skewers. There must have been kitchens somewhere in the Aerie that Huang had not yet seen, as once the tables were heavily laden with food an older man and a younger woman appeared in the chamber, their faces beet red and sweating, no doubt from an oven's heat, their clothes stained with flour, grease, and sauces. They took their place at the end of the table, and then the meal began.

The food smelled delicious, and for all Huang knew, it tasted so, as well. He couldn't say for certain, having been tied to the far wall, out of reach of anything edible. He considered pleading, but remembering what had befallen the drivers who had begged the bandits for clemency—had it really only been earlier that day?—he decided it better to remain silent. He crouched against the wall, and then when the muscles in his thighs and calves began to ache, slid down into an undignified but marginally more comfortable sitting position.

Huang's stomach rumbled, and his throat ached with thirst. The bandits worked their steady way through the meal, laughing and joking, clinking cups in toasts, singing songs, reciting jokes and obscene poems and infantile riddles.

Despite finding himself in this strange mountain stronghold, tied to the wall like a dog, Huang couldn't help but find all of this strangely familiar. Sitting outside a ring of fellowship, on his own. Then he remembered those nights on the convoy, and the jokes and songs and laughter of the guards and drivers. Was this really so different, after all?

Finally the meal came to an end, and Huang thought he could control his hunger no longer. He rose up on his knees as the bandits climbed to their feet, and held his hands out in supplication.

The bandit chief Zhao strolled over, patting his full belly with one hand, carrying a bowl in the other.

"We haven't forgotten you, Hummingbird," Zhao said, chuckling. Then he bent down and dropped the bowl clattering on the floor in front of Huang. "Eat up, now. You've got to keep up your strength. Tomorrow won't be *near* so relaxing as today, I assure you."

As the bandit chief strode away, Huang inspected the contents of the bowl. It was half filled with murky water, little puddles of grease floating on the surface around a half-eaten chicken leg, a hunk of stringy pork, and a partially gnawed fish head.

Huang longed for the undercooked rice and rancid fish heads of the convoy dinners, but he held his nose and ate the meager feast as quickly as he was able.

Huang was left to sleep tied to the wall in the chamber overnight. He slept fitfully, if at all, sprawled on the hard stone floor, shivering in his thin uniform. The next morning, the scar-faced Jue came and untied Huang from the wall, and put him to work once more. Of all the bandits, Jue seemed the friendliest. Or, if not friendly, then perhaps the least threatening. Perhaps it was the scar that, though ragged and gruesome on its own, in place made the bandit look as though he were always smiling. Taken with his round, almost babyish face, it made Jue seem almost like an overgrown child.

Friendly or not, though, he was a taskmaster when it came to assigning the bandits' prisoner chores, and Huang found himself run ragged through the course of the day, doing great piles of reeking laundry, cleaning the kitchen after meals—pots and utensils as well as floors and counters—and helping a pair of mechanically minded bandits move spare engine components out into the hangar where the airship was parked. It was during this last task that Huang was taken to the place where the breather masks and thermal suits were stored when not in use, a locked cabinet not far from the airlock corridor. He made careful note of the cabinet's location and watched attentively as the bandits unlocked and then relocked the cabinet door.

Huang's thinking was that, if he were able to get hold of a breather mask and thermal suit, having somehow slipped his bonds and eluded recapture, he might be able to make it out into the hangar and from there into one of the innumerous passages that opened onto it. With a considerable amount of luck, he might be able to find the old disused mining tunnel through which the cave complex had originally been discovered. If he found the tunnel, he might be able to get past the obstruction at the other end, and from there escape the mountain and the Aerie altogether.

But in the hours leading to the evening meal, Huang found a much more pressing need for a breather mask when he was given the task of cleaning out the Aerie's inefficient latrines. Hours spent up to his knees in offal and muck, trying unsuccessfully not to gag. When he was finally through, he was allowed to clean himself off as best he was able, but after dumping bucket after bucket of water over his head and changing from his soiled uniform into a set of ragged bandit cast-off clothing, he was still unable to get the stench of it from his nostrils. And when he ate the picked-over leavings and table scraps that evening, it all tasted of bile and dung on his tongue, so much did the lingering smell pervade his senses.

That night, he slept once more tied to the wall, shivering in his ill-fitting cast-off rags.

The following days passed much the same, with Huang greeting the day lying cramped and uncomfortable on the stone floor, spending the day doing various noisome and distasteful tasks, and ending with a bowl of scraps and greasy water.

As his body was busied with mindless, repetitive tasks, Huang's mind often wandered. He entertained elaborate fantasies of rescue, of a battalion of Bannermen rapelling down the Aerie's skylight, guns and swords in hand, to arrest or kill all the bandits—depending on Huang's mood when fantasizing—and liberate their lone prisoner.

Of course, in his calmer, more reasonable moments, Huang knew full well that it was likely that no one knew that he was the bandits' prisoner, since the hog-tied guards and drivers—if they'd survived even *this* long—would not yet have been found by a passing convoy. And even if anyone *did* know that he was their prisoner, the bandits' mountain stronghold was evidently entirely secret, and if its location *was* known, it seemed well enough fortified, naturally and by design, to withstand most any attack.

No, if Huang was to be freed from captivity, it would have to be by his own hand.

One night, when delivering the customary bowl of greasy water, leftover rice, and half-eaten scraps of meat, the bandit chief Zhao lingered in front of Huang. He still wore the red saber at his side and fingered its hilt appreciatively. Across the room, Jue and a few other bandits still sat around the table, finishing a jar of wine.

"Hummingbird," he said, like a man addressing a dog, "I must admit that this is one fine sword you've given me. I can't help but wonder where a simple solder of the Green Standard might have obtained such a blade."

Huang's fingers tightened around the edges of his bowl. As if he had *given* the bandits *anything*.

"Well, speak up, Hummingbird." Zhao nudged him with a booted toe. "How did you come by this sword, eh?"

When Huang spoke, it was in a voice barely above a

whisper, as he always used when answering the bandits. "A gift from Governor Ouyang."

"Did you . . . Did you say . . . Ouyang?" Zhao tightened his fist around the sword's hilt.

Huang looked up, meeting the bandit chief's eyes for the first time in the exchange. He nodded.

"Ouyang?" Zhao repeated. His lips drew into a tight line, and his eyebrows narrowed. "That *wretch*? That foul pile of *dung*?! *That* Ouyang?"

Huang answered instinctively, without thinking. "No, the governor-general is an honorable man."

Zhao's face flushed red, and his eyes widened. "Honorable? *Honorable*?!" He turned and snapped his fingers at those still seated around the table. "Jue, turn your head this way."

Jue shrugged but turned to face them.

Zhao looked down at Huang, stabbing a finger toward Jue. "See that scar? Do you? That's what Ouyang's *honor* is worth." He held up his own left hand, and for the first time Huang saw that Zhao's ring finger on that hand was missing after the second knuckle, ending in a knobby lump of flesh. "And my finger, in the bargain." He turned and pointed to a bandit who sat opposite Jue, one of his arms twisted into a crab's claw. "And his arm." He pointed to another of the bandits, who sat with a cup held frozen halfway to his lips. "And his sons."

Zhao turned his gaze back to Huang. But while Huang didn't answer, his expression no doubt made evident the lack of credence he held for Zhao's words.

The bandit chief narrowed his eyes. "What do you know of mines, Hummingbird?"

Huang shrugged, not even bothering to speak. It was easier to say what he *didn't* know about mines, which was essentially "everything."

"Miners work tirelessly," Zhao went on, his hand still on the hilt of the red sword, "day and night, season after season, to extract all the substances society needs to function." He held up his left hand, and began extending fingers one at a time, counting off. "Everything from heavy metals with which to fabricate buildings and vehicles, to hidden pockets of frozen water at the poles, to the chemical constituents of the very air we breathe. And it isn't only with the sweat of their brow and back that miners pay. No. Some miners lose limbs in mining accidents, some lose sight in an eye or the ability to hear, some bear scars from faulty machinery or badly mended broken bones. And nearly every miner has lost a family member down in the mines, whether father, brother, or son, mother, sister, or daughter. They work hard and are rewarded only with pain and misery."

Huang couldn't help himself. He scoffed and answered instinctively again, scarcely above a whisper. "What would *thieves* know of hard work?"

Zhao's hand on the sword's hilt was a white-knuckled fist, and he snarled while drawing the blade partway from the scabbard, eyes flashing. Huang tensed, expecting a killing stroke to fall at any moment.

"*I* worked in a mine." The bandit chief spoke slowly, deliberately, like he was talking to a child or an imbecile. "That's what I know of it. I was a miner until Ouyang forced me from it."

Huang's eyebrows shot up. "What?"

Zhao raised an eyebrow of his own. "You're *surprised*? How little you know." He glanced over at the bandits seated around the table, who were now following their chief's conversation with mounting interest, their expressions dark. "Most of those living in the Aerie were once miners." He motioned to Jue and the others with a dip of his head. "And the rest were cargo loaders, airship mechanics, and so on—skilled laborers every one. And all of us driven from our homes and jobs by the oppressive tactics of your *honorable* Governor Ouyang. The great governor-general, who harasses businesses that don't pay his bribes and favors those that do. And may the ancestors protect any miner or mechanic who makes the mistake of trying to organize his fellow laborers against the unfair bosses who paid the governor-general's bribes and haven't the money left over to meet the payroll. Those of us who survived encounters with the governor-general's strikebreakers still bear the scars, and we were the lucky ones."

Huang glanced over at Jue and the others, and saw that their eyes were half-lidded, as with remembered pain. The bandit holding the jar of wine slammed it down forcefully onto the table, sending a thin stream of liquid sloshing from the jar's neck.

"May Ouyang rot in hell," one of the bandits cursed in a harsh voice, and around him the other bandits dipped their heads in agreement.

Zhao drew the sword from the scabbard and held its red-tinted blade horizontally in front of him. The light glinted on the firebird engraved there so that it seemed to dance. Again Huang tensed, fearing the killing stroke, but instead Zhao just studied the blade closely, as though finding secret messages written on it.

"If I'd known this was once the governor-general's blade, I might not have picked it up." He glanced to Huang. "And had I known you carried *his* blade, I might not have spared your life, after all." He glanced to the other bandits and then back to Huang on the floor. "But I find I like the feel of the sword at my hip, and you've proven useful in doing the tasks none of us care to perform, so perhaps you both have your uses, at that." He lowered the point of the sword, directed at Huang's chest, and narrowed his eyes. "But if either you or the sword cease to be useful, Hummingbird, know that I've no compunction against snapping either of you in half and tossing you in the latrine."

With that, Zhao slammed the sword back into the scabbard, turned on his heel, and marched out of the chamber. When he had gone, the bandits at the table exchanged meaningful glances, shooting dark looks Huang's way, and then followed their chief out.

Left alone with his table scraps, Huang felt an icy lump of fear growing in his gut.

Huang needed to escape, and soon.

He had survived this long only at the bandit chief's whim, and it seemed certain that it was only a matter of time before Zhao's mood shifted and Huang found himself no longer a valued "pet" and instead ended up spitted on the end of his own sword.

The key, he was sure, was the locked cabinet of breather masks and insulated suits. If he could gain access to that, he'd be one step closer to making good his escape.

The problem, of course, lay in the word *locked*.

On three different occasions Huang had been ordered to assist the mechanics working on the airship in the hangar, and all three times he had stood by while the mechanics opened the locked cabinet and broke out the necessary masks and suits. He'd gotten a good look at the lock on two of the occasions, but seeing what he was up against hadn't made him any more confident of his chances.

The cabinet was secured with a combination lock. There were three wheels, each with ideograms engraved around its circumference. The lock was shaped like a stylized dog, the wheels forming the dog's belly and chest. As near as Huang could tell, the lock was forged steel, and therefore essentially unbreakable as far as he was concerned. The only way he'd be able to get it open would be to move the wheels in the proper combination to open the lock.

There were several problems with that plan. First, Huang didn't know the combination. If this lock was anything like the other combination locks he'd seen over the years, when the wheels were in the correct positions, the ideograms would spell out a word or phrase. Even if Huang knew the combination, though, he still had the second problem to contend with: he didn't know *where* the wheels were to line up. Combination locks of this type had a second level of security beyond the combination itself, which was that there were no marks to indicate where the entered combination should be aligned. If the wheels were off by only a few degrees, then the lock would remain unopened.

So all that remained for Huang to do was to find the combination, discover the proper wheel alignment, and get to the cabinet when no bandits were around to stop him.

Of course, if he got *that* far, he'd still need to get the heavy steel doors open, get into the airlock corridor, open *another* heavy steel door, get out into the hangar, reach one of the cave mouths, navigate the caves, find the disused mine shaft, and hope against hope that he could remove the obstruction blocking the shaft entrance.

And survive long enough once he was outside in the trackless wilderness that he could be rescued or reach civilization on his own.

All without the bandits catching him.

Easy.

Well, easier than cleaning the latrines again, at any rate.

Huang finally got his break a few days later.

All morning the Aerie had been abuzz with activity. It seemed that Zhao had received word of a particularly valuable shipment in a convoy spotted a short distance off. It was a merchant shipment, leaving Forking Paths and bound for the Southern Fastness. Since these were merchants and not imperial bureaucrats safeguarding the shipment, though, the merchant convoy was much better protected and armed than had been the Green Standard convoy of which Huang had been a part. Instead of just the dozen bandits who had accompanied Zhao on the earlier raid, therefore, nearly the whole complement of bandits in the Aerie would be taken along on this foray.

Huang was run ragged all morning, helping the bandits load and secure their arms and armament in the airship. Provisions sufficient for a two-day journey were stowed away in the gondola, and enough fuel to reach Tianfei Valley and back were rolled into the airship's hold in great steel drums.

Virtually all of the bandits were being employed in this foray—the cooks and mechanics, men and women, young and old. Only a few bandits, either too infirm or too injured to be of any use, were left behind at the Aerie. And Huang, of course.

When Zhao and the others left the relative comfort of the cave complex to load into the airship in the hangar, the bandit chief stopped to visit Huang. The prisoner had been tied up in his customary position along the wall in the dining chamber, and a day's worth of table scraps and a bowl of greasy water had been set in front of him like food left out for a dog locked at home while his masters went away for the day.

"No nonsense while I'm away, Hummingbird," Zhao warned, fastening the stays of his insulated thermal suit, his breather mask dangling from one ear. "Consider this a little vacation, a respite for a day or two from your normal chores. Generous of us, isn't it?" The bandit chief laughed, and then strode out of the dining chamber to join the others in the airlock corridor.

Muffled by the distance, Huang heard the steel door open and close. Now he was alone in the Aerie with only one or two bandits, and those so infirm that they were practically bed-ridden.

If ever he was going to have an opportunity to escape, it was now.

The first hurdle was the cord securing him to the wall. This was simple enough to manage, comparatively. Since the bandits had first captured him, Huang had been careful never to attempt removing the bonds or untying the knots while in their sight, but when he was left on his own, he had experimented with the knots as long as he still had feeling left in his overworked fingers. He'd found, after a few days' trying, that he could untie and retie the simple knots securing him to the wall with relative ease. He had always tied the knots securely once more before the bandits returned, to cover the evidence.

Now he had only to untie the knots and slip loose his bonds and he was free to leave the dining chamber and make for the locked cabinet.

The infirm and injured bandits appeared to be abed, so fortune was with Huang. He reached the steel door to the airlock, and the nearby locked cabinet, without encountering any resistance.

Now he had only to accomplish the impossible and unlock the cabinet.

It was not as impossible, though, as Huang had originally thought.

He still did not know the combination, but on two different occasions he'd heard the bandits say something about wanting gold while opening the cabinet. Once the bandit had paused with the lock in his hands, evidently having forgotten the combination, and the other bandit prompted him by asking, "Do you want the gold?" Upon hearing that cryptic phrase, the bandit smiled and nodded, and then spun the wheels and opened the lock. On the other occasion, the bandit had chuckled ruefully when opening the cabinet, saying, "I sometimes wish there *was* gold in here, and not just these damned stinking masks."

Huang's guess, then, was that the word or phrase that the ideograms on the wheels combined to form had something to do with gold.

As he lifted the dog-shaped lock in his hands, its tail a thick loop of steel that connected to the back of its head, he saw in short order that he was right. One of the ideograms engraved on the last of the three wheels was in fact the symbol for *gold*. Whatever the combination, then, it would include that symbol.

Which meant he was a third of the way there. Not counting the correct alignment, of course.

There were eight symbols engraved on each of the wheels, it appeared. Even though he knew one, that meant there were still sixty-four more possible combinations. And something like a hundred possible positions in which the wheels could be aligned. A brute-force attempt of every combination, then, would mean *thousands* of attempts. He'd eluded resistance this long, but even if he was able to stumble on the right combination and alignment before the airship returned, he was bound to be found out by one of the few bandits remaining at the Aerie in the interim.

So he would have to be smart.

He wished his brothers were here, who had a much better

head for this sort of thing than he did. Or his old fencing partner Kenniston. This was exactly the kind of puzzle that Kenniston used to do for fun. When they weren't fencing, Huang would most often be off drinking and making time with attractive young ladies, while Kenniston amused himself with riddles and puzzles. Kenniston could never beat Huang at elephant chess, but any other game that demanded logic to solve was Kenniston's own domain. But Kenniston was off somewhere being an elite Bannerman, while Huang was trapped in a bandits' hidden camp with the smell of dung perpetually in his nostrils.

One limitation of this kind of combination lock, Huang knew, was that the word or phrase spelled out by the wheels couldn't be random. It needed to be something actually used in spoken or written language. Which meant that he could eliminate anything that was gibberish with the symbol for *gold* at the end. That seemed to eliminate at least half of the options, if not more, assuming that the combination wasn't a real word that simply wasn't in Huang's vocabulary—which certainly wasn't impossible.

Maybe there was another clue in the things he'd overheard. The bandits had talked about wanting gold. Was that of any use?

Huang almost shouted with joy when he found the symbol for *want* on the middle wheel. He remembered himself just in time, or else he'd have attracted the attention of the bandits who, injured or infirm or no, would doubtless have been able to subdue him with pistols and rifles in hand.

So the combination was most likely a phrase, having something to do with wanting gold. Something *want gold* or Something *want the gold* or Something *wanting gold*. Two down and three to go.

The only problem was, none of the eight ideograms engraved on the first wheel made any sense. None of them, combined with the two known variables, produced anything about someone wanting gold. They just produced gibberish, all but one that said . . .

His breath caught when he realized what he was seeing.

The first wheel, turned to the only ideogram that made any kind of sense, produced a phrase that was actually quite clever, in retrospect.

I don't want the gold.

Huang couldn't help himself. He laughed. Here was a lock designed to keep someone out, and the combination was a phrase that meant that the person entering it didn't want the valuables within. Was that some kind of Zen Buddhist koan or just an ironic joke?

He had the combination, and it had taken him only . . . How long? It was hard to say for sure, but by the way his stomach was grumbling, it seemed to have been much longer than he'd realized. Hours, at least.

There was no time to waste. Huang began testing the

hundred or so different alignments. Unfortunately, here brute force *was* the only option, so Huang went to work moving the wheels into a position, tugging on the dog's steel tail, and then, when the lock failed to release, carefully moving the wheels another fraction and trying again.

And again. And again. And again.

When the lock finally popped and the cabinet swung open on squeaking hinges, Huang wanted to shout with joy. Then, on seeing the cabinet's contents, he wanted to howl in despair. It was more a matter of fatigue than stealth that he kept silent and did neither.

There were no insulated thermal suits in the cabinet, and only one breather mask. Worse, the mask was not hung carefully on a hook, but flung carelessly onto the floor of the cabinet. And it was easy to see why. The mask was cracked, and there were visible rents in the tubing.

Only then did it occur to Huang that he'd never seen more than two dozen of the masks and suits in the cabinet, and with nearly all of the bandits suited up and on the airship on this latest raid, there wouldn't be any extras left behind. The injured and infirm had been left behind because there weren't enough masks and suits to go around, not just because of their poor health.

Huang didn't have a choice. He'd have to make do as best he could.

He began by tearing strips from the cuffs of his ragged cast-off tunic. These he tied as tightly as possible around the gaps in the tubing. Then he tore another strip, wadded it up, and stuffed it into the crack in the front of the mask. It wasn't perfect, but with any luck it might hold for a while.

Slipping the mask first over one ear and then the other, he snugged it into place over his nose and mouth and then went to work on the steel door.

Huang managed to get both doors opened and closed without attracting the attention of the bandits. Precisely how, he would never know, but he presumed that they were either too deep in the complex to hear the noise or had just assumed that one of the other bandits who'd stayed behind had done it. Whatever the case, Huang was through the airlock corridor and out into the hangar.

The lights were off, and the only illumination in the huge space was the small bit of sunshine that trickled down from the chimney-light skylight overhead. The hangar was twilight gray like the desert at night with only one moon in the sky. Huang could just barely make out the oil stains on the stone floor where the airship was customarily parked, and the darker shadows of the passage mouths in the dark gray walls.

Huang's stomach grumbled, and he wished for the hundredth time that he'd had the opportunity to prepare before making the escape attempt. As he'd formulated his plans these last days, he'd decided that his best chance at survival lay in securing a supply of food and water before trying to leave the Aerie. However, the unexpected departure of the airship and bandits from the mountain had forced him to accelerate his schedule and had left no time to get supplies. He'd have tried to obtain some before making this last-minute attempt, but the kitchen lay on the far side of the complex from the dining chamber, and the quarters of the injured and infirm bandits lay in between. He'd brought with him the few scraps Zhao had left in his bowl, stuffed in his pockets, but he'd munched on these while trying to work out the combination and the alignment, and had none left.

At least he had been able to get a lantern before opening the airlock, finding one hanging on a hook near the door. He lit it now, and the greenish light of the chemicals burning within played across the floor and walls of the hangar.

Huang wasn't sure which of the passages was most likely to lead to the mine shaft, but one was as good as another. It was likely to be large enough for a man to crawl into, at least, since the miners had originally come this way, but it was a moot point since Huang *couldn't* get into any of the passages too small for a man to enter. So Huang simply picked the closest passage of sufficient size, a dark round shadow on the wall a short distance off, and went in. There was no point in waiting around for someone to discover him gone.

Huang checked the jury-rigged repairs to his breather mask, turned up the lantern's light, and entered the cave.

• • •

The breather mask failed before the lantern did, but it was a close race.

At first, Huang thought he was simply getting fatigued, his breathing becoming labored, his head starting to swim. He'd been descending the gently sloping passage for some time. He wasn't sure how long, only that it seemed as if his whole world had shrunk to a roughly cylindrical cave, the walls close enough that he couldn't stretch out his arms in both directions at once and had to take care not to bump his head on the ceiling, with nothing but dark shadows beyond the small circle of sickly green light cast by the lantern. His teeth had stopped chattering some time before, though his fingers and toes were numb with the cold, and his dry eyes stung.

He stopped occasionally, leaning against the wall of the passage, catching his breath before continuing on, trying to ignore the aches of his protesting muscles, the cramps in his legs. It was when he almost nodded off, sleeping standing up with his shoulder against the wall and the lantern almost slipping from his limp grasp, that he realized that he wasn't managing to catch his breath at all. Quite the contrary. His breath, and the air, were slipping away from him.

His hearing was all but completely muffled by the thin atmosphere, so he couldn't hear any hiss of air from the crack in the mask, but when he held the lantern up before his face, he could see a small cloud of condensation slipping away as the warmer air from the mask hit the colder air of the cave.

He wasn't sure how much time the breather mask had left, but it couldn't be long. His head swam, and the cave seemed to spin before his eyes.

Even if the passage *did* lead to the mining shaft, which seemed increasingly unlikely, he wouldn't survive long enough to make it there. He'd suffocate long before he reached the lower altitudes where he could survive without a mask.

He had no choice. He had to return to the airlock and the pressurized sections of the Aerie. Return to imprisonment and a life as the bandits' pet. It was better than suffocating and freezing to death, at least.

But even getting that far was hardly a certainty. Light-headed and dizzy, Huang turned and started back the way he had come, leaning heavily against the passage wall. Returning was more difficult than the descent, though, even leaving out the fact that he was now scarcely able to breathe, since now he was climbing against gravity's pull.

Still, the alternative was to stop climbing and wait to die, which hardly seemed an attractive option. So Huang continued, pushing one foot in front of the other, gritting his teeth with the exertion, climbing as fast as he could, hoping his meager supply of air lasted long enough to reach the airlock.

Then, of course, the lantern failed, and Huang found himself plunged into darkness. Which seemed, somehow, only fitting.

• • •

Afterward it seemed like a dream. Or a nightmare, rather, of cold and climbing and darkness. But though his memories of the event were muddled, he had a dim recollection of opening his eyes to sudden bright lights, lying on his back, and of a figure whose face was obscured by goggles and a breather mask leaning over him, looking more like some enormous insect than a human being.

There his memory stopped again.

The next thing he remembered was waking up back in the dining chamber. He was stretched out on the floor, lengthwise. When he tried to sit up, he found a heavy weight pulling on his neck, and found that in place of the braided cord that had secured him before there was now a heavy chain, the links as big around as one of Huang's fingers, welded to an iron collar fixed around his neck.

Huang struggled into a sitting position and went to rub the sleep from his eyes, then recoiled in horror. He held his hands before him, his eyes wide. On his left hand, his smallest finger was completely gone, and the next finger ended at the first knuckle. On his right hand, his middle finger ended at the second knuckle. All three terminated in lumps of puckered red flesh, over which clear adhesive bandages had been secured.

Huang's legs were stretched out before him. His feet were bare against the cold stone and felt strange. His heart in his throat, he looked down and saw that several toes on each foot were likewise missing, both feet swathed in clear bandages.

"Serves you right," said a harsh voice from above.

Huang looked up to find the gaunt-faced bandit named Ruan standing over him.

"Been up to me, we'd have left you there in the hangar to die," Ruan sneered. "But the chief didn't want to lose his precious pet, and in you came."

The bandit swung back one foot, and then kicked the chain that bound Huang to the wall, sending the heavy links swinging and the collar tugging painfully at Huang's neck.

"You won't be going too far with *that*, though, I don't think." The bandit's face slowly split in a devilish grin. "And try it again, if you can, and you'll lose more than a few fingers and toes to frostbite, you can be sure."

Huang looked back down at his hands, savaged by the cold. He felt incomplete, deformed.

"Leave him be, Ruan," came the voice of the chief, and Zhao stepped into Huang's field of vision. He crouched down on his haunches, to get a better look at Huang's injuries. "Healing nice enough, looks like." He glanced up at Ruan and then back to Huang. "Still, can't really blame him too much for trying to escape. I'd have done the same in his place. He brought harm to no one and nothing but himself, so what's the cost?" Then the chief smiled. "Besides, now he's one of us, eh?" He stuck his own left hand in front of Huang's face, and wiggled what was left of his severed ring finger. "A few fingers down and you fit right in, eh, Hummingbird?"

The chief laughed again, then stood.

"Come on, Ruan, let the pet get his rest, eh? We'll put him back to work soon enough."

When they had gone, Huang held his mutilated hands to his face, covering his eyes. Then his shoulders shook, first once, then again, then repeatedly, rhythmically. As he sat all alone in the dining chamber, chained to the wall, there was no one to hear the sounds of his weeping.

In the days and weeks that followed, Huang gave up any hope of rescue. He came to accept that his dreams of Bannermen storming the Aerie and liberating him had never been anything but fantasy.

Huang's life fell into a monotonous, grinding routine. He was woken every morning by the bandits, who unchained him from the wall and set him to work. He labored all day under watchful eyes, doing the most degrading, backbreaking work on offer in the Aerie. And then he ended his day chained once more in the dining chamber, watching the bandits eat and then making do with the scraps they left behind.

Still, as horrible and numbing as his situation might have been, it was not entirely bad. As harsh as his treatment was at the hands of some of the bandits, others of them treated him with more equanimity. The bandit chief Zhao, for one, seemed to care for Huang as he would a valued beast of burden, if not perhaps a cherished pet. He made sure that Huang got sufficient food and drink each day, and if ever Ruan or one of the others threatened to work Huang to the point of fatal exhaustion, Zhao would step in and insist that Huang be given some respite, or some lighter task at least. And not just Zhao, but some of the other bandits as well. Scar-faced Jue, for one, seemed to treat Huang almost as an equal, joking with him, working beside him instead of watching Huang sweat and strain from one side, even taking the trouble of asking Huang a bit about himself and where he came from. All of the bandits called him Hummingbird, as Zhao had insisted, but on the lips of some of the bandits the name sounded like a curse, while on others it was almost a term of endearment.

Which was not to say that Huang wasn't still eager to escape, however unlikely the prospects for it now seemed. But he was forced to admit, as time rolled on, that he might have been overly judgmental in his initial assessment of the bandits' worth. These were not men and women who had allowed themselves to become beasts, as he'd thought. These were people who had been driven by circumstance to be what they were, or so they thought. Huang could not bring himself to accept their reasoning and disagreed with their assessment of the governor-general, sure that they had simply fallen on hard times and looked for the most convenient scapegoat for their troubles. But Huang did admit to himself that they seemed sincere, if nothing else, and seemed genuinely to believe what they said about themselves and their lot.

Of course, they were his captors, so he hardly wished them well. But he found that it was somewhat more difficult to maintain thoughtless hatred of *men* than it was to despise beasts.

There came a time, some weeks after Huang's attempted escape, when again all the bandits but the sickest and infirm were required to go on a raiding foray. Since there were not enough bandits on hand for guards to be left behind to keep watch on Huang, it was decided that he would be brought along as well. The cracked and broken breather mask he had used was properly repaired and an ill-fitting thermal suit procured for him. He was chained to the bulkhead in the gondola, feet and hands bound, unable to move.

The raid, as it happened, was the most successful that the bandits had ever had, taking in more plunder than half a dozen other raids combined.

Whatever else they were, the bandits were superstitious creatures, and it was quickly decided that their good fortune was due to the presence of Huang in the airship's gondola. Though a contingent of bandits objected, Ruan chief among them, Zhao and the others agreed that their pet "Hummingbird" was somehow auspicious.

Immediately, Huang became the bandits' good-luck token. And, to Huang's dismay and over Ruan's objections, Zhao decreed that Huang would be taken along on all subsequent forays, to ensure continuing good fortune.

If Huang had entertained any hope of attempting another escape while the bulk of the bandits were away on a raid, those hopes were dashed. And so, like a cherished pet, he was brought along whenever his "masters" left home, however much he saw little more than the interior of the gondola. The one positive of the whole arrangement was that Huang was able, for brief periods at least, to see a sliver of sky through the streaked windows of the gondola. And that seemed, for a short while at least, almost like freedom.

Some weeks later, the airship was returning from a foray in the north when the disturbance was first noticed.

Huang was still chained to the bulkhead, as always, but in recent days he had been given a somewhat greater degree of freedom of movement, and though his hands were still bound before him, his feet were unrestricted. No longer forced to crouch like a dog against the bulkhead or sprawl on the cold deckplates, he could now perch on a stool bolted to the deck, which before had been beyond his reach. His eyes were protected by a pair of stained but serviceable goggles, and the breather mask that covered the lower half of his face had sprung leaks only once or twice in recent weeks. His thermal suit, finally, while overly tight in some places and hopelessly baggy in others, was perfectly functional, letting in only the slightest sliver of the cold that otherwise would have frozen him solid.

One of the principal benefits of being able to stand, though, was the ability to approach the windows and look *down*, to see the ground slip below them, even the clouds themselves when the airship rose high enough. So when the navigator raised the alarm, and brought Zhao and his lieutenants from their posts to the forward viewports to see for themselves, Huang was able to lean his head against the window, craning his neck as far around as possible, and catch a glimpse of what had aroused so much excitement.

It took a moment for the shadows and shapes and specks of color far below to resolve themselves into anything intelligible. And even when Huang realized what they were, he wasn't sure at all what he was seeing.

"Bring her down!" Zhao barked from the forward part of the gondola, and the pilot at the makeshift controls nodded grimly before pulling levers and flipping switches to begin the airship's descent.

"What is it?" called one of the bandits who couldn't get near the windows to see for himself.

"Atmosphere mine," Jue explained, brows knit above his goggles, his scar just visible over the line of his breather mask. "The one that went in two years ago. Looks like the miners are striking."

"I worked in that mine for a time," put in another bandit. "But it weren't no mine, it was a damned open grave!"

"Seems the miners agree with you," Zhao replied. He

lifted a pair of binoculars and turned to peer down through the viewport. "They're carrying signs, looks like. Calling for better working conditions. More safety checks. Higher wages."

"Feh," Ruan scoffed. "Why don't they just ask for wings, a pony, and their own private moon while they're at it? They're just as likely to get *those* as anything they're wanting."

"Well, seems like the Green Standard agrees with you," Zhao said.

Huang had straightened to hear the exchange, the shouted voices muffled by the thrum of the engines, but he leaned back to put his head against the window once more. The bandit chief was right! The yellowish green shapes down below *were* crawlers of the Green Standard Army. And the ring of antlike figures were uniformed soldiers, here and there fluttering the Green Standard on a pike. But who were the figures enclosed within, in their motley and rags? The miners?

Most of what Huang remembered from his military instruction was how to win in a game of elephant chess, when to deploy soldier and when chariot, how to block an opponent's horse and how best to flank a general, but those were merely pieces on a board, not living men in battle. Still, he remembered enough of military strategy, he thought, to recognize a classic containment maneuver. The small shapes at the outskirts of the ring of soldiers would be riflemen, properly braced against the ground, lying lengthwise with their weapons trained on the "hostiles" within the ring, to prevent them from breaking and escaping (but remaining careful not to fire on their own men). Then the soldiers in the ring would draw their weapons, favoring knives and swords, and advance slowly on the hostiles, closing the ring around them like a noose. With their avenues of escape closed off, the hostiles would be forced to stand their ground with enemies approaching from all sides. So long as the soldiers maintained numerical superiority, the hostiles would be hard pressed to stand against them.

But this was a tactic to be used in warfare, usually against a less-armed foe. Why would the Army of the Green Standard now be using it against simple miners?

"Bring her down, pilot!" Zhao shouted from the viewport.

"What have you got planned here, Chief?" Ruan's expression was suspicious.

"All the way," Zhao shouted to the pilot. "Set her down!"

"Chief?" Ruan grabbed Zhao's arm. "What's this to do with us?"

Zhao wheeled on the skeletal bandit, eyes flashing behind his goggles. "Those are our brother miners. We've no doubt worked side by side with them, or with those who have. Should we leave them to the tender mercies of Ouyang's thugs, just because there's no profit in it? Our *brothers*?!"

Ruan lowered his eyes, shamed.

Jue stepped forward, hand on the pistol holstered at his belt. "You heard the chief!" he shouted to the other bandits. "Shift yourselves, and make ready to hit sand."

As the bandits prepared to disembark from the airship, Huang glanced once more out the window, feeling his pulse quicken. Perhaps this was his moment to escape, after all? With the Green Standard Army so close by, he need only free himself from his chains and he could race to one of the crawlers, and to freedom. He had to keep careful watch for the opportunity and, when the time was right, make his move.

Still, as the bandits checked their firearms and loosed their swords and knives in their scabbards, Huang could not help but be plagued by a nagging thought. Why *were* Green Standard soldiers attacking a group of striking miners, anyway?

The airship touched down, and the deckplates vibrated with the pounding of feet as the bandits raced out the hatch and onto the red sands beyond. The last to leave was the pilot, who keyed in the sequence of controls to keep the engines idling, and then with sword in hand he followed his brothers out into the fray.

Huang was left alone.

Through the window, he could see that Zhao had ordered the airship touch down some distance from the mine where the soldiers encircled the striking miners, beyond the range of their firearms. If the crawlers had carried any heavier ordnance, it likely could have reached the airship's position even at this distance, but as no mortar shells had yet come whistling toward the airship, it seemed likely that the crawlers didn't carry heavy weapons or that the soldiers were too occupied to fire if they did.

With all the bandits now racing to aid the miners, Huang had only to rid himself of his chains and he would be halfway to freedom.

Provided, of course, he *could* rid himself of his chains.

Finally, Huang had to admit defeat. Even though he could move some distance in all directions, there were no tools or implements at hand that he could use to unfasten the collar from his neck or remove the chain that bolted the collar to the bulkhead. He was as trapped as he'd have been if he'd been left chained up in the Aerie, far from freedom.

What made matters only worse was his realization that the keys that Zhao used to secure the chain's locks were hung on a peg on the far side of the gondola, in plain view, but easily three times the length of his chain leash away. There was no hope that Huang could reach it, of course. But if only someone were to come along who *could*!

From his vantage point, Huang was unable to see where the bandits had gotten to, but imagined they were now busy mixing with the soldiers, taking the side of the striking miners; he could hear the distant thump of weapons fire. Huang gazed longingly at the keys, muscles straining helpless against his chain leash, when a noise from the open hatch startled him. Heart in his throat, hands twisted into fists at his side, he wheeled around at the end of his tether.

There were three of them, lurking beyond the open hatch with rifles in hands, bayonets gleaming at the ends of the barrels. Men in the uniforms of Green Standard guardsmen, their expressions grave, regarding Huang with naked suspicion.

It had been so many weeks since Huang had seen any faces but the bandits' that he was at first taken aback. Then he regained his senses and called out.

"Help! Oh, please, help!"

Having taken in Huang's chains, the soldiers now warily slid their gazes from one side of the gondola to the other, and then slowly mounted the steps and climbed through the hatch.

Huang went to speak again but realized his voice must be muffled by the mask, his appearance hidden by the goggles. Holding his bound hands up to his face, he was able to wrench the mask off and then slide the goggles down around his neck.

"My name is Humming—" Huang began, then choked, realizing what he was saying. He swallowed, remembering himself. Straightening as much as he was able, weighted by the heavy chain, he tried again. "My name is Huang Fei, and I am a Guardsman of the Second Rank in the Army of the Green Standard."

The trio of soldiers exchanged suspicious glances.

"I was taken prisoner by these bandits weeks ago, on the road to Far Sight Outpost."

One of the soldiers nodded slowly. Then, keeping his eyes

on Huang, he spoke out of the side of his mouth to his companions. "There *was* a convoy hit on that road, just as he says. But I didn't hear anything about any officer took prisoner."

"Please!" Huang held up his hands, showing the bonds, and then looked down at the heavy links chaining him to the bulkhead. "If it weren't as I say, why would I be chained up like this?"

The soldiers exchanged another glance, then shrugged. "Fair enough," one of them said. "What do you expect us to do about it?"

Huang was struck dumb for a moment by the casual indifference in the soldier's tone. It took him an instant to compose a response. Then he pointed to the keys that hung on the hook at the gondola's far side.

"Those!" He gesticulated to the keys wildly. "Bring them here. Unlock me!" He almost jumped up and down, so anxious was he, and he glanced nervously out the window, watchful of the bandits' return.

One of the soldiers shrugged again, dramatically, and then went and fetched the keys. While he crossed the floor to where Huang stood and went to work on the locks, the other two soldiers began poking through the barrels and crates lashed here and there in the gondola, glancing nervously from time to time to the open hatch.

Huang's full attention was on the chain securing him to the wall and the soldier who was taking far too long with the keys and locks to suit Huang's tastes. Finally, though, the last lock clicked open, and the collar fell away in two pieces. Huang was freed.

Huang rubbed his neck, which was covered with thick calluses from the constant presence of the collar for so many weeks. He went to thank the soldier who'd freed him, and found that he had joined the other two in opening and inspecting the various bins and crates lashed to the deck along the sides of the gondola. It seemed to Huang that the trio were searching for something without knowing quite what they were looking for. Then one of them held aloft a bejeweled necklace of gold that the bandits had taken in their last raid, his face split in a wide grin. The other two rushed to the crate where the necklace had been found, eagerly pawing through the contents.

It was only then that Huang realized what the soldiers were doing. They were ransacking the airship, searching for valuables. They were planning on *stealing* from the bandits.

Shaking his head in disgust, Huang rubbed his chafed wrists, and with a final distasteful glance at the bonds and chains that now lay scattered on the deckplates, he made his way to the hatch.

Once outside, Huang felt exposed, vulnerable. His hands ached for a weapon, and he thought to call back to the soldiers within the airship to see if any had a knife or pistol to spare him. But now that he was outside, he was able to get a clearer view of the ongoing melee near the mine, and what he saw stopped him in his tracks.

Though it was some distance away, the wind was still and there was no dust obscuring his view, so Huang was able to see it all clearly. The miners were unarmed, trapped within the encircling ring of soldiers. And the distant thump of weapons fire he'd heard had not been shots exchanged on either side, but instead was the sound of the soldiers in their entrenched positions opening fire on the unarmed miners, mowing them down. The only thing preventing the encounter from being a complete and immediate slaughter was the timely intervention of the bandits, who now attacked one side of the ring of soldiers, creating a break in the circle and allowing the miners a slim chance for escape.

The miners carried only signs demanding safety and better wages. Splints of wood from which hung banners painted in crude ideograms, nothing more. And the soldiers were firing on them as though they were a heavily armed enemy force.

Huang stood frozen, unable to move, not sure what to do. Surely *this* was not what it meant to be a soldier. Was this the life to which he hoped to return?

So caught up was Huang with the thoughts racing through his head that he almost failed to hear the sound of the three soldiers clomping back down the gangplank. He turned and saw the trio stepping onto the red sands, carrying armloads of plundered goods, their pockets bulging with jewels and gold coins and other trinkets, their bayoneted rifles slung from their shoulders.

The three came and stood beside Huang, watching the ongoing melee with evident admiration.

"Damned miners," one of them said, and spat in the dirt.

"Filthy beasts," another agreed. "They don't deserve no better than a bullet in the brain, if you ask me."

The third nodded. "They should know not to rise above their station. Keep to their place next time, I should think."

Huang narrowed his eyes, his teeth gritted, and looked from the smug, complacent soldiers, heavy laden with loot, to the miners caught in the crossfire, and the bandits who now risked life and limb to come to their aid. He remembered how the miners themselves must have risked life and limb in just the same way, every time they went down into the mines. He thought of the bandits he'd come to know, those who had kept him as a pet, who had lost limbs or loved ones in the thankless task of mining. These men and women had dug from the red soil the metals that made buildings and vehicles, and even the chemical constituents of the air he was now breathing. The bandits had been miners and had found themselves unable to improve their lot, so that now, as bandits, they fought back the only way they knew how.

"Damned bandits should have stayed out of this," one of the soldiers said with a sneer. "Now they'll end up as dead as the miners."

"Still," another said with a wicked grin, and pointed with his chin at the armload of loot weighing him down, "not bad for us, eh?"

Huang's blood boiled, and the world went red before his eyes. All thought of escape was forgotten. There was something else he had to do first.

Huang struck without thinking, without planning. One minute he was standing in the midst of the three soldiers, hands clenched into fists at his sides, and the next he hurled himself at the last soldier who'd spoken, throttling the man and knocking him to the ground.

The other two looked on with expressions of shock and anger but clung too tightly to their bundles of precious plunder to act quickly, which gave Huang all the advantage he needed.

Without delaying an instant, Huang reached down and snatched up the fallen soldier's bayoneted rifle, yanking it off the man's shoulder, and then swung around to train the rifle's barrel on the soldiers stills standing.

"Drop your loot and your weapons!" Huang snarled, bracing himself with one foot and tightening his finger on the trigger. "Do it and run, or I'll kill you where you stand."

The two soldiers looked to each other, confused, then back at Huang. The soldiers didn't bother to answer but opened their arms to let the loot fall, shrugged their shoulders to let their rifles fall to the dirt, and then took off running back toward the crawlers.

• • •

The bandits, once they'd broken through the ranks of the soldiers, had joined with the beleaguered miners and shared arms with them. The soldiers, now facing a combined force of bandits and miners, had seen the value in a strategic withdrawal, quickly losing interest in the encounter when the odds shifted enough that any of them might find his own life in peril.

A handful of the miners now returned with the bandits to the airship, evidently deciding to join the bandits' ranks. And they were not alone.

When Zhao and the others reached the airship, bruised and bloodied from their encounter with the soldiers, some supporting or even carrying their wounded fellows, they were surprised to find Huang sitting on the edge of the open hatch, a rifle across his knees, an insensate soldier sprawled in the dust before him.

"What's this now, Hummingbird?" Zhao looked from the fallen soldier to Huang with a slight smile tugging the corners of his mouth. "Our pet has slipped his leash, but instead of flying he stays and presents us with a mouse he's caught. Is that it?"

Huang stood and slung the rifle onto his shoulder. He noted that Ruan and a few of the others had their weapons at the ready, wary of any move Huang might make against them.

"I didn't fly because I have nowhere to go."

Zhao narrowed his eyes and jerked a thumb back over his shoulder, indicating the column of dust on the horizon that followed the retreating Green Standard crawlers. "What about that lot? They'll be back soon enough, in greater numbers, if I know their type. They won't want to tell the governor-general that they failed, so they'll return with enough guns to do the job right next time. You can always join them, since they're your sort and all."

Huang shook his head angrily. "They have nothing to do with me, Zhao." He chewed his lip thoughtfully. "If it's all the same to you . . ." He swallowed hard and nodded. "I'd just as soon go back to the Aerie."

Zhao arched an eyebrow. Beside him, scar-faced Jue wore an amused grin.

"But not as your damned pet," Huang went out, standing straighter, chin held high. "I'll be a bandit, if you'll have me."

A smile began to spread across Zhao's face. The bandit chief glanced at Jue, who only shrugged in response, and Ruan, who scowled angrily.

"Fair enough!" Zhao surged forward and clapped a hand on Huang's shoulder. "You're one of us now, ancestors preserve you." Zhao grinned broader. "But you're still Hummingbird, all right? Your other names are just too damned unpalatable."

Huang allowed himself a tight grin and nodded. "Hummingbird it is."

ACT III

●

DISSONANCE

EARTH SHEEP YEAR, FIFTY-SIXTH YEAR OF THE TIANBIAN EMPEROR

WEI WAS SNORING IN THE CORNER WHEN THE REP-resentative from the camp arrived, so it fell to Gamine to receive her.

"So you'll be performing both the homily and the revelation, then?" The woman glanced from Gamine to the aging mendicant propped up on cushions on the tent's far side, his eyes shut and his mouth open, tongue lolling.

Gamine smiled reassuringly. "No need to fear, sister. I discussed the topic of today's lesson with Master Wei over the morning meal, and I shall be happy to repeat it to the others."

The woman, old enough to be Gamine's mother—grandmother, even—looked at her and sighed with relief. "Oh, thank you, Iron Jaw. It's so much nicer when you . . ." She broke off and shot a guilty look at the old man. "That is, these last few seasons Master Wei has . . . Well, he's gotten . . ."

As the woman struggled to find the right phrase, Gamine came to her rescue. "Master Wei tires easily, of late."

The woman nodded eagerly. "Exactly." She took another deep breath and looked at the old man, his chest gently rising and falling, and shook her head sadly. "It happens with the aged, sometimes. They . . . forget things."

Again Gamine flashed her most comforting smile. "Perhaps. But then, perhaps Master Wei is only forgetting things not worth remembering, his mind on more . . . elevated matters?"

Unconvinced, the woman managed a weak smile. Then, bowing to the slumbering mendicant, and with a deeper bow in Gamine's direction, she drew back the tent flap and went to carry word to the rest of the camp.

Before the tent flap fell closed, Temujin lurched in, a half-full jar of wine in his hand. He stumbled, throwing his arms out in both directions in an attempt to regain his balance, sloshing wine onto the rug-covered floor. He made it a few steps across the tent, more a series of half-controlled falls than proper walking, and then collapsed onto a low stool beside a table.

"And what did that old sow want, as if I didn't know?"

"She came to ask about the service," Gamine answered.

"Of course she did," Temujin said with a sneer. He lifted the jar to his lips and sloshed most of what was left into his open mouth. Then he thumped the jar onto the table. "She's worried the old nick-ninny is too addled to do the job, is she?"

Gamine narrowed her eyes and pursed her lips. "She's concerned about Master Wei's well-being, I'm sure, just as the rest of us are, the powers preserve him."

Temujin wiped his straggly mustaches dry on the back of his hand and fixed Gamine with a squint-eyed stare. "Seems to me you make pretty free with this taradiddle of yours, hop-o'-my-thumb, even when there's no marks about to hear it. 'Powers' this and 'virtues' that and 'harmony' the other thing."

"And it seems to me that you are drunk, old man."

For a brief moment a proud smile started to spread across Temujin's face, and he began to nod, but then the smile slid into a frown, and he narrowed his eyes. "And what's it to you if I'm in my altitudes, at that, my little sprite? A man's due his rewards after hard labor, is he not?"

"And what hard labor would that be?" Gamine asked with a slight smile, amused despite herself.

"All this nonsense!" Temujin waved his arm in a wide circle, nearly toppling the jar to the floor, indicating the camp beyond the tent's thin walls. He wavered on the stool, listing from one side to the other and back, eyes half lidded. "I've pulled some long cons in my time, girl, but nothing so long as this gaff's been on. Three years now? And what have we to show for it but drafty tents and watery soups and a few hundred more mouths to feed? Where's the payoff we always talked about? Where's the big score? I'd swear if I didn't know better that you'd come to believe all this flimflam yourself."

"You're drunk," Gamine repeated, narrowing her eyes, her smile fading. "And a fool."

"I'm drunk." Temujin nodded, then jerked a thumb

toward the old man snoring in the corner. "And the old fumbler's lost his wits. And you?" He crossed his arms over his chest and stared down his nose at her. "You act like you forgot that all this is a dodge and started believing your own grift. So which of us is the biggest fool, hmm?"

That said, Temujin lurched to his feet, snatched up his wine jar, spilling the little that remained on the rugs underfoot, and then propelled himself gracelessly toward the tent flaps.

"The services start in a short while," Gamine called after him, her tone even. "Try not to bungle your entrance this time, would you?"

The old beggar spun on his heel like a weather vane, nearly falling over, and with his hand over his heart bobbed his head in a mockery of a bow. "As you wish, *Iron Jaw*. As you wish."

Temujin turned and stumbled through the tent flaps, leaving Gamine alone with her thoughts, the wine-sodden rugs, and the old man snoring indecorously in the corner.

Gamine climbed the steps to the wide platform atop the scaffold and looked down at the uplifted faces of the faithful gathered at the center of the camp. There were more of them now than ever, and more new faces joining them every day.

It wasn't just Gamine, Temujin, and Wei sleeping rough by the side of the road anymore. The camp had grown until it numbered nearly a hundred tents arranged in irregular concentric circles, the pinkish orange sands mounting in low drifts on their eastern sides. At the center of the circle, near the trio of tents that Wei, Gamine, and Temujin had made their own, was a roughly built scaffold, constructed of cast-off timbers, discarded aluminum sheets, and other odds and ends. Before the scaffold was a broad, open space, and it was here that all their followers now gathered.

Gamine remembered when she and Temujin had first joined Wei on his travels three years before, when they'd made do with a bare patch of dirt at the edge of market squares. Wei would preach his rambling sermons about the "powers," as he called them, figures drawn indiscriminately from fiction and religion, legend and mythology. Gamine would come onstage after the homily was done, professing her belief, and then proceed to demonstrate her virtue by reciting passages from novels, operas, and plays, as though possessed by the spirits of those characters. Scenes from *The Miner's Journey* or *Water Margin* or *The Journey to the West*. Or, depending on the makeup of the audience, she might assay a few scenes from the Briton myth-play *Robin Hood*, about a man who stole what the poor needed from the rich, or episodes from the story of the Vinlander culture hero Paul Bunyan, a woodcutter who supposedly stood against the invading armies of the Dragon Throne centuries before. Then, once Gamine had recited long enough to establish possession by the powers, Temujin would come forward to test her mettle and her resolve. It was nothing more than a pulled punch and faked reaction, but the act so impressed audiences that Gamine would forevermore be known to all of them only as the girl with the jaw of iron, or simply as Iron Jaw.

At first, they had simply gone from village to village as the mood struck them, staying only long enough to garner a few filling meals and comfortable beds from the newly converted, and then moving on to the next village when it began to appear that they might have overstayed their welcome. Temujin was primarily in charge of their movements in those days, using his well-honed instinct and practiced eyed to gauge the patience of those who supplied as charity that which the three drifters could never afford to buy. Wei, who was somewhat addled and out of touch even in his best days, simply did as he was told, and if he harbored any doubts about the man and girl who had joined him on his journeys, he never voiced them. As for Gamine, she paid careful attention, watching the audiences even more closely than they watched her, always working on improving the act. But as her timing and delivery improved, her position in their little grouping subtly begin to shift, so that in time she was giving instruction and orders as often as she was receiving them.

It wasn't clear at what point their trio grew. One day there were only the three of them, and the next they had gained a handful of camp followers. A few men and women from one village had elected to follow the three when they picked up stakes and moved on to the next town.

Temujin at first objected, with the grifter's logic that the only thing that followed a confidence man were stray dogs, the authorities, and his reputation, all of which would only bite him in the end. Gamine, though, pointed out that having the camp followers in tow would only help their grift when they reached the next village. Rather than Temujin and Gamine having to work to fan the flames of interest, the camp followers would spread the word for them, telling the locals in the next village all about the holy man and the miraculous girl with the iron jaw.

If she'd known then what would happen, would she still have pressed Temujin to allow the camp followers to come along with them? Gamine wasn't sure, but the question nagged at her, as did Temujin's accusation that she'd started to believe in the powers herself, if only a little.

But who could have guessed, in those early days, that the camp followers wouldn't have gotten tired of following them from village to village, from town to town? And more, that they would not be alone but would be joined by more followers, and more, until they were no longer a few travelers on the road but a whole caravan on the march?

What had begun as three people pulling a short con, in town after town, had grown in the intervening years into a full-blown religious movement. And though Master Wei was the nominal leader of the camp now calling itself the Society of Righteous Harmony, most all of the few hundred followers now looked to the girl they called Iron Jaw for guidance and direction, even when the old man wasn't off somewhere asleep or mumbling to himself.

Just as their handful had become a movement and the Society of Righteous Harmony had taken shape, the rough structure of their early performances had become gradually codified and regimented, so that it was now a strictly ordered sequence, followed with great devotion.

It was perhaps Gamine's own devotion that surprised her most, though. She and Temujin had joined up with Wei as a dodge, seeing an easy way to bilk meals, coin, and shelter from the farmers and villagers of the northern plains. But if Temujin was still motivated by a desire for a full purse and belly, Gamine's own motivations had shifted somewhere along the way. Perhaps it had started on the day that she realized she didn't feel guilty anymore. When she was up onstage with Wei, preaching the good word of the powers to people, it didn't feel like she was cheating or stealing; it didn't feel like a con. It had started to feel *real*. When she looked into the smiling faces of their listeners, heard the things they said about how belief in the powers had changed their own lives for the better, Gamine couldn't help but think that she was doing something genuine, something of worth. This wasn't a con anymore; this was a *service*. This wasn't an audience of marks, much less victims; this was her *congregation*. That she got meals and shelter out of it made it just that much more appealing.

As Gamine went through the rites—greeting the other members of the Society in their hundreds, hearing their antiphonal response, and then leading them in the ritualized movements and rhythmic breathing that supposedly helped the followers attain the mental and spiritual state necessary to receive the homily—she thought back to her years living in the Chauviteau-Zong residence. Thinking about Madam Chauviteau-Zong was sometimes confusing, since Gamine's thoughts about her former mistress were somewhat ambiguous. She still harbored thoughts of revenge, but her thirst for vengeance had waned in recent years. Instead, when she thought of her mistress's home in Fanchuan now, she most often thought about the lessons she'd learned there. The instruction Gamine had received from her tutors had, of course, covered the basics of organized religion, and she had been familiar with the creeds and credos of all of the major systems of belief from a very early age. But Gamine's familiarity with religion was like that of a person who had only heard a recipe described but had never tasted it. Or, as Temujin might say, like that of someone who had heard about another's injuries but never broken a bone. The two clearly had very different experiences with belief and very different views on the relative usefulness of religion.

Temujin, for his part, always said that he knew a con when he saw one, and he never had any patience for any church or holy man. Gamine had taken exception to that in the early days; after all, she said, many people had deep and sincere beliefs that guided their lives. Were all of them simply marks, victims of someone else's con?

But now, some years on, she couldn't help but wonder if perhaps Temujin had been right, and wrong, all at the same time. What if this *was* how religions began, and all systems of belief were in their early days nothing but grifts, just as she and Temujin had begun when first they met Wei? But, and more to the point, what if it didn't *matter*? What if a thing's beginnings weren't as important as where it ended? After all, she should know better than any, having no beginnings whatsoever. If belief began as a con but came in time to be a positive and affecting force in the lives of sincere people who used it to guide themselves to a better existence, did it matter that those who founded the belief didn't share those convictions? If it served a positive end, was it important that it had a negative beginning? Or a neutral beginning, if one was generous?

Gamine wasn't sure, but she was beginning to have definite suspicions.

When the faithful had completed the rhythmic breathing exercises and now stood with their hands folded before them, listening intently, Gamine crossed to the center of the platform and began the homily.

There were times when Gamine wished she had more to say. The camp's numbers had swelled recently. It had been not quite three years since a ground quake had disrupted the shipping routes between the northern lowlands and the valley provinces to the south, and almost two years since the drought began. Fire Star was being slowly transformed into another Earth, but it would be long generations before it was lush and green. The drought had ended, but a few seasons without sufficient water in the lowlands had meant the end of many farms. A small number of larger farming concerns were prospering once more—chief among them those owned by the Combine collective—but only at the cost of taking more than their share of the available water and then selling their agricultural goods at wildly inflated prices to the valley provinces. When the owners of the smaller independent farms tried to object, the Combine had sent word—and hefty "donations"—to the governor-general, who had in turn sent the Green Standard Army north to protect the Combine's interests.

Now many former farmers and plantation laborers had joined the ranks of the Society of Righteous Harmony, searching for some meaning in their lives. Master Wei had once provided that meaning through his daily homilies, but he was old and getting older, and more and more Gamine was called upon to perform all of the service herself, including the movements, the homily, and the revelation of possession alike. And while her homilies were perhaps a little more grammatical and less cryptic than much of what the old mendicant used to say, Gamine couldn't help but feel that her own messages were simplistic, perhaps even simple-minded. "Live in harmony with one another." "Take only what you need." "Trust the powers." But if Gamine's religious advice was less sophisticated than she might have liked, those in the camp seemed not to mind.

There were new faces in the crowd, Gamine saw. More people driven from their homes, come to join the Society of Righteous Harmony, desperate for some kind of meaning.

Gamine took a deep breath and did her best to sound as if she knew what she was doing.

Huang had been sure he knew what he was doing, but it was beginning to look as though he'd been wrong.

"Life isn't sport, Hummingbird. Sport has rules. In real life, the only rule is 'Don't get killed.'"

Huang rubbed his jaw, where a bruise was already rising from Zhao's last blow. The bandit chief held out his hand and helped Huang to his feet. Once he was standing, Huang knocked the red dust from his palms, brushed off his trousers, and then went to retrieve his saber from the place where it had fallen when Zhao kicked it from his hands.

"Try that one again?" Huang asked with a sly grin, and Zhao replied with a nod and a grin of his own.

The two men faced each other, a few paces apart, and raised their swords in defensive postures.

"Remember, now," Zhao said, waving the point of his saber back and forth before him, "no rules."

Huang nodded, his eyes wary and unblinking.

Their impromptu fencing strip was in the flat base of a narrow gulley. Once, perhaps billions of years ago, liquid water might have flowed here, carving this channel out of the living rock of Fire Star. But that liquid had dried up long ago, leaving only a dusty red ball of rock. When humans first arrived on Fire Star, a few hundred years ago, the only water to be found anywhere was locked in polar ice, buried beneath caps of frozen carbon dioxide. Miners still worked at excavating this frozen water, returning it to the surface, where it gradually thawed and flowed across the face of Fire Star once more. Someday, in the distant future, there would be rivers and streams again—if the plans of the scientists and artificers of the Dragon Throne were correct—and the lake at the bottom of the Great Southern Basin would grown into a proper sea, and perhaps even the northern lowlands might flood completely and become an ocean. But now the only water to be found here was what humans brought with them or pumped in from reservoirs somewhere far away.

"Come on, then." Zhao waved the red blade of his saber before him once more, taunting Huang to begin the attack.

Huang took a deep breath, let it out in a measured exhalation, feinted to the left, and then lunged forward, driving his own sword's point toward the bandit chief's chest.

In any proper fencing competition, the attack would have been a scoring maneuver, and Huang would have been declared the winner. He'd used the technique himself many times, and the only opponent who'd ever been able to counter the lightning speed of his feint and lunge had been his friend Kenniston An.

Zhao, though, did something completely unexpected, something that even Kenniston had never tried. Just as the point of Huang's sword drove toward him, Zhao leaned backward and fell *down*.

If he'd been thinking faster, Huang might have seen his brief advantage and taken the opportunity to change the direction of his thrust and stab downward, hitting the reinforced padding of the practice vest Zhao wore and scoring a hit. But seeing his opponent simply fall like a puppet whose strings had been cut unnerved Huang, and the confusion caused a momentary delay in his reaction.

That delay was all the opportunity Zhao needed to turn things to his advantage. Lying flat on his back, the bandit chief scooped up a handful of red sand and, without warning, *threw* it up into Huang's face. In the still air, there was no wind to blow the sand aside, and most of it pelted into Huang's face as Zhao had intended, gritting in his teeth, stinging his eyes, filling his nostrils.

Huang flailed back, momentarily blinded, tears streaming from his eyes. He pinched the bridge of his nose with one hand, trying to blink the sand from his watering eyes, while his other still held the hilt of his sword, its point aimed at the sky.

Before Huang knew what had happened, he felt himself falling to the ground, just as Zhao had done. But while the bandit chief's fall had been directed and deliberate, Huang's was simply the result of Zhao sweeping his legs out from under him with a sideswiping kick, knocking him off balance. Huang threw his arms out to either side, unsuccessfully trying to regain his footing, but it was too late. He thudded to the hard ground, his breath knocked from him. He'd lost hold of his sword somewhere and heard it clatter to the rocks a short distance off.

Huang felt a needle's prick on his exposed neck and squinted through the tears and the grit to see Zhao standing over him, the red-bladed saber prodding Huang just below the jawline.

"See, Hummingbird? No rules."

Huang's cheeks stung red with embarrassment, but he managed a weak smile and nodded. As Zhao helped him to his feet, Huang wondered whether he shouldn't send word to his parents in Fanchuan to clear out his old room and give away all his fencing trophies and medallions, considering that he'd been bested three falls out of four by a man with no formal fencing training whatsoever. Of course, Huang's parents probably thought he was dead by now, after so many years without any word from him, so such a message might complicate matters more than Huang would like. It wasn't that he bore his family any ill will; he just wasn't in any hurry to see them again. Someday, perhaps, but not soon.

Huang was retrieving his blade, and preparing himself for a fifth bout with Zhao, when a bandit raced into the gulley, bringing word from Ruan and Jue that the convoy had been spotted.

"That's enough play for today, I think," Zhao said, sliding his own red saber into its scabbard. "Time to be back at work."

As they walked up the gulley together, Zhao turned to Huang and fixed him with a familiar grin. "So tell me, Hummingbird: Which is more valuable, the soldier or the elephant?"

Huang shook his head, his expression rueful. He'd come to dread these little examinations, these past few years. "The elephant, I suppose," he said, knowing there was no point in fighting it.

Zhao narrowed his eyes, still smiling. "Why?"

"Because he can move two points, while the soldier can move only one."

Zhao raised a finger in triumph. "Are you forgetting the river?"

Huang sighed and shook his head again. "Oh, right. Well . . ."

The river, of course, was not any body of water, no more than the elephant was an animal or the soldier a man. Huang had never seen a river outside a lithograph or an elephant outside a zoo. Instead the river was the blank strip that divided an elephant-chess board into two sections, and the soldier and elephant two varieties of playing pieces.

"The elephant is a useful defensive piece, sure," Zhao went

on, "but he can only advance as far as the river's nearest bank. The soldier might only be able to move one point forward, but when he crosses the river, he's promoted and can move horizontally as well, making him a much more dangerous opponent."

"So the answer is the soldier?" Huang asked.

Zhao smiled. "What do *you* think?"

Huang was thoughtful. "I think it depends."

It hadn't been long after Huang had thrown in his lot with the bandits that he'd discovered that Zhao shared his passion for elephant chess, and in the quiet hours between forays, the two had taken to playing with a battered set that Zhao had brought with him to the Aerie, a relic of his previous life as a miner. Huang had originally expected to be able to beat the gruff bandit chief easily but had been surprised when Zhao had bested him four games out of five. Even now, years later, Zhao still won their games more often than he lost.

Zhao nodded. "It depends," he agreed. They continued on for a moment, drawing nearer the channel where the others had gathered. "And what does that tell us about men and machines in combat?"

Zhao had recognized Huang's talent for strategy in those early games and quizzed him on where he'd learned to play. Zhao himself had learned elephant chess from an old master who had ended his days working in the mines, but not before teaching a young miner named Zhao everything he knew about the game. When Huang explained that he'd been taught by his tutor, learning elephant chess instead of the military strategy with which he'd been tasked, Zhao had laughed. He said that Huang had learned more about military tactics than he'd realized from his strategy tutor, if only he'd learn how to apply it. And that had been the beginning of their impromptu examinations as the bandit chief tried to teach Huang how game tactics could be put into real-world practice.

Huang furrowed his brow, trying to apply the lesson about soldiers and elephants on the chessboard to men and machines in the real world.

"Perhaps," he finally answered, "it means that a crawler is a useful asset, but there are places a crawler can't go. A man on foot, in the right circumstances, can be a more powerful asset."

Zhao nodded, his smile widening. "Sounds right to me." He reached over and clapped Huang on the shoulder. "Now come on, let's see what trouble the others have gotten up to."

"So what do you think, Hummingbird?"

Huang and Zhao stood near the lip of the channel, looking down onto the lowlands below. They were shielded from view of those in the convoy, and although the crawlers were some distance away, Huang felt the almost unshakable urge to whisper, as though his words might be overheard.

Huang wasn't entirely sure at what point he had become the chief's sounding board for strategy, but it seemed to have been an outgrowth of their discussions about fencing and elephant chess. Zhao continued his little examinations, quizzing Huang about what the bandits should or shouldn't do in given circumstances. The chief seemed to like his answers more often than not, so much so that in time Huang had become something of a de facto strategist, consulted whenever questions of tactics arose.

"Looks like the intelligence we received was correct," Huang answered, peering at the line of crawlers in the near distance. "Minimal armament, no defensive posture . . . they aren't expecting any trouble at all."

"And why should they?" The voice was Ruan's, who crouched against the cliff wall of the channel a few paces off. His eyes were narrowed in his skeletal face, and he regarded Huang coolly. "What are they carrying that anyone could *possibly* want? Compressor components? Elevator cabling? Emergency rations and bales of undergarments? Why would anyone in their right mind even *consider* raiding such a shipment?"

"Ruan?" Zhao said, turning the bandit's name into a warning, with one word saying, *Do you* really *want to keep talking?*

"Well," Huang said with a defensive shrug, "I'm sure there's some use to which those things could be put. Doesn't the Aerie's air-filtration system need a new compressor?"

"That's as may be," Jue put in, shaking his head sadly, lips pursed and scar showing white against his tanned skin. "But our system uses an entirely different gauge than the mines do, and I don't think these parts could be adapted to fit." He gave a weary smile and added, "But *I* wouldn't mind a few dozen pairs of undergarments, myself. Would save on doing the wash."

Ruan shot the scar-faced bandit a sharp look, then turned to glare at Huang once more.

"Well, Ruan?" Zhao asked, crossing his arms over his chest. "Is there something you'd like to say?"

The skeletal-faced bandit glared for another moment at Huang, and then his expression softened, fractionally, as he turned to the bandit chief and shook his head reluctantly. "No. No, I suppose there isn't."

"Well, enough then." Zhao nodded and turned to Huang. "In that case, Hummingbird, I don't see any reason not to put your plan in motion. You want to send word to the men down the line that we're ready to move into position?"

Huang nodded, casting a quick uneasy glance in Ruan's direction. Then he saw Jue's supportive grin and smiled in return. He paused for the briefest moment, contemplative, and then hurried off to relay Zhao's commands to the rest of the bandits arrayed up and down the line of the channel, their weapons primed and ready.

As he made his way up and down the line, giving the bandits their instructions, Huang could hear their voices following after him. None told him to his face what they thought of him and his position in the organization, but as soon as his back was turned they were much more forthcoming.

There was one, though, who was not shy about expressing his displeasure, especially when Zhao wasn't around.

"You don't fool me."

Ruan blocked Huang's way, his skeletal face twisted in a sneer, his arms folded over his chest.

"I need to pass, Ruan," Huang said, his voice low but level.

"What you *need*," Ruan said, unfolding his arms to reach forward and prod Huang in the chest, "is to keep your rutting mouth shut."

Huang narrowed his eyes. A few years before, he had been the bandits' disgruntled prisoner, and Ruan had been quick to argue for his speedy execution. Since then, he'd gone from being a reluctant pet to being a valued bandit and was now even something of a prized strategist, a close advisor to the chief. It seemed that Zhao held him in the same esteem as he did Ruan and Jue, and in recent months Huang had even begun to suspect that he might have eclipsed even them, as the bandit chief came more and more to value Huang's own advice over all others, even when contradicted by his longtime lieutenants.

Huang wasn't sure what he thought of the change in his status, but it was clear to him what Ruan thought of it.

"We aren't your personal army, boy," Ruan said, poking

Huang again in the chest, "and if it was up to me, you'd be shoving your advice up your bunghole. Just how you've turned the old man's head away from profit I'll never know, but don't think for a minute that you've fooled me."

That the raids were more successful than ever, none could deny. With Huang's instincts at strategy and formal training in the use of weapons augmenting Zhao's tactics and more catch-as-catch-can alley-fighting style, the bandits had been gradually transformed from artless brawlers into formidable fighters, fierce and intelligent. But if the bandits' encounters were more successful, seldom suffering casualties in the course of their raids, the bandits found that they were bringing ever less profit back to the Aerie after each foray.

And worse, when they were back in the safety of the Aerie, the bandits had been forced to adapt to a much more frugal existence. No longer did they indulge in the feasts of former days, trenchers piled high with food and endless jars of wine. Now they ate rations of rice and salted fish, drinking their wine watered if at all, and only occasionally enjoying the luxury of duck, or pork, or that rarest of treasures, beef.

Many of the bandits felt they knew precisely what their problem was, and just who was the author of these troubles. The difficulty, they felt sure, was that they were no longer living like bandits; they were now living like soldiers.

And it was all the fault of the man they called Humming-bird.

"Look, Ruan," Huang said, keeping his voice low, "I don't

want to fight you. I just don't see any point in wasting our lives in the pointless pursuit of plunder."

"Pointless?" Ruan sneered. "Spoken like a true child of privilege who never worked a rutting day in his life."

Huang's hand twitched for his saber's hilt, but he kept his arms at his sides. He couldn't really blame Ruan for how he felt. Huang *had* changed things in the Aerie, these last seasons. But it wasn't as if Huang had set out to make the bandits' lives more difficult. What he had set out to do was to make their lives more *meaningful*.

"What good is it to get a few coins in your pocket," Huang said, "if the army can come along the next day and take them right back from you? We need to fight *smarter*."

Under Huang's guidance, Zhao's bandits were no longer driven by profit but by the desire to harass their enemies. It was because of Huang that the bandits now attacked military targets virtually to the exclusion of all others; and those few nonmilitary targets that found themselves the subject of the bandits' attentions were those most closely allied with the military's master, the governor-general—mine owners, shipping concerns, and so on.

Such a target was the convoy that the bandits now prepared to attack.

"This convoy is carrying matériel from the Far Sight Outpost north to the White Plains Station," Huang went on. "In case you've *forgotten*, it's White Plains that supplies the soldiers employed as strikebreakers all throughout the north.

Without the supplies carried by this convoy, the garrison will be left unable to supply the necessary manpower, and the mine owners will be left without a shield of armed soldiers between themselves and the men and women whose lives are threatened every day by the unsafe working conditions down in the mines."

"You may not have noticed it, boy," Ruan sneered, "but we're not working in a mine here, are we? We climbed up out of the dirt and found a better life. Why can't we just leave the others to do the same?"

Huang regarded Ruan for a moment, then shook his head. "I wouldn't let Zhao hear you talk like that."

"Yeah?" Ruan reached up and rubbed the sharp point of his jaw. "Well, seems to me there's a lot that Zhao won't, or can't, hear for himself. Like what a worthless waste you are, nor how you're mucking up our good thing here. Seems that Zhao thinks the sun rises and sets on his little pet, and damn anyone who doesn't agree."

Huang shifted uneasily, not sure how to respond.

"Seems to me, though," Ruan went on, "that Zhao won't always be around. And come to that, he won't live forever, will he? And if something *were* to happen to the chief, then . . . ?"

His lips drawn into a line, Huang shouldered past Ruan, shoving the skeletal bandit out of the way. "I don't have time for this," he said.

"I'd watch out, if I were you, *Hummingbird*," Ruan called

after his retreating back. "Zhao won't be around forever, after all. . . ."

When the main body of the convoy had drawn alongside the channel, Huang watched as a detachment of bandits surged over the rim, long knives flashing in the sunlight, bellowing at the top of their lungs. From entrenched positions along the edge of the channel, snipers opened fire with their long-barreled rifles.

That the sniper fire did little but *plink* off the light armor of the crawlers hardly mattered to Huang's plans, nor did the fact that the bandits on foot—for all that they shouted themselves hoarse and spent all their energy running and waving their swords overhead—could hardly do much damage on an individual basis against large vehicles in motion. The snipers and the knife-wielding bandits were, in Huang's carefully orchestrated plan, little more than distractions.

Even so, as distractions they fulfilled their tasks admirably. Faced with attackers on foot, the drivers of the convoy—as Huang had known they would—had slowed their crawlers' forward progression and maneuvered the large vehicles into a rough circle of protection. Then it was time for the next phase of Huang's plan to be put into action.

Huang remembered another convoy, another ring of crawlers, with himself in the role of defender. It seemed odd, though somehow fitting, to find himself now in the opposite role.

"They've moved the crawlers into position," Jue said, sliding back down the wall of the channel from his lookout post at the ledge, "just as you said they would. They can't be more than a dozen paces off the mark."

"Close enough." Huang spared a nod, then motioned to Ruan. "Your men ready with the detonators?"

Ruan scowled but responded with a curt nod. "Just waiting for the chief's word, is all."

Huang felt the barb in Ruan's words, even if no one else did. *Zhao is still in charge here,* the skeletal bandit was saying. *He gives our orders, Hummingbird, not you.*

Biting back the impulse to respond in kind, if perhaps less subtly, Huang turned from Ruan to Zhao, who stood with his eyes just above the lip of the channel wall, watching the bandits herd the crawlers into position. "The convoy is in place, Chief," Huang said in clipped tones. "Waiting on your orders."

Zhao allowed himself a grin and slid back down the channel wall to join the others at the base of the gulley. "Well done, Hummingbird." He turned to Jue. "Call the men to their fallback positions." Then to Ruan. "When the others are clear, order the detonators hit."

Needing no further instruction, the two lieutenants nodded and hurried off to carry out Zhao's orders.

"If this works, Ruan might never forgive you," Zhao said in a low voice to Huang, smiling slightly. Huang raised an eyebrow, concerned, and Zhao explained. "He always did like getting his hands a bit dirty, if you take my meaning, and this plan of yours leaves him with little to do but conduct traffic. If we can take out an armed convoy with a few well-placed explosives and a bit of theater, Ruan might find himself without an opportunity to slake that damned bloodthirst of his."

"Ruan's not bloodthirsty," Huang objected, feeling the need to come to his rival's defense despite what Ruan thought of him. "He just sees it as doing the job properly, and saving us the trouble of having to do it all over again later."

Zhao nodded slightly, clearly unconvinced. "Perhaps. But you might try to remember that *your* neck was once a job Ruan wanted to do properly, and you might want to wonder whether he thinks it still needs doing, at that."

Huang grinned. "I'll try to remember that."

The last of the bandits who'd harried the crawlers on foot was now leaping down into the channel, and to safety. The snipers continued to *plink* their shots against the crawlers' armor, but even they were retreating one by one from their entrenched positions to the safety of the gully's floor.

"That's the last of them," Zhao said in a voice scarcely above a whisper. Perhaps he, too, was afraid that the convoy might overhear, and spoil the surprise that awaited them. "Won't be long now."

As if in response, there came a low hissing sound from the direction of the ring of crawlers, as the first of the detonators began to strike alight.

"Get down," Huang said urgently, sliding back down the cliff wall, motioning to the few bandits on either side who had chanced a peek over the ledge.

Zhao hunched down beside him and covered his ears. Huang, remembering Zhao's long experience with these kinds of explosives down in the mine shafts, followed suit, squeezing his eyes to narrow slits for good measure.

They *felt* the explosions as much as heard them.

And then it was over.

Even at this distance, the bandits were pelted with a rain of red sand and shards of rock, even splinters of metal sheared from the crawlers themselves. Luckily few of those in the shelter of the channel received any noticeable injuries from the shrapnel, and these were bandaged easily enough. Huang just tried not to think too long about those who had been inside the crawlers and the risks to *them*.

When the rain of dust and debris slowed, and the cloud kicked up by the half dozen explosions cleared, Zhao and Huang chanced a look back over the channel's edge to see how well the plan had worked.

Huang's plan, it transpired, had outperformed anyone's expectations. It was just as well that there wasn't much of a market for the goods and materiel carried by the convoy, because little of it survived the blast. For that matter, the crawlers themselves scarcely survived the blast, with only twisted shapes of blackened metal and smoking ruin remaining where the sickly yellowish green crawlers had been only moments before.

The explosives had been plunder the bandits had won from another convoy some time before, but Zhao and the others had seen little use for the stuff before now. They had worked in mines, after all, and having been miners, they would always *be* miners in some matters. To them, explosives were of use in clearing rock, in blasting passages in the skin of the planet itself, and little else besides. Of course any number of them had lost fingers or limbs, or fidelity of hearing, or even loved ones to unintentional blasts, but they still did not think of explosives as potential weapons.

Huang, without any real experience with the stuff, couldn't help but see it as *both* weapon and tool. Buried strategically in the locations to which the crawlers were most likely to flee, in his estimation, the explosives would do to the convoy what no amount of weapons fire could ever accomplish, shredding them open like cans of rations, without putting a single bandit life in jeopardy.

Of course, the blasts *would* put the lives of the convoy's drivers and guards in jeopardy. Worse, it was likely to end them all together, snuffed out like candles in a gale-force wind. But there was the *slightest* possibility, Huang was sure, that the drivers and guards might escape the conflagration, by either taking to their heels, or being thrown clear of the explosion by the blast's concussive force, or any number of other hypothetical situations. That any of these hypotheticals was so improbable as to approach impossible was not a matter on which Huang dwelt. So long as it was *possible* that he had not just engineered the murder of dozens of people, he was able to sleep at night, if fitfully.

He resisted the temptation to think of the hypothetical dead as "innocent" people. Who was innocent, in the final analysis, after all? Zhao? Jue? Ruan? Hardly. Huang himself? Well, as much as he tried to avoid violence whenever possible, necessity had forced him into an impasse from time to time, and he could not deny that his own hands had come away dirty, as Zhao's colorful euphemism had it. But if he was responsible for ending one life to save another? Was that worth the cost? Were the lives of miners he would never meet worth the price of his own bloodied hands?

Huang wasn't sure, but the possible solutions to the equation plagued him by night and day.

Gamine's stomach grumbled, and she couldn't remember the last time she'd felt full. The midday meal was only a short time away, after she finished the morning services, but she found it difficult to work up any enthusiasm for her meager rations. Hunger seemed to be a constant companion these days.

It wasn't that there wasn't food. The Society of Righteous Harmony probably had more food at its disposal now than it ever had. Ever since they'd moved south and west to the outskirts of Yinglong in the Great Yu Canyon, supplies had been easier to come by. Yinglong had originally been founded as a farming community generations before, and though it had grown in the intervening years until it was the largest town north of the Tianfei Valley, it was still the center of a wide agricultural network. Most of the nearby farms were all Combine operations, but those who labored in the town's markets and transport depots were sympathetic to the Society and willing to cut Gamine's people deals on supplies and produce, sometimes going so far as to look the other way while Society followers "accidentally" made off with bundles without paying.

So there was more food on hand than Gamine had seen since she left the Chauviteau-Zong residence. The problem was that there seemed to be more and more mouths to feed with each passing day, and even their plentiful supplies could stretch only so far.

Gamine sometimes wondered just what it was about the Society that so appealed to these new converts. The early camp followers who had formed the first core of the Society had been the displaced and dispossessed, men and women with nowhere else to go. For them, the Society had been a kind of refuge, and they had found in the Society's teachings—first from Master Wei and then increasingly from Iron Jaw—a message of hope for a better tomorrow.

But many of these more recent arrivals were not cut from the same cloth as those early followers. These were not homeless refugees, searching for any kind of shelter and security they could find. These were men and women who left behind gainful employment to come and join the Society. Some even brought children, whole families closing up their homes in the villages and towns and opting instead to live in the ever-growing tent city of the Society of Righteous Harmony. In recent months, there had even been children born among those already living in the camp, new life beginning just as their parents had left old lives behind.

The camp was situated on the western edge of Yinglong, between the town's edge and the foot of the canyon walls, their knobs of rock rising above the dust and loose debris on the slope, the tops of the walls towering so high overhead that they could scarcely be seen from this vantage point. Sheltered between the canyon walls and the town, the camp was largely spared the ravages of the dust storms that blew from time to time across the canyon floor, excoriating everything in their path. But the high walls also meant that shortly after midday the sun disappeared from view, and the camp was plunged into shadow almost as dark as night, though the skies overhead were clear and bright. It was a strange, twilit existence in the camp, with the day being the brief interval between the sun rising over the spires of Yinglong to the east and passing beyond the canyon wall to the west, and the nights seemed never to end.

Perhaps this endless twilight had something to do with Gamine's strange moods. She'd read that people who lived at Fire Star's poles, mining frozen water from beneath what remained of the ice caps, had constant sunlight during the summer solstice, when the sun shone directly on them, and continuous darkness during the winter solstice, when the planet's axial tilt pointed the pole away from the sun's rays. In those seemingly endless days of eternal night, it was said that a person's psyche suffered, and that people fell into deep depressions that would not lift until the sun rose once more above the horizon. Was it any wonder that Gamine, who now saw the sun for just a few short hours each day, was similarly affected?

Gamine was tempted to lay all her dark moods at the feet of the towering canyon walls, and to ascribe her glum outlook on the ever-present shadows. But still she could not escape the thought that it was instead some premonition that so affected her, some presentiment of danger or misfortune waiting just around tomorrow's horizon.

Could it be Master Wei's ill health, perhaps, caught up to him at last? Could she be sensing the stealthy and relentless approach of death coming for the old man? He seldom climbed from his sleeping pallet these days, and when he spoke, it was only to ramble about people and places long gone, lost in Wei's childhood long before Gamine was born. Having taken leave of his senses almost entirely, he recognized nothing about his present surroundings, just looked around him with a fool's half smile and confusion in his eyes. He had taken to calling Gamine by the name of his long-dead sister and had decided that Temujin must be his own grandfather, and it seemed that he derived some comfort from seeing the two of them, however briefly. The others in the camp, when they chanced to visit Wei's tent, were likewise assigned roles from the old man's childhood—this one a farmer for whom Wei had worked in the harvest season, that one the magistrate in the village in which he'd been born—all of them made confused and unwilling players in this impromptu theater of unrelenting memories that took up the mendicant's twilight days.

But no. Gamine wasn't worried about death taking the old mendicant. If anything, death would be a kind of release for Wei, finally severing the last ties with the present away from which his mind and spirit had long before turned. With death, he would be allowed to move on to whatever waited beyond the veil of the living world. The Society, taught by Wei himself in more lucid days, held that the afterlife was a place of unalloyed joy and comfort, peopled by all of those who have preceded us in this life, and where each would be given their long-overdue rewards, everything they lacked for in life being given to them a hundredfold. There was no hunger in that blessed place, no pain, no loss, no loneliness, only endless satiation and comfort and bliss.

Gamine spoke about the afterlife in the homilies often, talking about the ways in which the powers rewarded those who had served them faithfully in life. She talked about the afterlife as much because of the evident comfort it brought to so many of the listeners as for any other reason. It was as if the simple act of hearing about the promise of deliverance in the afterlife helped the listeners forget, if only for a moment, the pain and strain of their torments in the here and now.

But while Gamine was happy to repeat Wei's words about the blissful afterlife when speaking the homilies to the assembled faithful, she did not believe in it herself. Or at least, not entirely. There was some small part of her, it was true, that fervently wished for there to be such a place of reward and rest, a part that looked forward to setting down the burdens of life and passing through the gate of death into a more serene place. But a larger part of her thought the whole thing was an empty promise designed only to comfort those who had nothing to comfort them in life.

Gamine hoped there was a life after life but suspected that if one existed, it would bear the same resemblance to Wei's simplistic wonderland that a landscape depicted by a master painter bore to a child's scribbled rendering of the same scene.

When Gamine had finished the revelation, performing the "iron jaw" routine with Temujin's drunken assistance, the sun stood atop the towering canyon walls above them. By the time she returned to her tent, to her simple midday meal of rice and salted fish, the sun was dipping behind the wall and out of sight, and the line of shadows marched inexorably toward the camp.

When she had finished eating, she left her tent and went to check on Master Wei. He was sleeping, for which she was thankful, since she often found it a chore to play the part of Wei's long-lost sister, listening to him rattle on about places and things that she had never seen, could hardly imagine. Tender scenes of the family gathering together for an evening meal, after Wei and his father had spent the day farming the family's allotment. Pilgrimages to holy shrines in distant provinces—to White Rock Temple, where the martyrs were put to the sword by the warriors of the Mexic Dominion in ancient times; to the Temple of Peace, which commemorated the place where the Guanpu Emperor set foot on Fire Star; and once even as far as the waters of the Great Southern Basin. Gamine hadn't been to any of those places, but even if she had, it would not have been beside a loving father or holding hands with a doting brother. She couldn't help but begrudge the old man these memories, as jumbled and confused as they were, and it was with a sigh of relief that she let the tent flap fall closed once more and turned away, leaving him snoring irregularly inside.

Before she was halfway back to her own tent, though, Temujin came stumbling up to her, eyes wild.

"Best shift yourself, my little sprite," he said, out of breath, his mustaches stained and matted by wine from the jug that sloshed in his hands. "Time to cut our losses and scarper, you ask me."

Temujin started to continue past her, but Gamine shot out a hand and grabbed hold of his arm. "What are you talking about? What are you running from?"

The old crook glanced back nervously over his shoulder and chewed his lower lip. "Constabulary, by the look of them.

Guardsmen." He shook his head. "Or maybe soldiers, at that—I couldn't rightly tell. But either way, it's men in uniforms with swords and guns, heading our way with a will, and that's never good news for those in our line of work."

"And what line is that?" Gamine cocked an eyebrow. "Preaching? Ministering to the needy?"

Temujin's lip curled in scorn, but after a moment he began to nod slowly. "Yes, that might be the best way to handle it, now that you mention it. Play it straight? We're what we seem to be and nothing more?" He scratched his neck thoughtfully. "All right, we'll try it your way. But I reserve the right to take to my heels if it goes south, and you're on your own lookout then."

Gamine released her hold on his arm. She decided not to explain that, so far as she was concerned, ministering *was* their line of work. That Temujin had taken her response as a suggested strategy just made him that much easier to handle.

"They're coming from the direction of the town, I take it?" Gamine looked back the way Temujin had come, where the light of the sun still shone on the ground.

Temujin nodded and took a long draft from his wine jar.

Gamine smiled, though in her chest her heartbeat began to quicken. "Then I expect we'd better see what they want."

They were soldiers, not guardsmen. That much Gamine was able to see right away. Bannermen, to be precise, the elite all-terrain military force. At their head was a man with an officer's rosette picked out in gold thread on the black fabric of his tunic, over his heart. His light eyes and pale skin suggested he was of Briton extraction, or perhaps Vinlander, but while his head was shaved in the Manchurian style, clean shaven from the forehead back to the middle of the scalp, the hair that fell in a braid down his back was fair, the color of straw, which gave him more the look of Deutschland or Norge or Sverige. Above his right eye was a distinctive cross-shaped scar, and a slight sneer tugged up the corner of his mouth.

The fair-haired Bannerman's hand rested on the hilt of the saber hanging at his side, a pistol hanging from his belt on the other hip. Though he'd drawn neither weapon, he watched Gamine and her people through narrow eyes that suggested it would take only a single wrong step on their part to prompt him to action.

"You're in charge here? The one they call Iron Jaw?" The Bannerman raised an eyebrow and gave Gamine an appraising look. "How old *are* you?"

"Old enough." Gamine crossed her arms over her chest. "Who are you, and what's this about?"

The fair-haired man nodded, lips slightly pursed, and spread his hands in a shrug. "Have it your way." Then he straightened and continued in a more officious tone. "I am Bannerman Kenniston, and I have orders to remove your people from this area."

"Remove?" said one of the Society followers standing

behind Gamine, sounding alarmed and insulted at the same time.

Gamine narrowed her eyes. "Just what do you mean by 'this area,' anyway?" She glanced from side to side, indicating the dirt at their feet. The shadow of the canyon wall now fell across her legs, its forward line falling on the ground just between her and the Bannerman. "Here?" She took an exaggerated step to one side, and pointed to the place where she'd been standing. "There?" She smiled. "I'm not sure I understand."

Gamine realized that she probably shouldn't taunt the man, considering that he and his dozen or so friends were all heavily armed, but somehow she couldn't help herself. There was something about his overly formal manner that reminded her of someone, and she simply reacted instinctually. It was a matter of moments before she consciously recognized the similarity to Madam Chauviteau-Zong's prim manner.

The Society followers behind her, though, saw only a bare slip of a girl standing up to a squad of Bannermen with a smile on her face. That story would be shared around the camp in coming nights, more proof that the powers shone upon Iron Jaw.

"There is no jest in my words, child," the Bannerman went on, "and I'm not playing a game. You've made some powerful enemies, and it's time for you to move on."

Gamine's smile began to fade. "What *enemies?*"

The Bannerman jerked his chin at the camp behind Gamine, where followers hung back, watching intently, partially hidden by canvas and twine that would do nothing to protect them if the squad should decide to attack. "How many of your people here left good jobs behind, these last weeks, eh?"

Gamine's lips drew into a tight line. The Combine. If it had been a snake, it could have devoured her leg whole before she saw it.

Many of the more recent converts in the camp had once farmed their own allotments, but after the drought and quakes they had been forced to find work as laborers on plantations owned by the Combine. When the laborers discovered that their lives under their new masters were not as satisfying as those they'd once known, many of them were hungry for something better, desperate for some meaning in their lives. And many had found that meaning, and that better life, in the Society of Righteous Harmony.

"I'm told," the Bannerman went on, "that just a few days ago there as was a mass defection of laborers from a Combine plantation near here, after one of their number attended one of your 'services' here and then carried back to the others what he'd heard."

"I can't imagine why the Combine would take offense. You can't tell me there aren't more people ready to take their place. There aren't enough jobs to go around."

"Perhaps," the Bannerman allowed with a slight smile. "But it sets a bad precedent, if nothing else. The Combine has been in touch with the governor-general himself, and word's come down that your little group has orders to pull up stakes and move along. You're not welcome here any longer."

"And 'here,' again, would be where?" Gamine took two theatrical steps to the left. "Is *this* far enough?"

The Bannerman's grin widened slightly, but his grip tightened ominously on his sword's handle. "You're no longer welcome in the Great Yu Canyon, child. You've been given five days to break camp, pack your things, and be on your way, or my men and I will be forced to act." He pulled the saber a fraction from its scabbard, the blade gleaming in the last sunlight spilling over the canyon wall. "And trust me, child, you do *not* want to see us in action."

Gamine met the Bannerman's gaze and felt ice dripping down her spine. She repressed the urge to shudder and tightened her hands into fists at her sides.

"We've never spoken against the Combine and have no desire to interfere with its interests."

"That's as may be," the Bannerman admitted with a shrug. "But I've got orders to move you, and so you're going to move."

At a signal from him, the other Bannermen all drew their weapons, the naked blades of their sabers gleaming in the dying midday light.

Gamine looked from the Bannerman to the Society followers who stood directly behind her, and the ragged circles of
tents stretching out beyond. The followers were looking at her
with expressions of expectant anticipation, eager to see what
she would do, how she would respond. After all, didn't the
powers speak to, and through, Iron Jaw? If the Bannermen
wanted a fight, couldn't the Society's divinely inspired leader,
invulnerable so long as the spirits possessed her, stand against
them with ease?

Gamine saw all these thoughts and more in the eyes of the
followers, and shrank from them.

"Very well," she said in a low voice, turning back to face
the Bannerman. "Tell your men to stand down, and I'll have
my people break camp."

Behind her, Gamine heard the followers gasp in surprise
and disappointment, but the Bannerman just nodded, his
expression unreadable. Letting his saber slide back into its
scabbard, he motioned for his men to sheathe their weapons,
and the brief confrontation was at an end.

Days later, the Society of Righteous Harmony was once more
in motion, migrating to the north, following the line of the
canyon walls. Their frequent companion, hunger, was now
with them always, the mealtime rations growing smaller with
each passing day. And not just hunger, but death followed
them, as well. A few days out of Yinglong, Master Wei finally

gave up the mortal world and moved on to the reward that awaited him in the life to come.

Wei was buried in the shadow of the Great Yu Canyon's walls, under a cairn of rocks prized from the slope. When she performed the funereal rites that Wei himself had devised, Gamine could not help but envy the old man, if only a little. His travails were at an end, while hers, she feared, were just beginning.

As the airship approached Mount Shennong, Huang idly sharpened the blade of his sword with a whetstone. The sword's blade was rugged, bearing scars and nicks, pitted here and there with age. It held a fine edge, though, and was nicely weighted for his grasp. Huang had taken it off an unconscious foe during a raid on a refinery some seasons before, and though it had yet to replace the red-bladed saber he'd been given by Governor-General Ouyang, which was still Zhao's prized possession, it had become familiar and comfortable in his fist.

The pilot signaled from the makeshift controls that the skylight entrance to the Aerie was within sight, and that they'd be touching down in moments. All the bandits on board the airship were relieved, looking forward to getting back into the protection of the Aerie and putting their feet up, if only briefly. This latest foray had taken them farther from home than most, nearly halfway to the Great Yu Canyon, and all they had to show for their trouble were a few crates of machine parts and the knowledge that they'd disrupted the activities of the Green Standard Army in the region for another few weeks at least.

Zhao had announced a brief respite, a vacation from their routine. Once the airship was landed and unloaded, he would order a feast prepared—"feast" in relative terms, nearly twice the normal rations—and a case of wine cracked open, and then the bandits would have a few days' vacation. They could all use the rest.

Even as the airship descended into the skylight, and they saw that there were no lights on in the hangar below, the bandits still did not suspect anything was amiss. The approach of the airship should have sent off proximity signals with the Aerie, alerting the few bandits who had remained behind on this last raid to ready the chamber for their arrival. But the space beneath them was dark as a moonless night, lit only by the thin sunlight streaming down from the thin chimneylike opening through which the airship descended.

"Maybe they've started their vacation early," Jue suggested, shouting to be heard over the thrum of the airship's engines.

Huang smiled, the expression no doubt completely hidden behind his mask and goggles. He gave an exaggerated nod instead. "I can't blame them," he shouted back.

Finally, the airship touched down, and the engines were stilled. As they gradually whirred to silence, the bandits opened the hatch and climbed out into the gloom beyond.

Sounds could not carry far in the thin air of the hangar,

but Zhao shouted for the ground crew to attend, all the same, cupping his hands around his breather mask like a trumpet and bellowing for all that he was worth. As it was, Huang, only a few paces away, could scarcely hear him.

Then the lights flared on, blinding bright. Huang squinted in the glare, his eyes struggling to adjust from the darkness of a moment before to the newfound brightness.

Huang saw immediately why the lights had remained unilluminated. The bandits who had remained behind, and were to act as ground crew, now lay bound and gagged on the cold stone floor of the hangar. Those who were not unconscious stared up at them helplessly. And Huang understood in an instant what could render such stout bandits helpless—a full platoon of Bannermen.

Three dozen heavily armed and armored Bannermen filled the hangar, well entrenched and with their weapons trained on the airship and the bandits now standing before it.

Huang never knew quite how the Bannermen had come to be in the hangar. The most likely explanation was that the military had successfully tracked the airship back to the Aerie after one of the bandits' raids, and had waited until the airship was away on another foray to storm the mountain stronghold and subdue the few bandits left behind, most of whom were too aged or infirm to put up much of a struggle. Then they had only to lie in wait for the airship to return, signaled by the proximity signals of the airship's arrival, at which point they would take up their positions in the hangar and ambush the bandits when they least expected it.

Of course, that being the case, why would they have dragged the bound and gagged ground crew into the hangar and left them on the cold stone floor?

Huang didn't have to wonder for long.

The bandits were still squinting in the bright lights, while the Bannermen's own eyes were shaded by dark goggles, their faces covered from the nose down by armored breather masks, with only their foreheads left visible.

The leader of the Bannermen, who had a cross-shaped scar above his right eye, carried a loudspeaker of some kind, which amplified his voice loud enough to be heard by the bandits even through the thin high-altitude air.

"Lay down your arms," the Bannerman shouted, his voice distorted and amplified by the machine, until it sounded like he was speaking in peals of thunder. "Surrender, and you may yet live."

Zhao, brandishing his red-bladed saber, stood his ground defiantly.

The lead Bannerman only shrugged, and in a single grisly motion whipped his saber from its scabbard and brought it point down into the back of the nearest captured bandit, who lay with his hands and feet bound, facedown on the cold stone floor beside him.

As the Bannerman swept his saber out of the bandit's back,

dark arterial blood sluicing from its blade, he again addressed the bandits through the loudspeaker. At his feet, the injured bandit jerked upon the floor, punctured lung struggling in agony for breath, his life pouring from the wound in his back.

"That's one of your number lost. How many more will follow?"

There were some sixteen bandits standing before the airship, and by Huang's estimation a full platoon of thirty-six Bannermen circling them on all sides.

"Oh, I almost forgot," the Bannerman with the cross-shaped scar said absently. "Can't have you running off, can we?"

At a signal from the lead Bannerman, one of his men raised a metal tube on his shoulder, and a torrent of fire gushed from its forward end, trailing black smoke. The mortar struck the airship just above the gondola. The envelope crumpled like paper, and had it been filled with an inflammable gas like hydrogen, the entire hangar would have gone up in the conflagration. As it was, the airship employed nonflammable helium, which did little more than pour from the massive rents in the envelope, filling the hangar. Had the bandits and Bannermen not been wearing breather masks, they would have squeaked at one another in comically high voices until they suffocated from lack of oxygen. The escape of the gas was all but unnoticeable, except for the evidence of the deflated, crumpled airship.

The gondola, though, was filled with breathable oxygen and caught fire immediately, burning like a magnesium torch, taking with it what little plunder the bandits had brought back from their most recent raids.

The force of the explosion knocked the nearest of the bandits still standing to their knees, and it was at this point that the Bannermen made their move.

Despite the cavalier way he'd dispatched the bound and gagged bandit at his feet, it was clear to Huang that the Bannerman did not intend to kill them all, at least not right away. If he had, he could simply have commanded his men to open fire on the bandits with rifles and pistols, all of them having had the opportunity to properly brace themselves against their weapons' recoil before the airship had even touched down. That he hadn't given any command of the sort, but instead had allowed a number of his men to meet the bandits with drawn swords in close combat, suggested he'd been ordered to take at least some of them alive.

More than likely, the Bannerman had been instructed to bring some of the bandits back to stand trial, or to be made examples of, preferably the leaders.

What that meant to Huang, aside from the fact that they might be better off dead if the alternative was to serve as the governor-general's example to other potential bandits, was that they had a fighting chance to escape. If the Bannermen were hesitant to open fire and rain bullets upon them, the bandits might just be able to fight their way clear. Just where they would *go* was still a cause for concern—with the Bannermen controlling the Aerie and the airship in smoking ruins behind them—but anywhere was preferable, at this point.

With some of the Bannermen retaining strategic positions along the hangar walls, their rifles primed and ready, their leader and a dozen or so of the others drew their swords and advanced on the bandits, their expressions unreadable behind black goggles and armored masks.

Huang drew his own sword and, taking his place at Zhao's side, prepared to meet the charge.

Swaddled in his thermal suit, hidden behind mask and goggles, Huang could hear only the distant echoes of battle sounds through the thin air. It was as if he fought underwater. When he moved, it felt like his muscles were several steps behind his thoughts, dragging sluggishly through heavy mud.

Since he'd taken over as strategist for the bandits, Huang had fought face-to-face only infrequently. He'd sparred with Zhao on a regular basis, teaching the bandit chief the formal fencing techniques he'd learned while Zhao in turn instructed Huang in the use of more dubious tactics. But those had been only practice matches, with the only blood drawn from nicks and scratches gotten by accident.

Now Huang found himself fighting for his life, with his sword the only thing between him and capture, or the grave. Perhaps even stranger, in fighting for his own life he might be forced to deprive an opponent of his.

Huang had never killed another in close combat, so far as

he knew. He'd injured other swordsmen, that was certain, as he had when the bandits had taken him prisoner when raiding the supply convoy to Far Sight Outpost, all those years before. But none of those injuries had been fatal, and many of those opponents had gone on to become close friends when Huang joined the bandits' number himself.

He'd been responsible for death before; at least, it was almost impossible to imagine that he hadn't. He liked to entertain the fantasy that all of those within the crawlers he exploded, or the mines he sealed off, or the refineries he blew to pieces, had somehow miraculously escaped just in the nick of time. It was a ridiculously implausible fiction, of course, but a comforting one, and it was a fiction that he clung to, particularly in the long, dark watches of the night.

In the present circumstances, though, Huang defended his life and liberty, and in doing so was faced with an inescapable decision—fight and live, or surrender and die. And in fighting, there was the very real likelihood that he would have to take another's life. Without any conditions or exceptions, without the chance that his opponent had secretly survived the encounter and sought medical attention. Without the slimmest possibility that he and his opponent might one day be friends, and that Huang would be forgiven for injuring him in close combat. No, he would have to kill, and see the life leave another's body, never to return.

The only problem was, Huang wasn't sure he could *do* that.

• • •

As it happened, Huang was not forced to discover whether he could kill. At least, not yet. He found himself facing a Bannerman who wielded his sword like it was a club, with considerable force but no finesse, and after parrying a few attacks, Huang was able to knock the sword from the Bannerman's hand. Then he'd simply stepped in and delivered a blow with a balled fist to the side of the Bannerman's head, sending him crumpling to the floor.

Tightening his grip on his own sword, Huang turned to see how his fellow bandits were faring.

Not well, it was quickly apparent. Already a handful of bandits were on the floor in various states of distress, some still moaning and twitching, some silent and unmoving. Those bandits who remained standing were holding their own, but the Bannermen's continued attacks were pressing them together in a knot at the center of the hangar, making it difficult for each of the bandits to fight without risking injuring their fellows.

Zhao was only a few paces away, crossing swords with the leader of the Bannermen. And though the cross-shaped scar over his right eye flushed red with exertion, it was clear that the Bannerman was far from exhausted, though the same could not be said for Zhao. The bandit chief turned aside the Bannerman's thrusts, but with less energy and enthusiasm with each exchange. And if the opponent whom Huang had faced was clearly ill trained in the use of the blade, the same could not be said for the Bannermen's leader.

There was something familiar about the way the Bannerman handled his blade, but Huang didn't have time to dwell on it. Another of the Bannermen rushed him from the other side, saber in hand, and Huang was forced to turn and face the attack.

While not as skilled a swordsman as the Bannermen's leader, Huang's new opponent was more adept than the fallen opponent who'd swung the blade like a club, and Huang was put to considerably more trouble to keep from being skewered on the point of the Bannerman's blade. At one point, Huang batted the Bannerman's blade aside and for an instant had an opening that would have allowed him to end the contest, but the only attack available to him would have required a killing blow. Huang hesitated, not eager to try his hand at murder, even if it would be justified in self-defense. Instead, he continued to trade blows with the Bannerman, parry and attack and retreat and attack and parry. Finally, he was able to score a painful but nonfatal wound on the Bannerman's upper arm, a long but shallow cut, freely bleeding, that caused the Bannerman to drop his sword and clutch his arm in agony. Huang followed with a kick to the Bannerman's midsection, driving the wind from him and forcing the Bannerman to his knees.

Huang turned back to see what assistance he might offer Zhao, just in time to see that contest, too, come to an end, though not in any way that Huang would have hoped.

Just as Huang was taking a half step forward to close the distance between him and the two opposing leaders, the Bannerman slashed down with his saber, the blade biting deep into Zhao's forearm and the hand that held the red-bladed saber. As Zhao's saber clattered to the stone floor, the Bannerman pressed his advantage, lunging forward and burying his own sword halfway to the hilt in the bandit chief's chest. Behind his grimy goggles Zhao's eyes widened, and as the Bannerman yanked his sword free once more, the bandit chief fell forward, face-first onto the ground.

Huang stood frozen for a long moment, watching the tableau before him, the Bannerman with the cross-shaped scar standing over the fallen body of the bandit chief, a man who in recent years had been as much as father to Huang as his own parent once had been, if not more. Then the Bannerman stepped over Zhao's fallen body as though it were only so much refuse scattered on the floor, and turned his attention to another of the bandits, who was fighting a Bannerman a few paces away.

Later, Huang would curse himself that he didn't immediately race after the Bannerman and avenge Zhao then and there. In the moment, though, his only thought was to help Zhao. Dropping his own sword to the ground, he rushed to where the bandit chief lay. Gingerly, he turned the bandit chief up on his side, his front already sticky with the dark blood that pooled beneath him.

"Zhao! Can you hear me?!"

The bandit chief's eyes rolled from one side to the other, half-lidded, and finally focused on Huang.

"Ouch," Zhao said absently, as though he'd just discovered a tiny splinter in his foot. "That hurt."

It wasn't until the bandit chief started shaking with laughter that Huang realized that Zhao was joking. But he didn't laugh long, since doing so forced him to cough, a pink-flecked foam gathering at the corners of his mouth just visible through the breather mask.

"Hold on, Zhao, we'll get you help!" Huang gripped the bandit chief's shoulders, trying not to stare at the sucking wound in Zhao's chest.

"No," Zhao said, and was once more racked with a fit of bloody coughing. "No help . . . Too late . . ."

The bandit chief lifted his head, glacially slow, as though looking for something, and then pointed to where the red-bladed saber lay. His eyes flicked from the saber to Huang, lids dropping farther.

"Sword . . ." Zhao said, his voice now barely a harsh whisper.

Huang straightened and went to retrieve the saber, then came back and crouched beside the bandit chief once more. He could only imagine that Zhao wanted to end his life as he'd lived it, with a sword in hand, but when Huang tried to press the saber's hilt into the dying man's hand, Zhao pushed it away.

"No . . . Hummingbird . . ." Zhao managed, but barely. "Yours . . . You lead . . . now."

Huang held the saber in both hands, shaking his head. "But Zhao, what . . ."

"Lead . . ." Zhao said, interrupting him. ". . . our brothers. Look after . . . them . . ."

Another racking cough caught the bandit chief, and his eyes squeezed shut with pain.

"Safety . . ." Zhao croaked, almost below the edge of hearing. "Lead them . . ."

And then the light went out of the bandit chief's eyes, and he was gone.

Huang straightened and stood at the center of the hangar, the red-bladed saber in his hand, while all around him the bandits fought for their lives.

Here and there on the hangar's cold stone floor were fallen combatants, bandit and Bannerman alike. But while the bandits were clearly giving as good as they got, the Bannermen had the advantage of numerical superiority, and it was only a matter of time before the bandits found themselves completely overwhelmed.

If any of them were to survive this encounter and escape death, capture, or worse, they would need to get out of the hangar and away from the Bannermen.

Huang realized he was waiting for someone to tell him

what to do. Even all the seasons he'd acted as strategist for the bandits, it had still been Zhao who had made the final decisions, and in the end Huang merely had to follow orders. He had been following orders his whole life, in one way or another. As much as he had liked to think himself the footloose free spirit when he was younger, carousing through the streets of Fanchuan, hadn't he just been his parents' dutiful son, even then? Oh, he might have preferred sport, wine, and women to his studies, but when his parents snapped their fingers and said it was time for him to go off and join the Green Standard Army, had he stood his ground or tucked tail between his legs and gotten himself fitted for a uniform? And in the brief time he was actually *in* the Army of the Green Standard, he was following orders then, as well. As the bandits' pet he'd had no ability to exercise his own will, and when he had opted to join the bandits' number he'd suborned his own will to that of the bandit chief, Zhao. But now, it seemed, there was no one left to tell him what to do.

Of course, Zhao *had* told him what to do, at that. The dying chief's last command, his last instruction to his prized lieutenant, had been for Huang to take his place as leader, and to lead the other bandits to safety. Huang was going to have to decide just *how* to accomplish that on his own. But now he found it difficult to remember the last time he'd made his own decision and followed it through.

There was the moment he turned on the trio of soldiers

who'd plundered the airship; he'd chosen the life of the bandit. And before that, when he'd attempted to escape from the Aerie, and gone through the hangar into the . . .

Into the cave system!

That was the solution. If there was any avenue of escape to be found in all of Mount Shennong, it would be in the winding tunnels carved in Fire Star's ancient past by gases escaping through molten rock. Years ago Huang had tried to escape from the bandits and back to his life as a soldier by fleeing into those same tunnels; now he would try to lead the other bandits safely away from soldiers the very same way. Hopefully this time his breather mask would survive the journey and he wouldn't asphyxiate in the process.

There was no time to lose. Only a fraction of the bandits still remained standing, and if any of them were to escape, it would have to be *now*.

"The tunnels, Jue!" Huang leaned close, speaking just loud enough to be heard. "We've got to reach the caves!"

The two bandits stood shoulder to shoulder, fallen Bannermen at their feet but more still coming to take their place.

"What about Zhao?" Jue followed Huang's haunted glance back to where the bandit chief lay lifeless on the floor, and then glanced down to see the red-bladed saber in Huang's fist. Then Jue nodded, his brows knit. "I'll pass the word."

"Wait for my signal, then everyone form on me. Got it?"

Behind his breather mask, Jue flashed the hint of a smile. "Seems simple enough. But you might want to include 'not dying' in the plans, as well."

With that, the scar-faced Bannerman turned and began slashing his way toward the nearest of the remaining bandits.

In a matter of moments, the word had passed from bandit to bandit. There were maybe ten of them still standing now, the rest fallen before the Bannermen's swords. There was no time to lose.

"Now!" Huang shouted as loud as he was able, then took to his heels, pounding toward one of the largest of the fissures in the hangar wall. The nearest sniper Bannermen were a good two dozen paces away on either side, which was why Huang had chosen this cave over other, larger ones. He only hoped it remained as large as they descended.

As Huang threw himself into the cave mouth, he heard a rifle shot *spang* off the wall just above his shoulder. The Bannermen were firing into the cave. Huang wasn't sure if the Bannermen felt they'd already captured enough bandits alive, if injured, and were ready to dispatch the rest of their quarry with firearms, or if they were simply unwilling to allow the slim chance the bandits might escape, and any hypothetical orders to take some of them alive be damned. Of course, for all Huang knew they'd never received any such orders, and had only closed with them in sword-to-sword combat because the Bannermen's leader had wanted a bit of sport.

It hardly mattered. Huang had reached the relative and temporary safety of the cave and now stood just within, helping the other bandits who followed do the same. One stumbled and fell, not from rifle shot but simply from exhaustion, just before the cave mouth, and Huang risked himself to rush back into the hangar and drag the bandit into the cave, while shots ricocheted off the walls and floor around them, kicking up fragments of stone that stung them like shrapnel. It wasn't until Huang and the other were safe within the cave that he recognized who the stumbling bandit had been.

"If we survive this," the skeletal Ruan said with a grimace that seemed almost like a smile, "remind me to thank you."

Others of the bandits never made it to the cave, felled by the Bannermen's rifles or cut down by sabers and knives as they ran past.

In the end, only a half dozen of them huddled in the shadows a few paces within the cave mouth.

"There's no more coming," Jue said, breathless, his hands on his knees.

"He's right," Ruan put in. "This is it. We should move."

"But where?" another bandit said, eyes wild, blood flowing freely from a cut above his left ear.

"The old mining shaft," Huang answered, his tone level but firm. "It's the only way out."

The other bandits exchanged glances, but Jue nodded. "He's right."

"Here they come." Ruan jerked a thumb back toward the hangar, where the lead Bannerman was now approaching, pistol in one hand and saber in other, toward the cave, his men following behind.

Huang spared a moment to glare from the shadows at the Bannermen's leader. He realized suddenly that he had lost any compunction against killing, and had no qualms against murder, so long as the person skewered at the end of his saber was the Bannerman with the cross-shaped scar above his right eye. But revenge would have to be satisfied some other time. Now he owed it to Zhao to get the few bandits who remained to freedom.

"Come on," Huang said, pushing past the others and continuing deeper into the cave. "There's no time to waste."

It seemed an eternity later, but was nearer a handful of hours, when the six bandits managed to remove the last of the rubble blocking the mining shaft's entrance, and looked out on a sight most of them had never thought to see again—the morning. The sun was just rising in the east and cast long shadows across the red sands. And from this vantage point, near the base of Mount Shennong, they could see what had been hidden from them the day before.

A short distance off stood two military crawlers, camouflaged from above by large canopies dyed the same rust red as the surrounding sands. From the skies, they would have been all but invisible, which explained why the airship had failed to notice them. The bandits could only suppose that the Bannermen had tracked them back to the Aerie after some previous raid, then come here in secret and waited for the airship to leave on another foray. Then the Bannermen must have scaled the slopes of Shennong itself and descended on lines through the skylight. Overcoming the ground crew and the other bandits within the Aerie, they had then simply lain in wait for the bandits' return.

They would never know the details for sure, but that seemed the most likely explanation, and it satisfied the curiosity of all concerned.

"So what now, Hummingbird?" Ruan rubbed his sharp chin, his cheeks seeming even more hollow than ever, his eyes sunken in dark rings.

Huang unslung his breather mask and let it fall to one side, then tugged down his goggles and left them hanging around his neck. "I don't have any desire to hang around here, do you?"

The other bandits shook their heads.

"So what do you suggest, Chief?" Jue asked. He'd already accepted Huang's leadership, though it was clear some of the others still harbored doubts.

There were only one or two Bannermen in evidence, maintaining a halfhearted picket around the crawlers, while the rest of their number were still in the Aerie above, tending to the prisoners and their own wounded, or in the cave system trying to track Huang and the others.

"We'll need a ride," Huang said.

He raised the red-bladed saber, given to him once long ago by Governor-General Ouyang, and again years later by a man who had sworn bloody vengeance against Ouyang's name, and pointed toward the crawlers. Then he glanced to the others, his lips curled in a grim smile.

"Why don't we take theirs?"

Gamine was officiating over the third funeral in as many days and wasn't sure how many of them she could handle.

The Society had reached the barren, hardscrabble highlands north of Forking Paths, where the northernmost mountains of the Three Sovereigns range could be seen squatting on the western horizon. On clear days, when the dust storms didn't limit visibility to their hands before their faces, they could even see the misty outlines of Bao Shan towering farther off.

Gamine knew that too many had died when she realized it wasn't the death that bothered her so much as the funerals themselves. But could she help it if the dry, barren ground underfoot seemed no more to want the dead Society followers than the towns and villages to the east had wanted them alive? Unable to burn or bury the bodies, they'd been forced to cover them in sad mounds of sand, which began to blow away and reveal the lonesome corpses beneath even before Gamine had finished reciting the burial verses.

If not for Mama Noh, who stood beside her always in recent days, supporting her both figuratively and literally, Gamine might well have left the dead to rot where they fell, without observance or ritual at all. But Mama Noh knew well how to perform, how to play a part, how to bend the face into the expected expression and go through the motions, even if within there was nothing but numb resignation.

The journey west from Yinglong had been difficult and had taken its toll on the Society of Righteous Harmony, but there were times when Gamine almost felt that, if that was the price of meeting Mama Noh and the rest of the Red Crawler Opera Company, then it just might have been worth it.

There wasn't enough food to go around, and less with each passing day. Most of those who had died in the western trek, whatever the immediate cause, had ultimately been defeated by hunger. The Society followers were wasting away, little by little, and it seemed only a matter of time before there was nothing left of them at all.

Yinglong had been only the first community to bar their gates to the Society and to force them away at the end of rifle barrels and blades. Word of the Society of Righteous Harmony preceded them, and in town after town, village after village, the authorities would greet them at threshold and order Gamine and her people to go back the way they had come.

The Society purchased what little food it could afford— and stole or begged what food it couldn't—from the farming communities it passed, but most of the operating farms were Combine plantations, and the foremen were always close at hand to drive the Society away. The Combine felt it had lost too many laborers to the siren call of Gamine's homilies, it seemed, and would not suffer any more to follow.

It had been as they were leaving the Great Yu Canyon behind altogether, heading out onto the highlands, that they first caught sight of the crawler.

Temujin had been sure it was the authorities, tiring of pushing them out of village after village and preferring instead to hunt them down and eliminate the nuisance once and for all.

Gamine had felt a serpent of dread coiling and uncoiling in her gut. She hadn't wanted to believe that Temujin was right but found it hard to dismiss him outright.

The Society was walking in an irregular column, some hundreds of them altogether, walking a few abreast, stretched out over nearly a mile. The crawler approached from the north, a black speck against the violet-tinged late-afternoon sky.

Gamine had suggested that, if it *was* the authorities come to eliminate them, there would be little point in running. Temujin objected that there was still no compelling argument against *trying*, at least.

Then the crawler slowed and stopped just ahead of the Society's column, and it became immediately clear that whomever they were dealing with, it was *not* the authorities.

The crawler was of antique design, and though time and

the elements had worn down the paint on the hull, its former brilliance was still evident. The crawler was painted nose to tail an arrestingly bright shade of red, like the glow of the sun just before it dipped below the horizon. None of the Society followers could ever remember seeing a military crawler using anything like that sort of coloration. Most military crawlers were painted bland, yellowish green shades, not in such bright red hues.

If the crawler was bright and arresting, though, it was nothing compared to the passengers it disgorged through its open hatches.

They tumbled, they juggled, they danced, they sang. Their clothes were a riot of motley in all shades and colors, their hair twisted in strange spires atop their heads, rings glinting in their ears and on their noses. And at the vanguard, approaching Gamine and Temujin like an advancing storm front, was the largest and most arresting of them all: Mama Noh.

She was a woman of prodigious size and uncertain ethnicity, with bangles around her wrists and ankles, hair piled in a towering hive rising from the top of her head, cheeks colored red and eyes lined with kohl. Her eyebrows and eyelashes had been completely plucked clean, with brows reapplied with paint high on her wide forehead, and the corners of her mouth were stained by the tobacco she always kept tucked between her cheek and gum, spitting out the tobacco-laced saliva into a dainty porcelain cup constantly through the day. The cup, which had once been something like white but which was now stained a deep golden brown, the color of a fresh-baked loaf, was emptied out onto the ground whenever it began to fill, and so Mama Noh left behind her a dotted trail of brownish expectoration in little pools wherever she went.

Gamine supposed that she fell a little bit in love with Mama Noh when first she saw her, even considering how scared she was of this outlandish interloper, but when Mama Noh opened her mouth, all doubts and reservations were forgotten, and Gamine was sure that she'd found a friend.

When they'd completed the most recent funereal rites and piled sand as high as possible over the body of the departed, the Society followers returned to their ragged circle of tents to begin preparing the evening meal. The sun rode low in the west while both moons hung overhead.

The Society ate their meals together these days, stretching their meager rations as far as they were able. Watery soups and thin stews were the order of the day, with the bowls filled with little more than slightly discolored water. At least they were served steaming hot, if nothing else, since fire kits to heat the pots were hardly in short supply.

The tents of the camp were arranged, as always, in roughly concentric rings, surrounding a broad clearing at the middle. At one side of this clearing was parked the red crawler that gave the opera company its name, and it was in the lee of the crawler that Gamine and Mama Noh sat now, with the other Red Crawler players mixed here and there with the Society followers.

"Your attentions seemed to drift in the observances, child," Mama Noh said, then took a delicate, lingering sip of her soup. She held the bowl to her lips and inhaled deeply. Though the provender was humble, still Mama Noh was one who seemed to savor every bite of life, no matter how small or unsatisfying. As she was fond of saying, Mama Noh was convinced that life was a banquet, and that most people, failing to realize it, were starving. "Perhaps, if the need should arise again, one of my people, or even I myself, might take this burden from your shoulders and perform the rites instead?"

Gamine set down her bowl, hardly touched, and shot a dark look at the players' matriarch. "*If* the need should arise?" She shook her head angrily. "*If?!* Lady, it is instead a question of *when*, or even *how soon*! If you ask me, we'll be lucky if we make it through tomorrow without having to bury another of our people. If we make it through two days running, I think I might just have to dance in celebration!"

Mama Noh held her bowl under her nostrils for a moment longer, her eyes half-lidded, as though the scent of the watery soup were the most pleasant thing she'd ever smelled. Then she gently set the bowl on the ground before her folded legs, her bangles jingling.

"Merely a suggestion, my dear child, merely a suggestion."

Gamine glowered, but after a moment her expression softened fractionally. "I'm sorry, Mama Noh. It's not . . ." She took a deep breath, forcing herself to calm. "I just can't help but wonder what we're doing out here."

"Journeying to the west, it was my understanding," Mama Noh said with a faint smile.

Gamine sighed. "But to where? We've heard that there are communities out past the Three Sovereigns that might be more welcoming, but are there really?"

Mama Noh's eyes narrowed, and when she spoke again, there was iron beneath her words. "They could hardly be less welcoming than those we left behind in the east, my child."

Gamine's eyes met Mama Noh's, and she nodded. The Red Crawler Opera Company, Gamine knew, had learned that the authorities in the villages and towns to the north and east seemed to have as little use for tumblers and players as they did for itinerant preachers and their camp followers. The Red Crawler had found itself driven out of towns, not just with rifle barrels, but with rifle shot, and had lost at least one of their number to injuries sustained when a riot broke out at one of their performances. Until they had encountered the Society of Righteous Harmony out on the highlands, the Red Crawler Opera Company had intended to return to Tianfei Valley in the south, however much the prospect failed to excite them— they had left the valley under a cloud some time before, when a few of their number ran afoul of the local authorities, after it was discovered that they were augmenting their earnings as company players with activities of a less savory and not entirely legal character. It might be some time before they could safely return to Fanchuan. Once they had met Gamine and her people, though, the Red Crawler had seen a new road open up before them, and they had requested to join their caravan.

The Society followers had taken to the Red Crawler people right away, and vice versa. The players were all gymnasts and martial artists, as all opera performers were required by necessity to be, and many of those in the camp now spent what little idle time they had studying the players' movements closely, gradually learning how to move as the players did. No one had ever said out loud that their intention was to learn to fight, but there were many in both the Society and in the opera company who'd had their fill of quaking when confronted by the authorities, and who rehearsed endlessly in their heads how they would handle such encounters differently in the future, knowing now what they did of life in the wilderness. Many in both groups, which was now quickly becoming one melded group, felt that the town fathers and farm owners who had driven them out had done so without a single thought as to what might befall the wanderers when they crossed from the arable lands to the east into the barren wastes of the west.

One of those who harbored dark thoughts about those who had harried them away from civilization was Gamine herself, however much she kept those thoughts to herself when addressing the others. In close company, though, when talking with Temujin or Mama Noh, Gamine felt more comfortable speaking her mind, and the topic of how things could have been done differently was a source of frequent discussion.

So it was that, when the evening meal was interrupted by word that military crawlers had been spotted approaching the camp from the west, Gamine's pulse quickened, and her hands tightened into white-knuckled fists at her sides.

"Mama Noh," Gamine said, rising to her feet, her expression dark, "I can't speak for you, but as for me, I am sick and tired of running."

The Red Crawler's matriarch set her bowl down gently and daintily wiped her fingers dry on a silk kerchief. Then she unfolded, surprisingly graceful given her prodigious bulk, and stood up beside Gamine.

"My child," she said, her tobacco-stained lips curling in a broad smile, "I believe you're reading my verses from the script again."

"Shall we go see what these approaching crawlers are about?"

Mama Noh threaded her arm through Gamine's. "You're in charge around here, dear. I just provide entertainment. Lead on."

• • •

Gamine stood with Temujin on one side and Mama Noh on the other as the crawlers approached through the evening twilight in a cloud of dust.

"You sure this is a good idea, girl?" Temujin took a sip from his wine jar, which these days was so diluted with water that it was a close cousin to the thin soups at mealtime. "I mean, mightn't we better head the other way, 'stead of standing here waiting for the hurly-burly to break loose?"

"Don't listen to him, dear child," Mama Noh said, patting Gamine's shoulder. "He's just speaking his fear."

"You're damned right I'm speaking fear, you great puff guts. I'm well and truly terrified, I am. I'm not sure what kind of past you've got with military types, but I've had a run-in or two with them in my day, and I'll tell you for nothing the main problem with them: they're all *armed*. You get a regular-day cove hot and bothered at you, and the worst he'll do is scream himself red or call for a guardsman. But upsetting a soldier's almost as bad as crossing a Parley, since they're both just as likely to pull a gun or a knife and end the matter with quickness."

"If a gun or knife might cease your endless complaining, you dour old warthog, it might well be worth the risk."

"That's enough, both of you," Gamine said sharply. She looked from one to the other, eyes flashing. "We're not alone here, you know."

She glanced back over her shoulder and saw the mass of

Society followers and Red Crawler people gathered behind them, watching with expectant expressions. Seeing them now like this, in the dying light of the sun, all sharing the same mixture of fear and apprehension, Gamine realized that they really had become one group, these last weeks. Whether they were laborers who had joined the Society after leaving behind unrewarding jobs on Combine plantations, or farmers who had joined because they'd lost their homes and had nowhere else to go, or opera players who had joined because their paths converged in the wilderness and the Society presented alternatives they might not otherwise have had, they were all now a part of the Society of Righteous Harmony, whether they fully accepted all the tenets or not. And all of them looked to Gamine for leadership.

The crawlers were only a short distance away now, and the yellowish green coloration was now unmistakable, even in the fading light. There was no question about it, these were military crawlers. They could not again hope to encounter another crawler painted bright red and full of new friends.

Everyone was looking to Gamine to lead them. In which case, it was time she started to lead.

Afterward, Gamine could not recall all of the speech she'd given there in the twilight, but she remembered enough to retain the essential gist.

The crawlers had ground to a halt only a few paces away,

the engines still idling noisily, sounding like dying monsters. Gamine had stepped forward and, in a loud voice, addressed those within.

Gamine spoke about how the Society had been forced out into this wilderness, far away from the civilized lands, but that the powers still had a purpose for them all. Still, they could not simply sit back and wait for their destiny to find them, but would have to get up on their feet, stand their ground, and fight to make their destiny a reality. And that stand, that fight, would start here and now. They were tired of running and would run no more.

Gamine doubted that any but Mama Noh and the other players recognized that so many of the turns of phrase she used were borrowed liberally from Song Huagu's *The Miner's Journey*, but if the players hid knowing smiles, the rest of the Society followers were entirely galvanized. And if any of the followers *had* recognized the phrases, they'd only have been even more convinced that the powers now spoke through the girl they called Iron Jaw. The Society was ready to follow Gamine anywhere she went, to take any risk she asked of them, for the sake of the powers and the special destiny that awaited them.

When Gamine had ended her speech, as if in response, the hatch of the lead crawler opened, and three men climbed out. They seemed weary, as though it was a struggle just to remain on their feet.

They approached Gamine, their hands empty. They were imposing figures but didn't wear uniforms, as Gamine might have expected, but ragged clothes more suited to common laborers. If not for the swords and pistols hanging at their belts, they might easily have been the sort of people who had stood and listened to Gamine's homilies outside any one of a dozen villages and towns in the east, or who had been convinced by her revelations that she was protected by divine hands.

One of the three had a round face, with a large scar crawling up from the side of his mouth, while another was so gaunt that he looked almost like an animated skeleton. The third, who walked in the lead, was a young man only a few years Gamine's senior, who seemed to be missing fingers on both hands, and while his clothes were as shabby as those of his fellows, the ivory-handled sword that hung at his side looked to be worth a fortune.

The three stopped in front of Gamine and her two advisors, just out of arm's reach. Then the young man smiled.

"So you're tired of running, are you? Well, I think my friends and I are tired of running, too."

ACT IV

•

UNISON

METAL MONKEY YEAR, FIFTY-SEVENTH YEAR OF THE TIANBIAN EMPEROR

HUANG WASN'T SURE WHEN THE NAME HAD FIRST BEEN spoken. It was an idle curiosity for him at best, and not something he spent any amount of time troubling over. But still he wondered, when there was little else to occupy his thoughts, at what moment they had first become the Harmonious Fists.

Their numbers had swelled since the ragtag remains of the bandit band and the battered camp of the Society of Righteous Harmony first encountered each other, out there on the highlands. Then, there had been perhaps a few hundred Society followers and a half dozen bandits, all told. Now the group numbered in the thousands and, what was more, nearly all distinctions between farm laborers and former bandits had been lost. Even the more flamboyant players of the Red Crawler Opera Company had blended into the mix, though they had retained enough of their colorful character that they were still relatively easy to spot in the crowd.

Huang could see them now, in fact. A few of Mama Noh's people were instructing a large group of Fists in the use of martial arts, practicing ritualized movements similar to those Gamine used in her daily services, but here with a more practical application than in summoning up the support of imaginary powers. And on the other side of the camp, separated by carefully regimented rows of tents laid out in a precise grid, Huang could see Jue with another group of Fists, training them in the use of the rifles that a raiding party had brought back from an attack on a military-supply convoy. From where he sat, atop the crawler that served him as both mobile command center and personal residence, Huang could faintly hear the *pok pok* sound of the rifles being fired, and now and then could see one of the Fists fly backward through the air, having failed to properly brace himself for the rifle's recoil.

Huang laid a hand on the ivory hilt of the red-bladed saber at his side and shook his head. He'd fired his share of rifles and pistols these last seasons, striking back against the forces of Governor Ouyang. But he still preferred close quarters with a blade in hand, for all of that. With a sword, he felt more in control, while with a firearm he felt he was simply servicing the weapon, which was itself doing all the work. It hardly mattered, though. They were all simply tools for doing a job. Sword, rifle, pistol.

And fist, of course. So when *had* they become the Harmonious Fists? Huang had to assume that there was some conflation between the Righteous Harmony of Gamine's religious ecstatics and the more physical immediacy of the former bandits' preferred mode of conflict resolution. Perhaps the newer recruits, those disaffected miners and former plantations laborers and dispossessed families who joined them in their dozens, had confused the two when hearing the garbled history of the uprising from those who were on hand to greet them. And so the often drunken, often brawling bandits who had come with the man called Hummingbird and the somewhat more serene men and women who followed the girl called Iron Jaw in seeking after righteous harmony had been commingled in the eyes of these newcomers as brawlers who sought righteousness, fists that fought for harmony.

Whatever its origins, in time the name had passed through the ranks, and then had been picked up by the villages and towns who were sympathetic to their aims, and then adopted by those who defended the very policies that Huang sought to defeat. And so, given enough time, the resistance that Huang and Gamine had begun, that day their two groups met on the highlands, had come to be known as the Harmonious Fists Uprising.

Huang's reverie was interrupted by a series of loud thumps on the roof of the crawler. He was being summoned. Taking a last look across the ordered ranks of tents—the people tending to the cooking fires, the men and women practicing their martial-arts forms or firing and reloading their rifles—he hauled open the hatch in the crawler roof and swung down inside.

"What do you *do* up there, anyway?"

"Look for somewhere else to sleep," Huang said with a sly grin. "The bed's much too crowded as it is."

In response, Huang caught a beaded cushion in the face. Rubbing his stinging cheek, he hissed in pain. "Ow. That actually *hurt*."

"Serves you right." Gamine looked up at him from the bed, wearing the unreadable and inscrutable expression he always found so frustrating. "If you put your faith in the powers, you wouldn't get hurt as often, now would you?"

One corner of Huang's mouth tugged upward in a smile, while the other corner remained unconvinced. Was Gamine kidding? She didn't actually believe that, did she? It was so often hard to tell with her.

"Come on, you," Huang said, kicking the side of the bed with his foot, sending Gamine jostling back and forth. "The others will all be here by now."

Gamine scowled at him and stuck out her tongue. In moments like that, she always seemed so much younger. When she addressed the Fists in the daily religious services, she was Iron Jaw, with an apparent wisdom beyond her years. And though Huang knew that she was only as old now as he'd been when he'd left Fanchuan and joined the convoy to Far Sight Outpost, years before, he often felt that she'd managed to cram more living into her relatively short life, and never felt like he was any older than she. But looking up at him now, with her hair tousled and her tongue out in a childishly peeved expression, just for a moment she looked like a little girl. A girl who commanded the respect and loyalty of thousands who considered her the anointed spokesperson of the supernatural powers, but a little girl nonetheless.

"Come on," he repeated, "we're late for the council meeting as it is."

Then the moment passed, and the little girl was gone. Gamine's tongue flicked back into her mouth, and her unreadable expression grew quite a bit more readable.

"You and your damned council," she snarled. "Well, go on, then, if you must."

"Aren't you coming?"

"When it suits me."

Then she turned away from him, tugging a quilted blanket over her shoulders, and waited for him to leave.

Huang sighed. He watched her back for a long moment, then opened the hatch that led from their improvised sleeping chambers into the remainder of the crawler's cargo hold, which had been set up as the mobile command center. He knew full well that there was no point in arguing with Gamine when the conversation took one of these turns.

Their romance has hardly been the stuff of poetry and ballad. It had begun without preamble one night, two lonely people finding comfort in each other's company. They had passed the night together, drawing more than warmth and release from the nearness, but comfort of a sort, and even something that might have been mistaken for happiness, however briefly. But that had been months ago, and now it was hard to remember a time when they had not been together.

Hummingbird and Iron Jaw. Iron Jaw and Hummingbird. The Harmonious Fists often spoke the names run together, as though they were speaking of one person and not two. And, so far as the Fists were concerned, the two might as well have been one person, considering how they spoke with one voice whenever addressing the group. Only the inner circle—Jue, Ruan, Mama Noh, and Temujin—knew that not only did the two disagree, and vehemently, but that they did so almost constantly. When not in the public eye, the two were in an almost perpetual state of disagreement, arguing about everything from which potential targets had the most strategic value to how their often meager provisions should be divided up among the Fists. The two understood the value of presenting a united front, and so publicly were always in accord; but behind closed doors their arguments were loud and long running.

The only time they spoke to each other with anything like tenderness was in the still-dark watches of the night, as they lay side by side in their bed, their bodies sheened with the sweat of their exertions, breathless. In these quiet, tender moments, they spoke to each other in low voices, gently, sharing secrets and confidences, baring their hearts and souls just as they had so recently bared their bodies.

But as with all things, these tender moments must end, and when the morning came, the two found themselves right back where they'd been, facing each other across a divide neither could seem to bridge.

Jue reached the command center just as Huang was exiting the makeshift living quarters he shared with Gamine. Ruan was already there, as was Mama Noh. Huang didn't notice Temujin at first; then he heard the gentle sound of his snoring from the far corner and looked to see the old man curled up around an empty wine jar.

"Her highness not coming today, is that it?" Ruan sneered, arms crossed over his chest.

"She'll be along presently," Huang answered, and found an empty chair at the table bolted to the deck. The room was long and narrow and had once been used to transport men and materiél to and from military outposts all over Fire Star's surface. Since falling into the hands of the Fists, when the bandits made good their escape from the compromised stronghold in Mount Shennong, it had been gradually transformed. Woven rugs lined the bare steel floors, bolts of cloth had been hung from the sidewalls, and lights affixed to the ceiling. Furniture had been procured, and the table was bolted in place to keep it from shifting when the crawler was in motion. A similar arrangement, with the addition of a simple pallet with bedding, completed the sleeping chamber in the adjoining section.

"Too busy communing with the powers, is she?" Jue chuckled.

"That's enough of your sneers and titters, you jackanapes." Mama Noh wagged a heavy finger at the two former bandits, her bangles jangling on her thick arm. Her brief history with them, and with Ruan especially, had been filled with acrimony. "The young mistress is entitled to her personal time and to do with it as she pleases."

"And if she pleases to spend her time talking to imaginary friends, that's her lookout, is that it?" Ruan's lip curled.

"The powers will not be mocked," came the voice of Gamine from the doorway. "Do you profess disbelief, Ruan?"

As Gamine came and took her place at the table opposite Huang, Ruan and Jue exchanged somewhat uneasy glances. While Huang was the de facto military leader of the Harmonious Fists, Gamine was their spiritual leader. Whether all of the former bandits had fully embraced Gamine's religious instruction was a moot point so long as they *said* that they had. But within the confines of the inner circle, the former bandit lieutenants felt more at ease speaking with derision of the confused and cobbled-together cosmology originated by the late Master Wei. When Gamine spoke up in the defense of belief, or castigated them for their lack of faith, it was often difficult to tell whether she was kidding or whether her unreadable expression hid the fires of true belief.

Of all of them, Huang was the most discomfited to be unable to read Gamine's true meaning. He'd known her only a relatively short time—not quite a year—but in that time had become as intimate with her as he'd ever been with another, both literally and figuratively, and while it sometimes seemed that their hearts had grown as close as their bodies nightly became, there were still parts of her mind that were closed to him.

"Now," said Gamine, folding her hands on the table before her, "I believe there were matters for us to discuss?"

While the others discussed supplies, training regiments, and possible targets for sabotage and preemptive raids, Gamine glanced from face to face, her own set in a mask of perfect attention, but always letting her eyes, and thoughts, linger on Huang.

There were times when Huang was so easy for her to read that it seemed he was made of glass. His hungers and appetites were always plain on his face, whether for food or drink or company or other pursuits. She could always tell when he'd rather be somewhere else, and could usually discern easily enough what he'd rather be doing. She could tell when something another said or did raised Huang's ire and was almost unerring in predicting how he would respond.

On the other hand, there were aspects of Huang's character that always left Gamine completely baffled. His choice of friends, for one, confused her to no end. Ruan was uncouth, with poor manners and even worse grooming habits, and whenever he opened his skull-like head to speak, a cloud of noxious breath came pouring out along with his words. Jue wasn't quite so bad, but he always seemed too easy to respond with one of his lopsided grins, and he was entirely too dismissive of the powers; while he, like Ruan, professed belief publicly in the teachings of Righteous Harmony, too often during the homilies Gamine would look over to see Jue rolling his eyes comically at something she'd said, or hiding a laugh behind his hand while she performed the revelations.

More and more, Temujin had withdrawn from his role at her side, in particular during the revelations, and Mama Noh and her people had stepped forward to fill the gap. It helped matters considerably to have more people trained in pulling punches and breaking falls, able to come up onstage and help demonstrate the efficacy of the powers' support. With the audiences swelling so rapidly in recent seasons, there had been mounting suspicion on the part of many of the new converts about the veracity of Gamine's demonstrations of possession, and when Temujin was too drunk to play his part, and either pulled his punches too soon, leaving huge amounts of daylight showing between his clenched fist and Gamine's supposedly iron jaw—or worse, when he pulled the punch too late and actually delivered a bruising blow to the side of her face—it did little to help the cause. The former opera players, though, were far more adept at stage fighting, and in recent months the revelations had become increasingly sophisticated and choreographed. Even better, some of the players now could take the stage and demonstrate that *they* could be possessed by the powers as well, with several apparent true believers resisting the punches and kicks thrown by a number of congregants selected ostensibly at random from the crowd.

There was little that separated the arts of the theater from the art of the con, Gamine had learned, except that theatergoers *knew* that they'd be paying when they walked in. And both theater and con were close cousins to religion. All three involved putting on a show for people, giving them what they thought they wanted, and then leaving them satisfied for as long as possible, while taking from them whatever coin the performer thought to be the best payment. In the case of the theater, and most often the con, the payment was in currency. In the case of religion, it could just as easily be currency as well, but at the same time payment could be in less tangible but no less valuable coin: devotion, loyalty, love.

Gamine and Temujin had started the Society as a racket, cadging food and lodgings and the occasional coin from gullible townsfolk and farmers all up and down the northern plains. In time, it had grown from a con into a movement, and if truth be told, by that point Gamine had more interested in the devotion of the Society followers than in any currency she might earn for her troubles.

Now she wasn't sure. Had she come to believe her own grift? She knew that she wasn't rendered invulnerable when she faked possession onstage. It would be ridiculous to believe that she did. But at the same time, something had moved her, or moved through her, to assemble a group of people that now numbered in the thousands. And weren't all of those true believers better off now than they had been as homeless wanderers or poorly paid farm laborers or disgruntled miners? Maybe there *were* such things as the powers, who simply moved in mysterious ways. Who was she to say that there weren't?

So what did Gamine want from those who followed her? What was it she required of those in the audience, those who viewed the theater and bought the con and believed the religion?

Faith. That was what she wanted. And while she and Huang shared so many hopes and ambitions, and while he gave her so much that she needed, that was the one thing he couldn't offer. When he looked at her, she knew, Huang didn't see Iron Jaw, best beloved of the powers. He saw Gamine. And that made all the difference.

Later, when the day was done, and after they'd exhausted themselves, Gamine lay beside Huang on the bed. She drowsed in the dim light, eyes half-lidded dreamily, and then turned to find him leaning on one elbow, looking at her intently, wearing nothing but a strange expression.

"What?" Gamine found herself suddenly self-conscious and rubbed her tongue over the front of her smile. "Do I have something stuck in my teeth?"

Huang laughed gently and shook his head. "No, though you took quite a bite out of Ruan earlier, so you might what to check and see if you've got any bits of his backside stuck in there somewhere."

Gamine replied with a grin. "He was being an ass—what do you think? He can't expect these people to pick up strategy as fast as he's teaching it. These are farmers, after all, not sol-diers."

"And Ruan was a miner once upon a time. Everyone has to adapt."

Gamine nodded with a shrug. "But why are you looking at me like that, then?"

"Like what?"

"Like you're doing." She punched him playfully in the arm, pushing him back a few inches.

Huang's smile broadened, and he looked at her in silence for a moment, and then shook his head as though shaking something loose. "It's just . . . I can never quite figure you out. It's almost like you're two people, one when that door is closed, and quite another when it's opened."

Gamine sighed a little wistfully. "Oh, I think I've been more than two people in my time."

Huang's look of confusion intensified. "Say that again?"

Gamine met his eyes. Her faint smile faded. "What would you say if I told you I spent my earliest years as a street urchin, with no family or home, without even a name of my own?"

Huang cocked an eyebrow. "I'd . . ." He trailed off, a little helpless. "To be honest, I don't know what I'd say. Why?" He paused, and studied her closely. "*Did* you?"

Gamine nodded. "That's one person, at least. The nameless waif on the streets, eating out of rubbish bins, sleeping in rough alleyways, with worse manners than a stray dog."

"Then you've come quite a long way, I'd say."

Gamine gave a lopsided grin. "And the long way 'round, at that." Then, in response to Huang's continued confusion, she went on. "When I was five years old, servants of the household of Madam Chauviteau-Zong plucked me off the streets, hosed me down and put me in a fresh set of clothes, and presented me to their mistress. She looked me over and said simply 'Gamine. She'll do,' and from that point onward I was part of the household. For the next eight years I lived in the Chauviteau-Zong estate, studying constantly, working endlessly, trained by the best tutors the mistress's great fortune could afford. Then, at the end of eight years, I was loaded into a carriage with Madam Chauviteau-Zong herself, which carried us to the residence of Governor Ouyang. There I was taken to a secluded room, and along with a number of other children of roughly the same age, subjected to endless examinations. In the end, I answered all the questions correctly and was the last child left standing, the rest having been escorted away by guards. It wasn't until those same guards escorted *me* out that I learned what had become of them. It seemed that, having passed all those examinations, I had fulfilled whatever usefulness I served for the mistress, and she was done with me. I was stripped of all my valuables and tossed out into the street."

Gamine left off talking, while Huang regarded her with a strange look in his eye.

"And that was the end of the second person I've been, I suppose. The pampered, well-educated ward of the Chauviteau-Zong estate. If I hadn't met Temujin soon after, who taught me the craft of the con, I doubt I would have survived very long, a cosseted pet set out in the wilds among all the feral beasts. And that, you could say, was the start of the third person who's lived in my skin. A year or more later, when we chanced upon Wei in the highlands, I first put my foot on the path that would lead to me being Iron Jaw, the fourth and last of my various incarnations." She paused, for the moment lost in thought. "Still, I can't explain any of it, in the final analysis. Even all these years later, I have no notion why Chauviteau-Zong should have taken me into her home, and had tutors instruct me, and servants groom me. It was as though I was being cultivated for some purpose, but in the end all that was asked of me was to pass the examinations at the home of the governor-general. Had all the other children been nameless sons and daughters of the street like me?" Gamine shrugged. "It hardly matters, I suppose."

Huang reached over and brushed a hand against her bare shoulder, his expression caring. "I've heard of your mistress and the games she played. My parents once spoke of Chauviteau-Zong and the others, when I was young. I don't think they imagined I could overhear, as I doubt they'd have spoken so freely if they had."

"What . . . What did they say?" Gamine's voice cracked a little, despite herself. She felt unaccountably unnerved. Part of her didn't want to hear any more on the subject, while another part wanted to hear nothing else. "About Chauviteau-Zong?" Gamine felt that she knew precisely what he'd meant by *games* but was almost afraid to ask.

"You've probably worked most of it out on your own, I'd imagine," Huang said, somewhat reluctantly. "Your mistress and those of her class, well-connected aristocrats with too much money and not enough to occupy their time, would find various things on which to wager. Who could purchase the fiercest animal? Who could fund the construction of the fastest-flying airship? Who could commission the most brilliant sculpture? And on and on. Eventually, they ran out of things with which to compete and had to find fresh ground. They started . . ." He paused and, with brows knit, regarded Gamine. Then he had to look away before continuing. "They decided to start wagering on people. But it wasn't enough to find the strongest man, or the fastest runner, or such like. Instead, they had to wager on the essential *qualities* of a person. As I understand it, the idea came of complaining at the quality of bureaucratic officeholders, and the statement by your mistress or one of her equals that . . . that a monkey could be trained to do just as good a job." He swallowed hard but still refused to meet Gamine's gaze. "The agreement was that whoever could take a stray child from the street and train them well enough to pass the highest level of bureaucratic examinations would win the wager."

"So the questions we were asked . . . ?"

Huang nodded. "The equivalent of a *juren*-level imperial examination." At last he turned and met her eyes. "At the age of thirteen, you could have walked out of that room in the governor-general's palace and gone to get a job in the imperial bureaucracy and had employment for life."

"And instead I was tossed into the street to fend for myself."

Huang reached out and put his hand on her shoulder, squeezing. "I don't imagine it's any help to hear it, but when my parents discussed the practice, they did so with disapproval. My mother in particular was horrified at the thought of children turned out into the wild like that. My father . . ."

When he trailed off, averting his eyes, Gamine pressed him to continue.

"My father," he finally went on, "said that the children

had come from the streets, and been returned to the streets, so while he thought the game was unseemly, he didn't think it did any real harm to them."

To her surprise as much as his, Gamine smiled and nodded. "He was right, I suppose." She chuckled, and seeing Huang's confused expression, explained. "I used to harbor a mighty thirst for revenge, and at night would plot all the ways I would make the old woman pay for mistreating me. But now I wonder whether I shouldn't thank her, instead."

"Thank her?" Huang repeated, disbelieving.

"Certainly. Had Madam Chauviteau-Zong not taken me in when she did, I'd likely have died while still a child. Instead, at her expense the tutors equipped me with all manner of useful skills and knowledge, however much I didn't recognize it at the time."

"But in throwing you out in the street again, wasn't she just putting you back in harm's way? After all, you said that if you hadn't met Temujin, you'd have died then, instead."

Gamine offered a smile. "Well, then I suppose I need to thank *him*, too."

The night wore on, but neither Huang or Gamine seemed much in a mood for sleeping. Gamine's mention of revenge had sparked thoughts of vengeance in Huang's mind, and he smoldered with it, even some time later.

"What's bothering you, Fei?" Gamine said, laying a hand

on his chest, with her head pillowed on his arm. No one but Gamine called him by that name, these days. To everyone else, he was only and always Hummingbird.

"It's just . . ." he started, then broke off. "I don't know, Gamine." He knew that he was the only one to call her by *that* name, which seemed only fitting. Even Temujin had taken to calling her Iron Jaw like everyone else, but not without an undercurrent of derision. "I just keep thinking about what you said about your mistress, and plotting revenge against her."

"Mmm?" Gamine smiled. "Why, do you have any suggestions?"

Huang chuckled and shook his head. "No, it's just . . ." He took a heavy breath. "I've vowed vengeance myself, and I don't think I could shake it off as easily as you seem to be doing."

Gamine leaned in closer. "You're not planning on thanking this person, I take it?"

Huang's eyes flashed darkly, and his mouth drew into a tight line. "No," he said, managing to keep his tone level, but barely.

After a pause, Gamine said, "So who is this person, then, to have angered you so?"

Huang shook his head in frustration. "I don't know his name. Or even what he looks like, come to that. Only that he has a scar over his right eye in the shape of a small sideways cross, and fair-colored hair. He was the Bannerman who killed my friend, the bandit chief Zhao. I . . ."

Huang left off, his eyes stinging.

"What is it?"

"It . . . it was my fault," he finally admitted. "I was facing another Bannerman and had the opportunity to defeat him and go to Zhao's aid, but I was squeamish at the thought of killing and let the opportunity pass by, waiting for the chance of a nonfatal wound. If I'd taken the earlier opportunity, I wouldn't have been too late to save Zhao, and he'd still be alive today."

Gamine pushed back from him and rose up on her elbows to look him in the eye.

"In which case you might not have fled your mountain, but remained there and continued in the life of the bandit?"

Huang, wiping his eyes, could only shrug. "Perhaps," he allowed.

"And if you had continued in that life, who is to say that the *next* time you encountered the military he wouldn't have fallen, or you, or both? And then you'd never have met me and the rest of the Society on the road, and this revolution of ours would never have begun, and none of these people who have flocked to our side would have anyone to fight for their interests. Is that preferable?"

Huang gave her a hard look, silent but unconvinced.

"It's a hard thing to lose someone close to you, I know," Gamine went on. "For all that he was a crazy old man, I find that I still miss Master Wei from time to time, and not just because when he was still alive I could take a break from the homilies from time to time. But that doesn't mean that you can just wallow in self-pity over the loss. Nor lose yourself to thoughts of revenge. It's like Master Wei always said, 'However difficult the road, there is a plan, and the powers always have a purpose for us.'"

Huang's eyes narrowed, and he bared his teeth in a sneer. "Save your 'powers' nonsense for the audience, *Iron Jaw*. I don't need it, any more than I need your talk of 'purpose' and 'plans.'"

Tugging his arm from under her shoulder, Huang rolled over, and lay on his side facing away from her.

A moment passed, and then he felt Gamine's hand on his shoulder. A slight gesture, a brief attempt at contact. "I don't know if it means anything to you, but I think I met your Bannerman once myself. Just around the time that Wei died. He was the one to drive us off from Yinglong. Light hair and a cross-shaped scar over his eye. Said his name was . . . Kingston, perhaps? Something Briton-sounding like that, I believe. I'd probably recognize it if I heard it again."

Huang tensed and pursed his lips. He mouthed a name, not speaking it out loud, as if afraid to have his suspicions confirmed.

He remained silent, and still, and after a few long moments he felt Gamine pull her hand away. Then, much later, he eventually found slumber waiting for him in the quiet darkness.

• • •

The next day, an airship was spotted not far from the camp. Huang, having some experience with aircraft, had carefully selected the camp's current location at the base of a ravine, where the updrafts made it difficult for any airships to pass directly overhead. As a consequence, they were mostly protected against attacks from above. And given that the land rose sharply on either side, they were more or less hidden from the view of anyone approaching on the ground. But they were still visible to craft flying far enough from the ravine to avoid the updraft but high enough to see clearly over the edge of the rise, and it was in this narrow band that the airship appeared to have passed.

The ravine was far enough from any military garrisons that it would take some time for a detachment to reach them, and the intelligence network of the Harmonious Fists had received no word of any battalions on maneuvers in the region. So they had a small amount of leeway before word from the airship reached the military authorities and troops were dispatched. But that leeway was not overly generous and would not last forever, so it was time for the camp to be on the move.

Since the uprising had begun in earnest, the year before, the Fists had been playing a game of cat and mouse with the forces of the governor-general. Thankfully, the Fists seemed to take turns—sometimes as cat, sometimes as mouse—so that they were not constantly on the defensive. But the times when they played the role of the pursuer were limited to those occasions when the military forces were outnumbered or outgunned, or could be outmaneuvered. Even with their numbers swelled to some thousands, there simply weren't enough of the Fists to make a stand against the combined might of the Green Standard Army and the Bannermen alike, with their airships, crawlers, and heavy artillery in tow. And so the Fists had to select their fights carefully, and know when it was time to play the mouse and go scurrying for cover.

Now was a time for mice, not cats.

There were five crawlers in all in the camp—the red-painted crawler that had given Mama Noh's opera company its name; the two crawlers in which Huang and the others had escaped the Bannermen who had ambushed them atop Mount Shennong; and two more captured in the course of their skirmishes with the military this last year. These newer, captured crawlers were in fact piecemeal assemblages from more than a half dozen different vehicles, since in each encounter the Fists had inflicted considerable damage on the military crawlers before the enemies abandoned them and fled. But while they were somewhat unsightly monsters, which in motion sounded even worse than they looked, they were perfectly functional and offered much-needed help in hauling the Fists' stores of provisions and arms, with some small amount of room left over for those Fists who were too injured from recent encounters to move under their own power, mothers with newborn children, and so on.

The Fists in motion made for a motley caravan: Five

crawlers traveling in a line, with thousands of men, women, and children following beside and behind on foot. Along with them came the livestock they had captured, bought, or stolen over the seasons—goats that provided the milk the Fists drank, pigs that were fattened until they were ready for the table, even crates of chickens prized for their eggs while they still laid and for their flesh when they didn't. In addition to the crawlers there were innumerous handcarts and wheelbarrows, rickshaws and wagons, all of them pulled and pushed by nothing more sophisticated than human muscle. On the move, the caravan kicked up an incredible amount of red dust, which was the main reason that Huang preferred to travel at night whenever possible, ideally under cloudy conditions or high winds.

Unfortunately, the military airship had been sighted in the early morning, and to wait until nightfall would put the Fists at an unnecessarily large risk, when the chances of pursuit and attack were already so high. And although the winds were high, the skies were cloudless and clear. Hardly the most auspicious of beginnings.

There was no choice. Huang convened the inner circle in the command center, but not to invite debate, only to relay his orders. The Fists were to strike the camp immediately and prepare to head out before midday.

With any luck, they'd been well on their way and difficult to track by the time the military arrived. If not? Well, it was best not to dwell too closely on the alternatives.

• • •

The ravine in which the camp nestled was north of the western extremity of Tianfei Valley. While the others loaded the crawlers and carts, broke down tents and scaffolding, Gamine and Huang pored over maps of the surrounding terrain.

"The airship retreated to the north, toward White Plains Station," Gamine said, indicating the place marked at the top of the map.

"No." Huang shook his head. "That size airship isn't rated to fly so far afield. It must be operating out of somewhere closer by." He studied the map, then pointed to a hill much nearer their present location, marked with the ideograms for *airfield*. "There. Red Sands Basin. It's small, with only a single company of Green Standard soldiers on site. I doubt the airship's radio is powerful enough to reach any farther than that, so for the time being we can assume that they're the only ones who know our position."

"Won't the operators at Red Sands just relay it on to White Plains Station, or even Far Sight Outpost?"

Huang grimaced, then gave a curt nod. "Yes. But they're far enough away, even by airship, that I'm not too worried about their response just yet. It's the troops at the airfield that worry me."

"Just a company, though?" Gamine looked up from the map and met Huang's eyes. "That's just four platoons, isn't it? What is that, two and a half hundred soldiers?"

Huang nodded. "Just about."

"We're more than two thousand strong. Why should you be worried?"

Huang shook his head in exasperation. "Two thousand, yes, but all infantry, and many of them only poorly trained. In a standing fight, we might just handle two hundred fifty professional soldiers, but only if they forget to bring their heavy armament from home. And if they bring crawlers with mounted cannon? We might as well forget about it. It wouldn't take more than a handful of mounted crawlers to wipe us out entirely."

Gamine crossed her arms over her chest. She was tempted to say that the powers would protect them but knew that Huang wouldn't respond well. And even she wasn't sure if she'd have been joking to say it.

"So where are we going, then?" Gamine finally asked. "If you're right, it won't take long for troops from Red Sands to get here."

Huang scowled and leaned in to study the map more closely.

To the south and east stretched Tianfei Valley, where the three valley provinces were strung like beads on a necklace—too populated and well guarded. To the north and east was the Great Yu Canyon, where the highlands dropped precipitously down thousands of feet to the canyon floor far below—even if they could reach the canyon, there was no way down, and they'd be forced to divert days to the north just to get in. To the west were the highlands, with the Three Sovereigns mountains in the distance, and Bao Shan rising beyond—the high, rocky ground would offer little protection for a caravan on the march, and they'd be easy targets. All that was left was the south and west.

"Forking Paths," Huang said, indicating the mazelike tangle of ravines and box canyons that started just to the southwest of their current position. "It's close enough that we might be able to get into the maze before the troops catch up with us. And if we can do that, there's a good chance that we could lose them."

"And if we don't?" Gamine asked.

Huang looked up from the map and gave her a humorless smile.

"In that case, we better hope they forgot to bring their crawlers and heavy arms along, is all I can think."

Gamine and Huang walked alongside their crawler as the sun dipped toward the western horizon ahead of them on the right.

"What's wrong with you?" Gamine asked, glancing sidelong at Huang. "You keep fidgeting."

Huang scowled and flapped his hands in front of him. "My fingers itch, if you must know."

Gamine narrowed her gaze. "*Which* fingers?"

Huang glanced over at her, wearing a frustrated expression.

"Which do you think?" He held up his left hand, his scowl deepening.

On his left hand, Huang was missing all of his smallest finger and part of the next, while on his right hand his middle finger ended at the second knuckle. The three fingers were tipped with lumps of red scar tissue that had hardened into solid callus in the years since his injury. One night, during one of their quiet, tender moments of sharing, Huang had explained how he'd lost the fingers and what their loss had come to mean to him. The lost digits were a symbol of his connection to the bandits, most of whom had been scarred or disfigured in some way down in the mines. And so Huang never lamented the absence but carried it as a badge of honor.

Still, there were times when Huang complained of phantom pains, of twinges and itches in the fingers that were no longer there. And since they were gone, there was nothing to scratch, and nothing to ease the discomfort.

Gamine pursed her lips. "You know what *that* means."

"Not *this* again," Huang answered, rolling his eyes. "Look, it's nothing more than severed nerve endings misfiring, sending false signals through my nervous system. There's nothing *mysterious* about it."

Gamine shook her head. Once, she might have agreed with him. She'd been just as analytical and rational as a child, and in her time as a confidence artist she'd learned that the simplest and most reasonable answer was almost always the correct one.

Still, these days she couldn't help but feel that there were sometimes meanings beyond the obvious, and explanations other than the most reasonable.

"Have you forgotten already?" she asked. "Whenever you complain of your phantom pains, disaster or tragedy always follows. It isn't just a question of misfiring nerve endings. The pain is a precursor to danger, a signal to alert us of some approaching threat."

"Oh, come on," Huang said, his tone exasperated. "One time the 'disaster' came only a few hours after my phantom pains, I'll admit, but another time it took weeks until the 'prophesied danger' came about. In our world, it doesn't take any special foreknowledge to predict that something bad will *eventually* happen. It's just a matter of time."

Gamine saw from his expression that there was nothing to be gained from pressing the issue. He was certain that it was nothing more than coincidence and no cause for concern. For her part, though, Gamine was far from convinced. Something bad was coming, she knew it now.

"Look's like luck is with us, Chief," Jue said, handing Huang the binoculars, hanging on to a railing to keep from jostling off the crawler's roof. "Or against us, if you want to look at it that way."

Huang squinted through the glasses at the column of men and machines marching at the head of the plume of red dust.

"Looks like four squads," he said, "maybe five."

"I make it at five," Ruan said, scowling.

Jue nodded in the skeletal bandit's direction. "I counted five, as well, Chief."

Huang lowered the binoculars. "That's no more than eighty soldiers, altogether." He sighed. "Which *would* be lucky, if only . . ."

He trailed off and glanced behind him at the Fists' convoy. It would have been lucky, if the Fists had reached the safety of the Forking Paths by now. As it was, they were still woefully short, and the caravan was ill prepared to defend itself.

"Come on," Huang said, moving toward the hatch to clamber back down into the crawler. "Let's tell the others."

Moments later, rejoining the other members of the council, Huang recounted what they had learned about the pursuing soldiers, and what that suggested for the caravan's chances for survival.

"They shouldn't be on us yet, should they?" Mama Noh asked.

Huang shook his head. "No," he answered. "They shouldn't."

Given the distances involved, even with the relatively slower speeds the Fists' caravan was able to manage, they should have reached the Forking Paths labyrinth long before the soldiers arrived. Given the small number of troops, and the speed of their arrival, the only answer was that they had been on maneuvers in the area and had been radioed by the airship or by their command at Red Sands Basin to divert to the caravan's location and engage.

"How close are we?" Gamine asked.

Huang knew all too well what she meant. "The head of the caravan has almost reached the entrance to the Forking Paths." He sighed, tensing his hands into fists at his sides. "If the body of the caravan could get within the maze of canyons, our chances of eluding capture go up exponentially."

"I don't see those squads giving us that kind of chance, chief," Jue said.

Ruan scowled and shook his head. "They'll be here too soon for that."

Huang nodded. There was only one solution. It wasn't a good one, but it was the only choice they had.

"What?!" Temujin was the first to respond, but his shout of disbelief gave voice to the wide-eyed expressions all of them wore.

"It's the only way," Huang said somberly. "Some of us will have to stay behind and delay the soldiers, to give the rest of the caravan time to get safely within the labyrinth." He stood up and moved to open the crawler's side hatch. "Come on, there isn't any time to waste."

Huang leaped down to the ground, followed by the others, as the crawlers of the Harmonious Fists continued their slow but inexorable journey to the southwest. Squinting against the swirling clouds of dust, the leaders of the Fists regrouped, concluding their hasty council.

"I want two hundred of our best-trained fighters," Huang said, "ready to march out and meet our pursuit."

"And I want a drink," Temujin said, looking more sober than Huang had seen him in ages.

"I'll get our best marksmen pulled out of line and armed," Jue said, ignoring the old man's feeble joke.

Ruan rubbed his chin. "I can think of a few dozen good hand-to-hand fighters I've been working with."

Huang shook his head. "Won't be enough. We'll need more."

"I may be past my own prime, dear ones, in matters martial," Mama Noh said, straightening the hem of her skirt, "but I'm sure my people wouldn't hesitate to put their own skills at your disposal."

"That helps." Huang nodded. "And we'll need you leading the caravan, Noh. Can you catch up with the lead crawler?"

Mama Noh looked back over her shoulder at the yellowish green crawler inching along, barely above a brisk walking pace. "I'm not quite *that* far past my prime, Hummingbird. But must I command from that rattletrap? Couldn't I just as well lead the way in *comfort*?" She pointed to the red-painted crawler, following close behind, which had been her own home for years.

Huang smiled. "I don't think that should be a problem."

Mama Noh flashed him a grin and a wink, wished the others luck, and then hurried off to send the opera players over and to take her place in the red crawler.

"Temujin," Huang said, turning to the old man. "Can you take the lead crawler, instead?"

The old man scratched beneath his beard, scowling, but finally nodded. "My hindquarters must be made of less sensitive stuff than the great Noh's, since if the choice is riding in the crawler or standing out here in the dust with you lot, the question as to which is more comfortable hardly needs answering."

The old man exchanged a look with Gamine and then hurried off to catch up with the crawler, still rumbling toward the Forking Paths.

"Having the players onside gets us close," Huang said, "but we could still use more bodies."

"What about me?" Gamine said.

Huang looked over at her, his eyebrow raised.

Gamine gave a sly grin. "I can handle myself in a fight."

Huang gave her a worried look. "Look, Gamine, this isn't the kind of fight where punches will be pulled, you know?"

"No, *you* look." Gamine crossed her arms over her chest and narrowed her eyes. "I may not have been a soldier or plied the bandit's trade, but at the same time I'd guess that none of you spent an hour every day throughout your entire childhood being trained in self-defense, did you?"

Huang quirked a smile and shook his head.

"Just where *did* you grow up, anyway?" Jue asked, giving her an appraising look.

Huang and Gamine both glanced his way and smiled. "It's a long story," she said, and Huang nodded in agreement.

"Your *followers* won't be too impressed if their 'Iron Jaw' comes back injured," Jue replied.

"Or dead," Ruan put in, scowling.

Huang shot him a sharp look, then turned back to Gamine wearing a concerned expression. "Are . . . are you sure about this?"

Gamine fixed him with a grin. "What choice do we have? After all, what will my followers think if I *don't* stand and fight?"

Huang reached out and placed a tender hand on her shoulder. "Be careful, will you?"

"Don't worry." She reached up and rapped on her jaw with a knuckle. "Best beloved of the powers, remember? They won't let me down."

A short while later, as the Fists readied themselves for the soldiers' first assault, Gamine wished that she actually felt the confidence she'd affected with such bravado when volunteering for the duty. For that matter, she wished that she really *were* rendered invulnerable by supernatural powers. Looking at the soldiers now arraying themselves against the Fists, Gamine felt certain that a jaw of iron would come in handy in very short order.

The soldiers arrived with a crawler, but fortunately for the Fists it did not appear to be equipped with heavy armament. And despite the fact that the soldiers all carried rifles, they were approaching over such level and hard-packed ground that there were few places for their snipers to brace themselves against recoil, which reduced the chances that the Fists would all be picked off at range.

The Fists, for their part, had the advantage of terrain on their side. While the soldiers were forced to approach, with no cover but the crawler to hide behind, Huang had selected a narrow defile for the Fists to make their stand. The defile, a passage between two sheer cliffs, was a naturally formed gateway into the Forking Paths labyrinth. The distance between the two sides was no more than a half dozen paces, the width of seven or eight of the Fists standing abreast.

Huang ordered a handful of snipers to be positioned just beyond the defile, facing the approaching soldiers. Lying low on the ground, with their feet propped against the base of the cliff walls themselves, the snipers were well positioned to target the approaching pursuers and open fire.

Had the snipers been able to fire unobstructed on the soldiers, the encounter would have been a short one. Unfortunately for the Fists, the platoons' leaders had anticipated the strategy, and ordered the soldiers marching on foot to form a single-file rank behind the crawler, letting its large, metal bulk shield them from rifle fire. The snipers, unable to draw a bead on the soldiers, contented themselves with firing at the crawler itself, but their shots only plunked harmlessly off the crawler's armor plating, and in time Huang ordered them to hold fire to keep from wasting ammunition.

The crawler was designed for desert maneuvers, with its treads set wide apart, the body slung low. As a result, it was ill equipped for use in the mazelike canyons that stretched beyond the defile and, worse yet for the soldiers, looked too wide even to fit through the passage itself. While it served to shield the marchers behind it from the Fists' snipers, when the crawler reached the defile, its usefulness would be at an end.

Then, of course, the Fists themselves would be put to the test. Which was what Gamine was afraid of.

In such close quarters, rifles would be of little use, and handguns fired on the run would only result in sending the people firing the weapons falling on their backsides. And so the Fists and soldiers alike would be forced to resort to bare hands, feet, and handheld weapons.

There were over two hundred Fists arranged on either side of Gamine on the far side of the defile from the soldiers. These men and women represented the best-trained fighters the Harmonious Fists had at their disposal, most of them battle-hardened miners, farm laborers, and former bandits, but more than a few erstwhile townsfolk and householders who had joined the Fists after hearing Gamine preach. Gamine couldn't help but wonder if any of them were counting on the powers to protect them in the coming battle, and whether she should say anything to them if they did.

A short distance off stood a dozen or so members of the Red Crawler Opera Company. Some held swords, or knives, or other more exotic bladed weapons Gamine could scarcely identify, while others leaned on staves taller than they were. Some carried no weapons at all but wound lengths of leather cord around their fingers, increasing the weight and impact of their clenched fists.

To the other side stood Jue, directing the snipers who now waited with ill-concealed anticipation, their fingers hovering on their rifles' triggers. A short distance off, Ruan spoke with a group composed of former bandits and rough-hewn miners, limbering their arms and legs, discussing some final points of strategy.

At her side stood Huang, his red saber drawn and in his hand, the late-afternoon sunlight glinting off the firebird engraved on the blade. Behind them were gathered dozens upon dozens of Harmonious Fists, looking to their two leaders for the signal.

The military crawler was almost at the defile. Any moment now, the soldiers would come rushing around it on either side, weapons drawn. Some would no doubt fall to sniper fire right away, from the guns positioned on either side of the passage. But the soldiers following behind, provided they moved fast enough, would be able to close the distance quickly enough to attack the snipers with swords and knives and keep them from firing again. Gamine glanced again at the steep cliff walls and wished for the hundredth time there had been a way to scale them and position rifles high overhead, but with the time and resources available to them, it simply hadn't been possible. As it was, the Fists could only hope to fell the first wave of soldiers before their snipers would be forced to put down their rifles and engage hand to hand like the rest of them. Then it would simply be a test of skill, number, and advantage. Did the Fists, a motley and ragtag group of men and women from all corners, trained ad hoc by runaway soldiers, former bandits, and exiled opera players, really have the skill necessary to defeat the soldiers? Or would the Harmonious Fists Uprising end here and now?

Gamine looked over and found Huang looking her way, a strange expression on his face. Then he reached over and threaded his fingers through hers.

"You ready, Iron Jaw?" he said, smiling. Only this time, when he used the name, there was no derision implicit, no mockery.

She smiled and tightened her hand around his. "I'm ready, Hummingbird," she answered with a determined grim.

Huang nodded and, dropping her hand, turned to face the others. "This is the time, people. Stand ready. When the soldiers attack, don't wait for further orders, but do what you've been trained to do." He glanced back at Gamine, asking with a look whether she had anything to add.

Gamine took a deep breath and straightened. "Brothers and sisters! Look what we have accomplished, these last seasons.

Time and again we have harried the forces of Ouyang—disrupting supply chains, preventing his ability to torment the mines and farms of the north. Those miners, those farmers, those laborers, they are our friends, our families, our sons and daughters and brothers and sisters. You have followed us this far. Think what more we can yet do, if given the chance. But to continue the struggle, we few must stand awhile, to give the rest of our people the chance to get to safety. We must stand awhile, and fight. And while we might ache, and while we might bleed, you should remember that the powers are always with us, and that with them on our side, we can never be defeated."

Then, eyes flashing and hair streaming in the wind, Gamine raised her hand in a fist, high overhead. As one, all of those standing before her raised their own fists in response. For some, it was a salute; for others, an invocation for the powers; for others, simply a gesture of defiance to the authorities who had so long oppressed them. But whatever the significance to the individual, as a group they held their fists high and bellowed a loud, wordless shout of challenge to the approaching soldiers.

Gamine glanced over at Huang. He regarded her, his expression a strange mixture of sadness and respect, and then nodded. Turning to the others, he cupped his hands around his mouth like a trumpet. "All right then, you heard her. Let's *fight!*"

• • •

The encounter was short, but it was bloody.

None of the soldiers in the platoons managed to make it more than a few steps through the defile. In the end, each of them had been brought down, whether by sword, or bullet, or knife, or staff, or punch or kick. None of them had succeeded in getting past the ranks of Harmonious Fists and pursuing the caravan into the Forking Paths.

But if the Fists had succeeded in stopping the soldiers' progress, it had come at a heavy price. Because few of the soldiers were felled by the first sword to be turned their way or the first punch thrown at them. These were professional soldiers, highly trained and well armed, and it did not take them long to realize that they were fighting not for the distant objectives of the governor-general and his cronies but for their very lives.

There were some eighty soldiers in all, and more than two hundred Fists standing ready to stop them. And when the last of the soldiers fell, more than half of the Fists had already gone down, never to rise again. Fewer than one hundred remained standing, when it was all said and done, and all of those bruised and bloodied, many of them severely wounded.

Ruan and one of the other former bandits had taken charge of securing the crawler, and after forcing the hatch had found only the driver within. When they emerged, grim and bloodied, Huang refrained from asking whether the driver had surrendered before they "did for him," as Ruan euphemistically called it, or whether the driver had fought to the last. It hardly mattered, Huang supposed; they all had blood on their hands, one way or the other.

Since the crawler was too large to fit through the defile, Huang had ordered it driven into the passage, wedged between the cliff walls on either side, to block other, smaller vehicles from following. Then they had disabled the crawler's engine and smashed the axle underneath to pieces.

The soldiers they left lying where they'd fallen, but the Fists' own dead were gathered together at the center of the passage and arranged as neatly as possible; then Gamine read the funeral rites over them.

Huang, who had directed the efforts of the Fists throughout the battle, found himself almost completely incapacitated in the aftermath. He was not seriously wounded, having gotten only a few grazed knuckles and some shallow cuts and scratches, but his arms and legs felt like they were made of lead, and there was a gnawing pain at the pit of his stomach. He retched, leaning against the canyon wall and vomiting and vomiting and vomiting until there was nothing left to come back up, and then was wracked with dry heaves until he thought his abdomen must be a single giant bruise.

His hands were dirty, caked with the red sands, but were surprisingly free of blood. He realized that it would be perhaps more fitting if they were stained red, like a character in a revenge drama in one of the Red Crawler Opera Company's performances. Then those around him would be able to see externalized the mark that Huang now felt darkened him from within.

He had killed before, of course. Since the night when his hesitation had cost Zhao his life, Huang had never shrunk from taking another's life, if it meant preserving his own life or those of his friends. He had in the past year defeated any number of soldiers in single combat, had fired off detonators when Bannermen were close enough to be caught in the blast, and on, and on. But those had been one or two deaths at a time, half a dozen at the most, and each time Huang had felt the sting of those deaths just as keenly, and had been forced to spend long nights reminding himself that the safety of his friends was worth the cost, however high.

Now, though, Huang was forced to revisit the equation, and had difficulty making the cost balance the gain. Thousands of the Harmonious Fists would sleep in safety tonight, hidden within the mazelike canyons of the Forking Paths, because he and the others had prevented the platoons from following. But not only had their safety been purchased at the price of the soldiers' lives, all eighty of them cut down in an afternoon, but the lives of more than one hundred Fists had been paid in the bargain. More than one hundred Fists, representatives of the same people whom Huang had dedicated himself to protecting. But in leading them in this charge, he'd not done well by that one hundred, had he? How well had Huang managed to protect *them*?

Huang struggled to regain control of himself. He dusted his hands on his trousers and straightened. Gamine was concluding the funeral rites for the fallen, and the others were preparing to move out. With luck, they would catch up with the rest of the caravan by morning, and then they could get busy finding a more secure hiding place, one that would be more permanent—at least until the military found them again.

Standing and listening to Gamine, Huang was surprised at how level and confident her voice was. She stood straight, her gaze level and her voice strong, and seemed to bear no ill effects of the carnage they'd just witnessed.

When she had finished, she turned and caught Huang's eye, and gave him a wide smile. Huang did his best to smile in return, but the most he could manage was something nearer a grimace.

A few days later, while the others busied themselves establishing some kind of order in the camp—now set up in a box canyon with high, steep walls, hidden at the center of the Forking Paths labyrinth—Gamine sat in the command center, lost in thought. Before going off to supervise the Fists establishing a picket around the canyon's entrance, Huang had asked the other members of the inner circle to convene after the midday meal, but so far Gamine was the first and only one to arrive.

Never simple or straightforward, her relationship with Huang had been even more strained than usual these last days.

Ever since rejoining the caravan after the encounter at the defile, Huang had been withdrawn, sullen, slow to respond when she addressed him and silent when she didn't. Given that their normal mode of interaction, at least in close company, was sniping and bickering, she hardly minded the change. But he had pulled away from her in the night as well, sleeping well over on his side of the bed, making no advances on her and rebuffing any advance she made. And without the heat and exhaustion of passion, there were no quiet, tender moments to follow, and no baring of souls and sharing of thoughts. Gamine felt more alone than she had since the days before she met Temujin, when she had been forced out into the streets of Fanchuan, friendless and abandoned.

Now she had thousands who hung on her every word. And, with the success of the past days, her followers were even more convinced that she was anointed by the powers. Certainly the Fists were grieved by the loss of a hundred of their brothers and sisters, but the fact that their two leaders, Hummingbird and Iron Jaw, had escaped the encounter unscathed served as inescapable proof of their beliefs.

And did it? Gamine couldn't help but wonder. She was not invulnerable, of course. It was ridiculous to think otherwise. She could fall and be hurt just like any other young woman. But even with years of self-defense training by the tutors of the Chauviteau-Zong household, she was ill prepared for actual combat, so how had she managed to make it through a pitched battle against professional soldiers with scarcely a bruise or scratch to show for it?

Had Wei been right all along? *Were* there powers who spoke to and through her, and who shielded her when her cause was righteous?

Her train of thought was interrupted when the hatch opened, admitting a shaft of blinding light and a cloud of dust. Then Temujin stumbled in and closed the hatch behind him.

"Drunk already, old man?" Gamine said, a touch of scorn in her voice.

Temujin shook his head, and a smile peeked from behind his mustache. "Not yet, more's the pity. I'm sorry to report that one of the casualties of the recent unpleasantness has been our supply of wine, inexpertly stowed in a rush by lackwits and nick-ninnies who wouldn't know a good job of packing if it crawled up and bit their privates clean off. So in our mad dash from ravine to canyon, the jars were jostled and tossed rather too violently, and as a result the whole of our wine supply ended up as nothing but a few bits of broken crockery and a mess of soggy straw." He slumped his shoulders and let out a ragged sigh. "Oh, by the Eternal Blue Sky, what I wouldn't do for a *drink*."

Gamine pointed to the pot of tea cooling on the far side of the table. A cup sat before her, untouched.

"No. No, no." Temujin shuddered. "Tea is one thing, but this stuff? It must be down to the water we carry, but I swear that every pot of tea I've touched for weeks has smelled of nothing but sweaty feet."

Gamine grinned. "Where do you think they get the water from?"

Temujin cocked an eyebrow, momentarily horrified, and then chuckled. "Very funny, my little sprite. Mock an old man in his dotage. See if you don't get your just rewards when you reach my venerable age."

Gamine's smile faded slightly. Then, after a pause, she said, "Sometimes I wonder if any of us will live so long."

Temujin regarded her thoughtfully for a long moment. "You thinking about them as died the other day, facing the soldiers?"

Gamine was surprised. "Well . . . no, actually, I wasn't. Just that this sort of life doesn't seem well suited for longevity." She paused. "But . . . should I be thinking about them?"

Temujin narrowed his eyes. "*Shouldn't* you? I mean, don't misunderstand, we're all very grateful that you lot kept those soldiers off our backs—and their swords and bullets out of us, for that matter. But listen, hop-o'-my-thumb. Don't you feel the least bit bad about the fact it was your own words that led those boys and girls to their deaths?" He shivered again and hastened to add, "I'm not saying you should have done a single thing different, mind. And I know I've always taught you to keep a nice distance between you and the marks, and not to get too invested in their fortunes and misfortunes. But still . . . one hundred people, girl. That's . . ." He trailed off, holding his hands palm up in a shrug, a helpless gesture.

Gamine thought it over. "I suppose so. But if you think about it, all those people met their deaths knowing that they'd be rewarded in the next life, so really we should be happy for them, shouldn't we?"

Temujin's mouth fell open, and the whites shown around the corners of his eyes. "*Happy* for them, is it?" He sounded shocked, even horrified.

Before Gamine could answer, the hatch opened again, and Ruan and Jue trundled into the crawler, followed closely by Mama Noh.

"Anything to drink in here?" Ruan asked, kicking off his shoes and putting his bare feet up on the table.

Gamine smiled at the bandit's inadvertent joke, and then glanced to Temujin to see if he had caught it. But the old man only fixed her with a hard stare, then looked away.

Huang was the last to arrive at the command center. This was the first time all of the inner circle had gathered together since they'd arrived in the box canyon, the first time since they all stood together beside the caravan as the soldiers approached.

Since they reached their new hiding place, Huang had been working almost tirelessly. It was the only way he'd found to escape the thoughts that plagued him, but only for a moment here or there. No matter how hard he threw himself into the task at hand, memories of that day in the defile always came back, clinging to him like persistent ghosts not prepared to leave this life behind. When he slept, it was fitful and brief. Those hundred Fists paraded before him, followed by the eighty soldiers, then all the others who had fallen before his blade. And Zhao, and the drivers and guards of the convoy that had carried him away from Fanchuan years before, and all the other men, women, and children he'd seen die over the years since—those whom he had killed, and those who had died because he had been unable or unwilling to help them. Which was worse, to kill or to stand by passively and watch another die? And if he murdered to save another, what did that make him? Savior, or murderer? Or both? Or neither?

Huang had been troubled enough by his thoughts in silence. He had decided it was time to share his troubles with the others.

"I can't help but think that these victories might not be worth the price we're paying," he said as soon as the hatch swung shut behind him, not bothering with pleasantries.

The others exchanged confused glances—all but Gamine, who met his unwavering gaze.

"All this killing, all this dying, and for what?" Huang leaned on the table, his hands balled into fists. "We started this uprising because we were tired of running, because Ouyang and his cronies had made life difficult for us and ours, and we were going to stand up and fight back. But what have we gained? The workers at some mine or other might be spared a brutal reprisal by strikebreakers for a time, and get better working conditions, maybe even better wages. And perhaps a few farmers get enough water to irrigate their crops when the Combine plantations are pushed back inside their boxes a little, without the army to help them drain the reservoirs dry. But in the long run, will any of it do any good? We stop a supply convoy, and there's going to be another one along, sooner or later. We keep the army from beating down one group of striking miners, and they'll be taking it out on another group going on strike somewhere else the following week. We can't be everywhere, all the time. The only way we're effective at all is in *hurting* Ouyang and his people, and that means killing them, which means us dying as well. Is all of this—these tiny gains and minor, momentary victories—worth all of that death, on their side and ours?"

The others muttered to one another, and then one by one glanced from Huang to Gamine.

"What about your oath of vengeance against Zhao's killer?" Gamine finally asked, her tone level, conversational, her hands folded in her lap. "Is that, too, no longer worth the price?"

Huang's cheeks flushed red, and his eyes flashed. "That's different," he barked. "That's a matter between him and me. No one else has to die or kill to pay that debt."

Gamine pursed her lips and nodded thoughtfully. "All right, fair enough. So what are you saying? That we should abandon the uprising and simply give up? Just go home and let the governor-general and his forces do as they will?"

Huang slumped in his chair, scowling. "I . . . I don't know. I'm not saying that exactly . . . but perhaps." He straightened fractionally, holding his chin up. "Perhaps we should, at that. Maybe everyone would be better off if we did."

"And shirk our holy responsibility?!" Gamine exploded out of her chair, pounding her fists on the table. "We have been given a sacred duty to accomplish, or had you forgotten?"

Huang looked up at her, raising an eyebrow. "Given by *whom*?"

"You know damned well, Fei!" She bared her teeth. "You might not believe, but the others do, and I'm telling you that if the powers demand that we pay a price, we *will* pay it, or be damned for the disobedience."

"Damned?" Huang repeated, looking almost bemused. "Gamine, have you forgotten that you and Wei simply made all of that up? You don't actually *believe* that nonsense, do you?"

Temujin kept his gaze fixed on the table, while Mama Noh looked daggers at Huang, but Ruan and Jue looked to Gamine, seeming eager to hear her response.

They were disappointed if so, since Gamine's only response was to throw open the hatch and storm outside into the sunlight and dust.

The long silence that followed was finally broken by Jue. "Hummingbird, are you saying . . . ?"

"Not now, Jue!" Huang shouted, cutting him off. Then he, too, jumped up and stormed out, though instead of through the hatch he exited into his sleeping quarters, slamming the door behind him.

The others in the inner circle were left at the table, Ruan and Jue on one side and Mama Noh and Temujin on the other, exchanging uneasy glances.

"Well," Ruan said, lacing his fingers behind his neck and leaning back in his chair, "*that* went well. . . ."

Huang was pacing the small confines of the sleeping quarters, still seething, when Jue let himself in without knocking.

"What is it?!" Huang snapped, whirling on him.

Jue gave him a lopsided grin and held up his hands palms forward, an attitude of conciliation. "Just wanted to have a quick word, Chief." The grin widened, and the scar up the side of Jue's face flushed slightly red. "If you want to spar, though, that's all right by me."

Huang's expression softened fractionally, and he shook his head. "Sorry, Jue." He sat on the edge of the bed, elbow resting heavily on his knees. "It's just . . ." He trailed off and gestured toward the door. He didn't need to say any more.

Jue nodded. "It's a tough business."

"Well, I suppose no one said an uprising would be easy."

The scar-faced man chuckled and shook his head. "Oh, that's tough, too, Chief, but I was talking about women."

Huang leaned back and looked up at him, confused.

"I had a wife once, you know. Long time ago, now. Back before I got this"—he pointed to the scar lining his cheek— "when I still worked down in the mine. Married a local girl, father was one of the loaders on the job. She'd been around miners all her life, so she didn't mind my rough manners and rougher look. But it still seemed like we'd make a row damn near ever day, for one reason or another. Little things, too, like whether I'd left the teapot lid on or off, or closed the curtain when I left for the mine in the morning, or fed soupbones to a stray dog in the yard. Day and night we'd fight, it'd seem. But you know what? It was never about anything that mattered. It was always little things, you see, the mindless trivia of our waking lives. But when it came to the things that *really* mattered, the really important stuff? On those we never fought, never a once. Always of one mind, one accord, we were. That's how I knew we were meant to be together. Two people can disagree about every little thing they want, but if they agree down to the core about the things that really matter to them, they can weather anything."

Jue left off talking for a moment, looking into the middle distance.

"Where is she now?" Huang asked, finally breaking the silence.

Rubbing the corners of his eyes and licking his lips, Jue gathered himself before answering. "With the ancestors,

I expect. Or with the powers, if your lady's to be believed."
He turned to meet Huang's gaze. "Died in childbirth, Chief.
Lost her and the baby, all the same day. Afterward, there was
nothing for me but to work. Then I took it in my head to complain when an accident killed five loaders, my wife's father with
them. I agitated, kicked up a strike, and when Ouyang's thugs
came to break up the party, they decided to widen my smile
before leaving me for dead." He reached up, and absently ran
his finger along the line of his scar. "Some of the others found
me and patched me up. It didn't take long to decide I'd had
enough of mining and might want to try my hand at a different trade. I hooked up with Zhao, learned to use a sword and
fire a rifle, and then . . ." He shrugged. "The rest you know."

Huang regarded his friend, wearing a pained expression.

"Tell me, Jue, do you think I'm wrong? Is the prize worth
the cost we're paying? Should the uprising continue, and my
guilt be damned?"

Jue sucked at his teeth thoughtfully. "Well, I don't know
so much about prizes and costs, I suppose. I'm a simple man,
Chief. Someone takes something from me, I take something of
theirs. Someone hurts me or mine, I hurt them. But it seems
to me that if we're not in it, there'll be a lot of folks paying
all sorts of prices—pain, suffering, death—without getting
anything back in the bargain. If we're in there swinging, the
regular folks at least have some chance of making a go at it,
without Ouyang and his thugs getting in the way."

Huang nodded but didn't speak.

"Anyway," Jue said, shrugging. "That's not what I wanted to tell you, Chief. See, I've got this idea how we could put a hurt onto Ouyang, without our people taking much risk." In response to Huang's raised eyebrow, he continued. "Well, you know how important the Grand Trunk's supposed to be, right?"

It took nearly a week to turn Jue's plan from bare notion to reality.

It was simple, really. Almost deceptively so.

The Grand Trunk was the principal artery that ran from one end of the Tianfei Valley to the other, the line upon which the three valley provinces were strung. All vital trade, travel, and commerce in the valley happened along its length, with people and goods constantly moving back and forth. The designers of the road had planned well and positioned it far from the valley walls on either side, clearing the largest of the nearby rock formations and outcroppings, leaving no convenient hiding places for a raiding party to wait in ambush. As a result, the road was virtually impregnable from attack by bandits or revolutionaries alike.

But one point along the Grand Trunk was not quite so well protected, and while it was not as vital a part of the roadway as those stretches between the cities of Fuchuan, Shachuan, and Fanchuan, it was still absolutely essential, being the primary link between the Tianfei Valley and the north. The only other avenues out of the valley were by airship, which was prohibitively expensive for most commerce and casual travelers, and the far end of the Grand Trunk, where it terminated beyond Fuchuan, near where the northern plains began. But Fuchuan was many, many days' travel away at the best of times. The main conduit for goods, produce, men, and materiél between the valley in the south, and the highlands, mines, and military garrisons of the north and east, was through a passage that connected the terminus of the Grand Trunk with the eastern end of the roadway leading to the Forking Paths.

At this junction, the cliff walls closed on either side, towering a mile high, but less than half a mile apart. Since the onset of the uprising, the narrow pass would likely be well guarded, patrolled regularly by military forces. A direct confrontation on the ground would no doubt be a costly one for the Fists.

However, Jue wasn't a soldier, but instead thought like a miner. And from a miner's perspective, there was a simple solution to the problem, not from below, but from above.

Two teams had set out from the Fists' hiding place in the Forking Paths, heading east toward the junction. But rather than approaching on the roadway, the teams split up, one scaling up and out of the canyon maze to the north, and the other to the south. They would travel on foot and approach the cliff walls of the Grand Trunk junction from above.

The journey was almost two days of hard slogging. The teams didn't communicate by radio—for fear that their transmission would be intercepted—but at set times of day signaled each other with mirrors that reflected the light of the sun for dozens of miles, and at night employed lanterns for the same purpose. Even with binoculars they were just able to discern the flashing lights and pick out the sequence of flashes that they'd agreed upon.

By the evening of the second day they were in position—Huang with his team atop the northern cliff wall, Jue and his on the southern.

All those selected for this mission, except Huang, had been miners before they joined the Harmonious Fists. And they were well familiar with the heavy equipment they had lugged on their backs these last two days. Huang had only to give the order, and they went to work.

The drill was first. With one man to steady and two more to turn, the bit gradually bore deeper and deeper into the rock atop the cliff face, making only a low, barely audible hum. When the bit was fully extended, the bore went down almost six feet. Then they retracted the bit, moved the drill a few paces down, and started again. Finally, when the night was half gone, there were a dozen holes, each as deep as a man was tall, in a perfect line a half dozen paces from the cliff's edge.

Then the explosives were carefully unpacked and moved into position. They had been the most harrowing aspect of the two-day trek from the Fists' camp, with Huang always fearful that one of the bearers might slip and jostle the explosives too hard, and then they would all go up in one enormous blast. But they'd made it this far without incident, and with great care the former miners managed to get the explosives lowered into each of the bored holes and carefully packed into place.

Next the miners ran wires from each of the packed explosives, up the height of the bore hole, and then across the top of the cliff, a hundred paces to a rocky outcropping behind which the detonator had been positioned. Then, with precision and care, they wound each wire to the detonator contacts and carefully locked the trigger in the safety position.

When the last of the wires were attached, all that would remain would be to wait for Jue's signal that his team had finished the same work on the opposite wall, and they could retreat to safety and blast. Carefully placed, the explosives would shear off the front of the cliff faces and send them tumbling down to cause an avalanche. Rock falling from one side or the other would not be sufficient to block the roadway, cutting off the Grand Trunk from the Forking Paths and the highlands beyond—but an avalanche falling from *both* sides would do the job nicely.

The morning sun was just peeking up over the eastern horizon, and still Huang had not received Jue's signal from only a little more than a half mile away. Huang had been able to check on the other team's progress through the night, even if all he could discern were indistinct shadows moving against the night sky, and they had once or twice exchanged signals with flashing lights. Huang's last signals had gone unanswered, but now as the sun was rising, he should have been able to see Jue's team plainly at this distance. Come to that, a loud shout would likely be sufficient to reach them, if they weren't concerned about alerting any military forces that might be patrolling the roadways below.

Try as he might, though, with the naked eye or aided by the binoculars, Huang could catch no sign of Jue and his men. Could they already have completed the work and retreated to safety? Should Huang order his men to fire the explosives? What if Jue's team hadn't yet finished, and starting an avalanche on the northern cliff face only alerted the military to their plans, and the soldiers attacked before the southern face could be blown? Then the mission would have been for naught.

Huang gritted his teeth, trying to work out what to do next, as the men began affixing the last of the wires to the detonator.

The sound of pounding feet shook Huang from his reverie, and he looked up to see a small group of men rushing toward them, sabers in hand and lips twisted in rage. Bannermen!

As the squad of Bannermen rushed his team, all Huang could think was that their approach to the cliffs had not been as stealthy as he had hoped. The military forces patrolling the base of the narrow passage below must have spotted the Fists and ascended the cliff walls to intercept. That they hadn't attacked before Huang's team had drilled the bores and planted the explosives suggested that the Fists had been spotted relatively recently, but that was hardly a point of pride. As it stood, the last of the wires had not been fixed to the detonator, and Huang could not blow the cliff face if he wanted to, whether the explosives were in the bores or not.

It occurred to him to wonder whether Jue's team, too, were under attack, but then one of the Bannermen rushed him with saber drawn, and Huang was forced to put the question aside for the moment.

Huang had been taught, when fencing, always to watch the eyes of his opponent, not the blade. The blade could lie, feinting one way then coming back to attack another, but the eyes never could. So it was that a moment passed, and Huang had already parried a graceful thrust, before he got a good look at the Bannerman attacking him.

The man had thin, delicate features, his fair hair shaved to the top of his head, the rest worn in a braid down his back. Above his right eye was an cross-shaped scar, and a familiar sneer curled his lip.

The Bannerman lunged forward again, and Huang batted the saber aside as he danced backward.

"Kenniston An?!" Huang's eyes widened in shock.

The Bannerman paused for a moment, raising an eyebrow, surprised. "Huang Fei?" His smile broadened, but the point of his saber did not waver. "Well, this *is* a surprise."

Some part of him had known, Huang realized. Some part of him had known since Gamine had vaguely remembered the name of the scarred Bannerman, only a syllable or two different from that of his childhood friend. Or earlier, perhaps, when he had recognized the bemasked and goggled Bannerman's fencing style, just before Zhao fell before his blade. Some part of him had always known.

"Your parents said you were dead."

Some part had known, but Huang had not admitted it to himself before now.

"I'll have to inform them that they were premature. Of course, once we're done here, it's not as if they'll be *wrong*."

His closest friend from childhood, with whom he had studied the blade year after year, who had gone off and joined the Bannermen while Huang was still a boy—Huang's oldest friend was the Bannerman who had killed Zhao, the man whom Huang had come to see as a father.

"What's the matter, Fei? Aren't you going to say anything?"

Kenniston An. The only person who'd ever been able to defeat Huang in a fencing match. Now standing facing him, a sword in hand, and murder in his eyes.

"Did these people addle your brains before turning you against your own kind, Fei? Or did you only fall in with them *after* you lost your senses?"

Huang didn't bother to respond. What was there to say? He wouldn't, and couldn't, ask for mercy. He'd sworn an oath of vengeance, with Zhao's lifeblood still staining his hands, that he would one day find and kill the bandit chief's killer. He wasn't sure he could go through with killing his oldest friend, but he would be *damned* if he would ask Zhao's killer for mercy.

"Oh, well. I'll give your parents your best wishes, eh, Fei?"

Huang, silent as a stone statue, launched himself at Kenniston, whipping his sword over his head in a vicious downward stroke. The Bannerman sidestepped and blocked the stroke, then pivoted and brought his own sword in a sideways arc at Huang's midsection.

Dancing back frantically out of the sword's path, Huang put a few paces' distance between himself and Kenniston, then fell into a ready stance. He'd tried taking the offensive and would now try a defensive strategy.

Kenniston feinted right, then reversed to the left and lunged, right arm thrusting the saber forward, left arm thrown back for balance. Huang spun his own sword's point in a circle around Kenniston's blade, turning it aside and sending up a shower of sparks as the two swords slid against one another.

Huang riposted, turning his wrist and pushing his saber forward toward Kenniston's heart, but the Bannerman swung his own sword's point around in a circle, like a windmill's blade spinning, and swatted Huang's blade aside. Then the two fell back a pace, took ready positions, and started again.

Kenniston was winning. The conclusion was inescapable. Huang's muscles ached with the strain of parrying so many blows, and his legs were beginning to cramp. He'd been able to spare only brief glances around and saw that his men were holding their own against the Bannermen, but they were beginning to flag. The Fists had just hauled heavy drilling equipment two days overland, and then worked all night to bore a dozen holes in the living rock of the cliff. The Bannermen, though, had just scaled the cliff walls and seemed more than a little flagged themselves.

But Huang had fenced for too long, against too many opponents, to have any illusions about his chances of besting Kenniston An. The Bannerman would defeat him, and soon.

There was one weakness to Kenniston's strategy, though, Huang realized. The Bannerman was fighting as though this were a competition bout, for all that he intended to end the match by burying his sword in Huang's chest. But Huang knew that this *wasn't* a competition bout. This was real life. Life wasn't sport, as Zhao had always said. Sport had rules, but in real life the only rule was Don't Get Killed.

Huang remembered the other things that Zhao had taught him, as well.

As Kenniston thrust his blade forward in a killing blow, Huang saw an opportunity and took it. He fell backward, the sword's point passing harmlessly just above him.

Before Kenniston could shift his weight and turn his sword's blade downward, Huang broke all the rules of competitive fencing. Scooping up a handful of red sand, he threw it up into the Bannerman's face, the grains pelting Kenniston in the eyes, nose, and mouth.

As the Bannerman staggered back, sputtering and trying to wipe the sand from his stinging eyes, Huang pressed his advantage. A sweep of his legs knocked Kenniston off his feet, and in an instant Huang had leaped up, planted a foot on Kenniston's neck, and plunged his sword down toward the Bannerman's face, the point stopping only inches from Kenniston's eyelid.

"Stop struggling or you'll have more than grit in your eye, An."

Through tear-streaming eyes, the Bannerman looked up at Huang. The arrogant sneer had left Kenniston's lip.

"Call off your men, An."

Kenniston managed a defiant expression.

Huang lowered the point of the red-bladed saber, now only a finger's width from Kenniston's eye. "Call off your men," he said, his voice level, "or I may just drop this sword."

Kenniston snarled, then rolled his eyes to the side, toward

where his men were struggling with the Fists. "Stand down, Bannermen! Stand down!"

Huang didn't bother to look to see that they complied but listened as the Fists shoved their opponents away from them.

"You killed a man I cared about, An," Huang finally said, through his teeth. "Killed him like a rabid dog, on the orders of your master."

Kenniston seemed genuinely confused. "Well, I kill a lot of people, Fei, but none who don't deserve it."

Huang seethed. "Like miners striking for better pay and safer conditions? Do *they* deserve it? Or farmers who just want water for their crops, so they can feed their starving families? Do *they*?"

Kenniston, his eyes now bloodshot red, arched an eyebrow. Even sprawled on the ground with Huang's boot on his neck and Huang's sword poised above him, the Bannerman managed to look bemused.

"Is *that* why you've joined up with this Harmonious Fist nonsense, Fei? Because of a few dirty miners and farmers? Just what sort of nonsense have this Hummingbird and his mistress, Iron Jaw, filled your head with, anyway?"

Huang opened his mouth to answer, then bit back the words. He narrowed his gaze. "Nonsense, An? Is it nonsense to think that people shouldn't be starved or killed just for wanting justice, fair treatment, and a better life for their children?"

Kenniston scoffed. "Ancestors preserve us, you're *delusional*. People have to work for what they need, and earn a better life. It can't just be *handed* to them."

"But if it's taken away from them," Huang snarled, "it can sure as hell be handed *back*."

Kenniston blew air through his lips, dismissively. "Spout what nonsense you will, it won't do any good. All of this will be over soon, and your uprising will be a thing of the past."

"What do you mean?"

"You didn't think the governor-general was going to let this go on forever, did you? The emperor has agreed to his request for fresh troops and advanced siege engines, which should be arriving anytime now."

Huang spared a quick glance at his men, who were gathered together a short ways off, warily watching the Bannermen who slouched on Huang's opposite side.

"Ouyang has just announced a new offensive," Kenniston added, "and it's only a matter of time before all of you go the way of your scar-faced friend from across the canyon."

Huang tightened his grip on the sword's hilt, and the sword's blade began to vibrate with his tension. "What . . . what did you say?"

Kenniston smiled and rolled his eyes in the direction of the opposite cliff wall. "We spotted them last night and took care of them before coming to this side to see to you. If not for the fact that we spotted your signal light in the darkness, we might not have known you were up here at all."

Huang gritted his teeth. "What did you do with them?"

Kenniston's smile slid into a sneer. "Hadn't you heard? Governor-General Ouyang has given strict instruction that no insurgents or agitators are to be taken prisoner, but executed on the spot." The Bannerman's shoulders twitched in the ghost of a shrug. "I was simply following orders, Fei."

In his imagination, Huang saw the sword plunge down into Kenniston's brain, saw himself driving the life from the body of his oldest friend. He could almost hear the sound of it, of metal wrenching through flesh, could almost smell the metallic tang of blood spurting onto the dry sands.

But while he could imagine it, he could not accept it. Revenge or no, for Zhao or Jue or who knew how many others, it was a price he was not willing to pay.

Instead, he raised his sword and lifted his foot from Kenniston's neck.

The Bannerman smiled, expecting that he was being released. The smile faded as Huang swung his foot in an arc connecting with Kenniston's jaw, shattering the bone and rendering the Bannerman unconscious. He fell back onto the hard ground, alive but insensate.

Then Huang turned and pointed with his blade toward the other Bannermen. "Now, all of you, listen closely." He poised the blade over Kenniston's heart. "Let us leave in peace, or your leader is only the first of you to die."

The Bannermen exchanged glances. They scowled but agreed to Huang's terms.

The trip back was no longer than the journey outward had been, but to Huang it felt like an eternity. Not only had their plan failed, but they'd lost many good people, Jue chief among them. In the end, they hadn't even bothered to fire the explosives and collapse the northern cliff face, as with the southern cliff untouched it would have been a pointless gesture and, worse, a waste of resources. Instead they had retrieved the explosives, carefully repacking them and carrying them back for use at some later time.

For two days the Fists traveled, descending into the Forking Paths and then making their way back to their hidden camp, careful to elude any pursuit. They moved in silence whenever possible. The Fists hardly minded. Huang had been in a dark mood ever since the encounter with the Bannermen atop the northern cliff, and it was growing darker with every step. If the choices were silence or hearing just what black thoughts swirled behind Huang's smoldering gaze, the Fists were quite content to choose silence.

Gamine was performing the revelation when Huang and the others returned from their mission. She was on the scaffold, having finished delivering the homily to the assembled Fists, and now one of the opera players, ostensibly selected at random from the crowd, was helping her demonstrate the divinely powered invulnerability that had earned her the name Iron Jaw.

The player was just in the act of swinging his punch, which would be pulled less than an inch from her jaw, when Huang looked up and met Gamine's gaze. What she saw in his eyes, at that moment, so startled her that she jerked her head up, mouth open in surprise. The movement shifted her position just enough that the player's swing didn't stop just short, but connected with full force, impacting on her jaw like a load of bricks.

Gamine's head snapped back, and she stumbled backward, stars shooting in her eyes. The player rushed forward, urging apologies, while the audience of Fists gasped as one.

Within moments, Gamine had regained her composure. She resolutely resisted the urge to rub her sore and bruised jaw while delivering the final benediction to the Fists, after a brief explanation that the powers had wished to demonstrate her devotion to them by momentarily withdrawing their support from her, and that in standing steadfast and taking the full blow without flinching, Gamine had passed their test. Then she had hurried from the scaffold to hear what was behind the dark look in Huang's eyes.

Seated around the table in the command center, the inner circle listened attentively as Huang related the story of the last five days, of what had befallen them above the Grand Trunk junction, and what had happened to Jue and the Fists in the other team.

Gamine listened carefully, occasionally prodding the tender spot on her jaw, where the flesh was already purpling into a vicious bruise.

Finally, Huang related what his former friend had told him about the troop buildup and siege engines, about the new offensive, and finally about the standing orders that no Fists were to be taken alive.

"Do you believe him?" Mama Noh asked suspiciously.

Huang nodded. "Whatever else he is, Kenniston An is not a liar. He may have exaggerated somewhat, but what he said is essentially the truth."

"And you're sure that you weren't followed back?" Temujin put in nervously.

Huang shook his head. "We took special care, and there was no sign of pursuit." He paused and placed his fists on the table before him. "But we can't hide in here forever. It's only a matter of time before an airship passes overhead or a soldier stumbles into the canyon, and then they'll be upon us."

"And then they'll just kill us all," Ruan said, his brow knit, his mouth drawn into a tight line, leaving him looking even more like a skeleton than ever. Of all of them, save perhaps Huang, he seemed to be taking the news of Jue's death the hardest.

"Yes." Huang gave a curt nod and flicked a glance at the skeletal bandit. "And then they'll kill us all." He let out a ragged sigh. "Some of us might manage to escape again, at the cost of still more of our people's lives. But then they would find us again, and some would escape, at the cost of still more. And on and on. We can continue to play cat and mouse with them from here to the Great Southern Basin and back, but like Kenniston said, it's just a matter of time. The governor-general, with the emperor at his back, has an effectively inexhaustible supply of men and arms to send after us. And what have we got?"

"We've got righteousness," Gamine said, speaking for the first time since they'd gathered together. "We've got the hope for harmony. And we've got the powers."

"Ancestors, not this again," Ruan said, rolling his eyes.

Huang gave her a hard look. "You talk a lot about special destiny, Gamine. Was Jue bleeding out his life far from any home he ever knew *his* special destiny?"

Gamine opened her mouth, then shut it again. She took a deep breath, then let it out gradually through her nostrils. "Jue's death was a tragedy. I . . . I don't know, perhaps he *did* have a special destiny, but your friend Kenniston—"

"No friend of mine!" Huang seethed.

Gamine nodded by way of apology. "But when *Bannerman* Kenniston killed him, he prevented Jue from fulfilling his destiny. Maybe destiny isn't just something that happens but is a plan we're supposed to *make* happen." She paused and looked around the table at the others. "I don't know about the rest of you, but I don't think it's *my* destiny to be hunted and killed by Ouyang and his thugs, do you?"

Huang pressed his lips together and splayed his hands palm down on the table, inadvertently accentuating the missing digits.

"So just what do you plan to do about it, my little sprite?" Temujin scratched his neck thoughtfully.

"I think we need to stop running, stop hiding, and take the fight to Ouyang, where it belongs."

Across from her, a smile began to spread across Huang's face, and he inclined his head slightly. "Iron Jaw, for the first time in a long time, you and I are in complete agreement."

There were twelve of them crowded into the red crawler, all together, as it trundled down onto the Grand Trunk from the west. They were taking a chance passing through the same junction Huang had tried to attack the month before but held out hope that any forces in the area would only give the crawler a cursory search, should they be stopped. As it happened, they reached the city walls of Fanchuan before encountering any authority, and by that point they were on familiar ground.

Mama Noh rode in the cab, with Temujin in the driver's seat beside her. Ruan scowled from a seat in the rear, while Gamine and Huang sat on cushions on opposite sides of the converted cargo hold, which the Red Crawler Opera Company had for years used as a makeshift living room, storage area, and rehearsal space. In addition to the five surviving members of the inner circle, there were four of the original opera players and three former plantation laborers who had picked up enough tumbling or could sing well enough that they could pass for performers in a pinch. An even dozen who had left the relative safety and comfort of the Fists' camp in the Forking Paths and come to Fanchuan, capital of Fangzhang province, on a last-ditch attempt at final victory.

It was not common knowledge that the Red Crawler Opera Company was a part of the Harmonious Fists Uprising. From the beginning, Gamine and Huang had recognized the potential usefulness of having a small number of Fists who could come and go through towns and villages without raising undue suspicion. And since the red crawler had been a familiar sight in the Tianfei Valley and the outlying provinces alike for years, it was not difficult to establish identification with the authorities, if need be.

The plan was the simplest yet, brutally so, but with the largest risk and the most significant potential benefit. And it depended upon the twelve people within the crawler convincing the authorities in Fanchuan that they were precisely what they appeared to be, a group of opera players returning to the capital after several years performing in the outer provinces.

Temujin had been selected to sit beside Mama Noh because,

in his long years working various grifts, he had successfully passed himself off as everything from a bureaucrat to a peddler and all points in between. He was likely the most skilled liar in the bunch, though Mama Noh insisted that her skills were somewhat superior, but that she called it acting.

Huang felt certain that Gamine could out-lie both of them if the need arose, but he didn't see anything to gain from pressing the issue.

The guardsman at the city walls, after questioning Mama Noh and Temujin for three quarters of an hour, finally stamped his chop on their admittance papers, and the crawler was cleared to enter.

The easy part was behind them. Now things would get *difficult*.

It had taken several weeks to put the early stages of the plan into motion. One of Mama Noh's most trusted people, who had been with the opera company for long years, had been sent out on foot to Fanchuan. The woman had joined a caravan of travelers passing through the Grand Trunk conjunction, and on reaching the Tianfei Valley had stolen away in the night to circle Fanchuan and approach from the east, to allay any suspicion. Once within the city, her task had been to establish contact with those who had employed the Red Crawler Opera Company in years past, and to arrange for a suitable engagement for the players.

The realities of their circumstances meant that no communication had been possible with the player between the time she left the box canyon and the time that the red crawler arrived in Fanchuan, but Mama Noh's faith in her had not been misplaced. By the time that Gamine, Huang, and the others climbed down the hatch into the bustle of the capital city, the player had arranged a suitable booking for the company, beginning less than a week away.

The player's instructions had been short and simple, but everyone was endlessly impressed that she'd carried it off. After all, it could not have been easy to book an engagement where the only criterion dictated who was to be in the audience. But with a broad smile, the player was able to report success. She had managed to convince the agent to commission the performance without ever raising suspicion. The following week the Red Crawler Opera Company was engaged to perform at the Hall of Rare Treasures, the residence of Governor-General Ouyang himself.

Huang knelt in the forecourt, working the edge of his red-bladed saber back and forth across a lightly oiled whetstone. The blade's leading edge shone mirror bright, reflecting the daylight that streamed around the edges of a shuttered window. It'd already had the keenness of a razor when he'd started sharpening, hours before, and now he was doing little more than polishing the blade. But it gave him something to occupy his hands, though sadly the same could not be said of his thoughts, which still raced in tight circles in his mind.

He'd scarcely walked through the front door in several days, preferring to remain indoors, but in this he was not alone. Mama Noh's envoy had been able to secure lodgings for the company in the less fashionable district at the extreme south of the city in Southern Gate District, and the ersatz players all tended to remain inside and keep to themselves as much as possible. Even when there wasn't strategy to be discussed, plans to be reviewed, or maneuvers to be carefully practiced, Huang and the others preferred to keep out of the public eye as much as possible. Still, they could not remain indoors forever, and from time to time they were forced to go out into the city, either singly or in pairs, to fetch provisions or scout their routes to and from the governor's palace, or simply to indulge vices left too long unsated.

When Huang had ventured beyond the walls of their lodging, he had found Fanchuan a much different place than the city he remembered. It seemed to have changed considerably in the years since he had been gone, but then it was hard for him to know whether it was really the city that had changed or he himself. After all, he'd been little more than a child when he was last inside the walls of Fanchuan, and the boy who he'd been was now long gone.

Still, he could not deny that there were definitely things about the city that were different. And he was not alone in noticing them.

"This isn't a city," Ruan said as the door banged open and

he strode into the forecourt. He slammed the door shut behind him. "It's a rutting military stronghold!"

Huang only glanced up, continuing to work the saber back and forth across the whetstone. "More soldiers about?"

Ruan scowled. "I lost count!"

The skeletal bandit was right. The city did seem to be crowded with soldiers. Both Bannermen and those who served under the Green Standard, the soldiers loitered on every street corner, and crowded every teahouse and tavern. The hanging gardens in Sun-Facing District, not far from the Hall of Rare Treasures, had been pulled down, completely trodden under, and converted into a makeshift garrison, with ordered rows of tents housing hundreds, even thousands of troops. And whole rows of houses in Green Stone District had been seized by the authorities and converted into barracks.

"You *still* sharpening that rutting thing?" Ruan looked sidelong at the blade in Huang's hand. "If you keep it up, you won't have enough sword left to stitch on a button."

Huang looked up from his work, lips curled in a sneer. "Don't you have work of your own to be doing, Ruan?" Somehow, he managed to make the other man's name into a curse.

To Huang's surprise, Ruan didn't respond in kind but instead looked down at him with what appeared to be genuine concern. "You doing all right, Hummingbird?" He folded his arms over his chest and regarded Huang closely. "Not like you to snap like that." He paused and then glanced uneasily toward the main body of their lodgings. "It's not some sort of . . . *woman* trouble, is it?"

Huang couldn't help but chuckle. He shook his head. "No, nothing like that."

Ruan sighed, looking relieved. So far as Huang knew, the skeletal-faced bandit had never been in a relationship with a woman that lasted longer than a single night, if that, and the intricacies of longer-term relationships were obviously something with which Ruan was far less than entirely comfortable. "What then?"

Huang took a heavy breath and laid his saber across his lap. "I don't know," he said quietly. "Perhaps I'm just anxious about our mission. I keep thinking about having to . . ." He paused, searching. "About having to eliminate Ouyang."

Ruan pulled a face, like he'd just tasted something bitter. He shook his head. "No, no. Don't dress it up in pretty words like that. It isn't *eliminating* we're about. It's *killing*." He narrowed his eyes, looking closely at Huang. "Can't bring yourself to say it, maybe you shouldn't be doing it. Killing's a man's work, and no place for the squeamish."

Huang picked up his blade and began running its edge once more back and forth across the whetstone. He opened his mouth to answer, then closed it again, remaining silent.

"You know," Ruan went on, pointing to the sword in Huang's hands, "for the longest time I wasn't sure you knew how to use that thing. Oh, you could swing it around, of course, all sorts of fancy dancing. But it was forever and a day before I saw you actually stick it *into* anyone." He chuckled ruefully. "Fact, Jue and I had a bet running for a while as to whether you'd ever be blooded or not."

At the mention of Jue, Huang felt his face tighten and saw that Ruan, too, was lost in a sudden reverie, remembering their fallen brother.

"I've never killed if I could help it," Huang finally admitted after a long silence. "For a time, I thought I could avoid it. Then there came that day we stood at the mouth of the Forking Paths, and it was the lives of the soldiers or the lives of our own. It was a choice that I could make, and would make again. But later, when I stood on the cliffs overlooking the beginnings of the Grand Trunk, and had Zhao's murderer in the dirt before me, I couldn't—" He broke off, his eyes stinging. He tightened his hand around the saber's hilt in a white-knuckled grip, his lips drawn into a line.

Ruan stepped forward and laid an uncharacteristically tender hand on Huang's shoulder. "You're not a murderer, Hummingbird. There's no shame in that. You're a soldier and kill only when someone needs killing. You may have put off your uniform and taken up the bandit's life, but you're still a soldier down where it matters."

Huang looked up. He'd never heard Ruan talk to anyone this way, much less him.

"If not for Zhao," Ruan went on, "I would have killed you

the day we met, out there on the sands. I thought you needed killing." He paused, his expression unreadable. "I was wrong, though. And I'm glad I didn't kill you."

Ruan squeezed Huang's shoulder for a moment, then turned and walked away into the lodgings, leaving him alone with his saber, the edge mirror bright and razor keen.

Gamine hadn't seen Temujin in the better part of a day and was beginning to worry.

"He's probably off somewhere drunk," Mama Noh said.

"I'm sure of that," Gamine answered. "The question isn't *if* he's drunk, the question is *where*."

When they had first arrived in Fanchuan, there had been some concern early on that Temujin, with ready access to spirits, might fall back into his accustomed habits and in some drunken moment reveal the Fists' true identity and their plans to the authorities, however inadvertently. To the old man's credit, though, he seldom drank in taverns, but tended instead to purchase jars that he brought back to their lodgings to drink in peace. Whenever he was out of Gamine's sight for too long, though, she couldn't help but worry.

Just as she was checking the storeroom, half expecting to find him sprawled out insensate on the cold stone floor, she heard the sound of Temujin coming in through the front door. She met him in the dining area, to find him already unstoppering an oversized jar of wine.

"You look surprisingly sober," Gamine said with a smile, sliding into a chair across the table from him.

"That, hop-o'-my-thumb," Temujin said with a grin, "is a problem that will quickly be rectified." With the jar open, he didn't bother with a cup but drank straight from the spout. He set the jar back down on the table and wiped his mouth with the cuff of his sleeve. "There's not a few in this town that wouldn't benefit from a bit of tipple as well, if you want to know my opinion."

Gamine gave him a puzzled look. "What do you mean?" She'd seldom ventured outside the lodgings since they arrived, having the inescapable fear that she might run into someone who knew her from some former life, either as the prized pet of the Chauviteau-Zong estate or as the young grifter on the make. Most of what she knew of the current state of the city came from the reports the others carried back, Temujin among them.

"I've been in and out of this town since I was younger'n you, and I've scarce seen it so tense. People agitating on the streets about the governor, the papers full of stories of crime and murder and worse."

Gamine nodded thoughtfully. From what the Fists had learned since arriving the week before, there appeared to be considerable unrest among the populace. There were stories about the Harmonious Fists and the uprising in the news of the day, but surprisingly less than any of them might have

expected. Instead, the broadsheets and criers were more interested in stories about the Parley gangs, which were taking
advantage of the authorities' distraction with the uprising in the
north; an unrelenting crime wave had followed in all the valley
provinces. And, perhaps most surprisingly, time and again the
Fists heard stories about the public agitating for Ouyang to
step down, and for the governor-general's policies in the outer
provinces to be reversed, in particular his new offensive with
its "No Prisoner" tactic.

As difficult as it was for the Fists to believe, a considerable percentage of the public *supported* the uprising and were
pushing for the farmers, miners, and other laborers to be given
precisely what they were demanding.

Gamine tilted her head to one side, hearing faint strains of
music from beyond their lodging's walls. "What's that?"

Temujin cocked his head, listened for a moment, then
shrugged. "Oh, just another funeral procession. Passed it on
my way back. Seems folks die pretty often here in Southern
Gate, don't they?"

Gamine chewed her lower lip, lost in thought. She remembered what Master Wei had taught about what awaited the
faithful after death, how there would be no hunger and no
pain, no loss and no loneliness, only endless satiation, comfort, and bliss. She thought of all those Fists who had fallen,
these years past, in their struggles against Governor-General
Ouyang. Had they woken to find themselves in that kind

of paradise, free from earthly worries and woes?

Thinking of Ouyang, though, reminded her of their mission and the task that lay before them. She wasn't sure which was worse, the thought that *nothing* lay beyond death, in which case in killing Ouyang she would be consigning him to oblivion, or the thought that *something* lay beyond death, in which case she would be sending him to his punishment or reward, whichever the case might be. And if there was some life after life, some continuance beyond the veil of death, was she running the risk of denying herself entry by staining her hands with Ouyang's blood in cold, calculated murder? Because that was what it would be, she had come to realize. Not the heat of battle, defending herself and her people from attack, but the clinical, calculated taking of another life, killing someone who had no inkling that death was coming to him.

"Old man?" Gamine finally said, breaking the silence. "What do *you* think waits for us after death?"

Temujin quaffed another draft from his jar, his eyebrow cocked. "More of the same, is what I figure. If you ask me, and you did, death is just the life we'll find on the other side of the Eternal Blue Sky. Like passing through a mirror. Jenghiz Khan and the Mongols of old had themselves buried with their prized possessions, their animals, swords, and gold, so they'd have them ready to hand when they sat up on the other side. If it was good enough for them, I figure it's good enough for me." He took another pull from the jar and wiped his mouth on his sleeve. "But I don't spend too much time worrying about death, hop-o'-my-thumb. Life is trouble enough."

It was the day of the Red Crawler Opera Company's scheduled performance at the Hall of Rare Treasures, and everything was in readiness. The thirteen Fists had been drilled on the plans until they could each recite not only their own role backward and forward, but those of all the others as well.

None of them were under illusions about their own chances of escape. If everything went exactly according to plan, the odds were still against *any* of them living to tell the tale. They would be attacking the governor-general when he was at his most vulnerable, within the safety of his own home. While they had a better-than-average chance of succeeding, and reaching Ouyang before his guards intercepted them, the place would be ringed with still more guards. And although the guards were stationed to keep people *out* of the governor's residence, when the alarm was raised about Ouyang's murder, the guards would be in a perfect position to keep the Fists *in*.

And even if they *were* able somehow to escape the governor's residence, elude the guards, and make it out into the city, Fanchuan was packed from one wall to the other with Bannermen and Green Standard guardsmen. Most would be willing to cut down the Fists where they stood for the promise of a free round at a tavern, and if the authorities put a bounty on their heads when issuing their descriptions, it was likely that the Fists wouldn't make it a dozen steps before being hacked to pieces.

But each of the Fists knew what they had been getting themselves into when they'd agreed to go on the mission.

Which wasn't to say that they didn't have doubts.

"Won't be long now," Gamine said, sipping her tea.

Huang took a deep breath and let out a ragged sigh. "Only a few more hours," he said, and nodded.

Silence stretched between them, while somewhere in the dingy lodgings water dripped slowly, drop after drop after drop.

The relationship between Gamine and Huang had cooled these last weeks. They now slept separately, and when they spoke it was only of strategic matters. Still, that morning, with their appearance at the Hall of Rare Treasures only hours away, the two found themselves dining alone in their lodgings, while the others were preparing the red crawler, or tending to the props and costumes, or having a final ramble through the city streets before the mission began.

"Have you heard?" Huang said at length. "The Council of Deliberative Officials has issued an official writ of censure against Ouyang, demanding his resignation and the reversal of his policies in the north. Apparently they've begun an investigation into charges of corruption, calling in representatives from mining interests and the Combine to testify, and will be bringing the matter before the emperor himself."

Gamine shook her head slightly, a faraway look in her eye. "No," she said, barely above a whisper. "I hadn't heard."

Huang nodded and let out another ragged sigh. "It's only a matter of time before Ouyang and his cronies are ousted." He paused, and then quickly added, "If, of course, we weren't planning to . . . you know . . ." He trailed off and lowered his gaze.

"Huang?" It was the first time she'd called him anything but Hummingbird in some long while. "What do you think happens to us? When we die?"

Huang looked up and met her eyes. "I . . . I'm not sure, Gamine. Sometimes I think there may be something afterward, but usually I think that things just . . . end." He paused thoughtfully. "I think that life is just life, without anything before it and without anything to follow. This is existence"— he waved his arm in a wide arc, indicating the room around them, the city beyond, the planet beyond that—"all of this, and it's existence that matters. It matters what we do in life, and it matters how we live, not where we might go after we die. The only important things are how we treat one another, what kind of people we are, and what we do."

Gamine looked at him in silence for a moment, her eyes glistening. "I . . . I want to believe that Wei was right, and that a reward awaits us, but I still can't escape the doubt." She chewed her lip. "What if this *is* all that there is. Does it make any sense to throw our lives away?"

Huang pressed his lips together. "Killing a man whose

effectiveness is at an end, and who is bound to stand for his crimes before the emperor, regardless of what we do? Is that what you mean?"

Gamine was still for a moment but nodded. "We wanted to help people. But what we've done already has spurred others to help them instead. First the people, now the Council of Deliberative Officials."

"So what's to be gained from all of us dying, when life is all that matters?"

The two looked at each other in silence.

Then the stillness was broken by a crash from the doorway, and they turned to see Temujin standing there, his face a red ruin, his belly covered with the blood his hands could not staunch.

"D-Diggers . . . P-Parley," Temujin croaked as Gamine and Huang helped him up onto the table and eased him into a prone position. "T-Thompson . . . Mary . . ."

Huang looked to Gamine for answers, and she nodded, her expression dark. "Thompson Mary was part of the Diggers Parley. We ran afoul of her and her gang in Fuchuan before we headed north onto the plains and met Wei."

Temujin reached up a bloody hand and grabbed hold of Gamine's upper arm. "Tavern . . . I was in . . . the tavern."

Gamine nodded and put her hand over his, mindless of the still-warm blood. "What happened, Temujin?"

Huang did his best to staunch the flow of blood from the old man's wounds, but they were too deep, and too many. It was only a matter of time.

"D-Diggers," he said, his voice raspy and harsh. "Found me. Thompson Mary . . . came . . . said she'd seen me . . . on the street. Recognized me . . . Remembered . . . me. From Fuchuan. S-said . . . said she owed me . . . for her arrest."

Gamine squeezed her eyes shut for a moment, but the tears flowed down her cheeks unbidden. "Oh, you tiresome old man." Her voice cracked, and she squeezed his bloody hand on her arm.

"Gamine," Huang said, in a voice barely above a whisper, "there's nothing we can do for him."

Gamine nodded.

The old man's cheeks and forehead were now blanched, almost as pale as ivory, drained and bloodless.

"Sorry, hop . . . hop-o'-my-thumb . . ." Temujin coughed, and pink foam flecked in his mustache. "D-Didn't mean . . . to queer . . . your plans. . . ."

Gamine reached out her free hand and brushed it against the old man's forehead, which already felt clammy and cold. "You always said a grifter's got to know when the con's run its course and it's time to leave, didn't you, old man? Well, I think maybe it's time to pack up and move on."

Temujin looked up at her, his eyes watery and weak, and a faint smile tugged up the corners of his mouth. "Do . . . Do you mean it . . . sprite? No more . . . of this . . . flimflam?" He sputtered, racked with painful coughs. "Ooohh . . . to get back on the road . . . and to work the old gaffs . . . again." His smile broadened, and his gaze rolled from Gamine to Huang standing next to her. "Bring your man along . . . why don't you? He . . . He's a right enough cove . . . for all . . . of that. . . ."

Then he coughed once more, but it was a death rattle. His eyes rolled up in his head, and his body went limp.

Gamine stood holding his lifeless hand for a long, long time, silent and unmoving.

Finally, when she was at last ready to let go, she and Huang had a long talk.

When the others returned to the lodging, ready to load into the red crawler and head to the Hall of Rare Treasures, Gamine and Huang were there at the entrance to greet them.

"What's all this?" Ruan said, pointing with his chin at the sheet-wrapped bundle on the table. Mama Noh didn't have to ask; her hand flying to her mouth and her horrified expression made clear that she knew precisely what, and who, it was.

"Temujin's past caught up to him," Gamine said, her voice hoarse but her eyes dry and clear. "There were costs he still had to pay." She glanced over at the bundle on the table, and then back to the others. "It's nothing to do with our mission. But everything to do with what we'll do next."

The others exchanged confused glances.

"That's what waits for all of us—today, tomorrow, or a hundred years from now." Huang pointed a finger at the body on the table. "Now, I can't speak for the rest of you, but as for me, I'd rather tomorrow than today, and a hundred years from now instead of tomorrow."

Gamine took a step forward and raised her chin. "We came to the city and now find that the man that we intended to kill is virtually dead already, his power lost, his influence all spent. The people are against him, but worse than that, the bureaucracy is, as well. Right now he controls only the military, but to turn that against the people or the government would only anger the emperor, and with the emperor's support withdrawn the military will be lost to him, as well."

"Our plan was to kill Ouyang," said Huang. "To kill him to benefit our friends and family, to make for them a better world. But it would cost our lives to do so. We all know that. If that better world is already approaching through the efforts of others, is it worth even one unnecessary death?" He looked from one face to another. "Besides, if we let matters take their course, Ouyang's policies will be reversed, including his offensive against the Fists. But if we kill Ouyang, who is to say that his successor will not decide that Ouyang had been right all along, and press even harder for our complete extermination?"

The others began muttering to one another behind their hands.

346 • CHRIS ROBERSON

"So what are you saying, Hummingbird?" Ruan crossed his arms over his chest. "What do you expect us to do?"

Huang smiled, and glanced at Gamine before answering.

"We expect you to *live*."

In the end, only a handful of those who had come aboard the red crawler returned to the box-canyon camp, to convey the last orders of Iron Jaw and Hummingbird. Mama Noh and the other players, along with one of the laborers who requested to join their company, loaded up and left Fanchuan by the eastern gate, heading toward Shachuan, where they hoped new engagements awaited them.

Ruan carried back word to the Fists. They were instructed to break the camp, divide their supplies and resources as fairly and evenly as possible, and disperse back to their homes, or to fresh lands if they preferred. The only injunction on them was that they were to lay down their arms and not engage the military. The soldiers, so Ruan was to tell them, would soon enough be busy elsewhere.

As for Iron Jaw and Hummingbird? Gamine and Huang, once they saw to the funeral rites for Temujin, said a quiet farewell to each other and then faded off into the city, going their separate ways.

And with that, the Harmonious Fists were no more, and their uprising was over.

•

CODA

•

METAL SNAKE YEAR, SEVENTY-EIGHTH YEAR OF THE TIANBIAN EMPEROR

HUANG FEI ARRIVED AT THE HOUSE OF THE ETERNAL Blue Sky as the sun was beginning to set, the last rays peeking around the rooftops of the Green Stone District. It was full summer, and the day had been warm, but as the daylight faded a slight chill could be felt in the air.

The doors to the house were open, and already the happy rumblings of the crowd gathering inside could be heard. All of the leading lights of Fanchuan had been invited—not only bureaucrats and merchants, but artists, musicians, and writers—and the benefit promised to be the social event of the season. All the proceeds were to go to the House of the Eternal Blue Sky, Fanchuan's leading home for orphans and wayward children, but Huang could not help but suppose that some of the funds might end up redirected to the other enterprises of the House's founder.

The matriarch of the House was a tireless advocate for

poor children, and in addition to looking after her charges who were residents at the house—attempting to find homes for them where possible, and training them for productive and happy lives once they grew to adulthood—she was constantly lobbying the authorities to provide greater protections for the poor, in the city and in the outer provinces alike. It had been years since Huang had seen her, but the news of the day was full of stories of her efforts and of her recent successes in convincing the Council of Deliberative Officials to petition the new governor-general to enact more stringent penalties for those who abused and misused the children who had no home but the streets and back alleys of Fanchuan.

When Huang had received an invitation to the benefit, he'd reacted with a mixture of excitement and apprehension. He was excited to see her, apprehensive about how their reunion might play out.

As he crossed the threshold into the House of the Eternal Blue Sky and saw the smile on the face of the house matriarch greeting him, that apprehension melted like ice tossed into a fire.

"Huang!"

"Madam Borjigin," Huang said with a formal bow, but before he'd straightened she'd knocked the wind from him, wrapping her arms around him, squeezing him in a vice grip with her ear pressed against his chest, her eyes shut tight.

"It's been a long time, Huang," Gamine said, lingering

for a long moment before opening her eyes, still holding him tightly. Then her eyes opened and she pushed away, holding him at arms' length. "You look good!"

Huang smiled and ran a finger down the softening line of his jaw. "My wife insists that I don't eat enough, but I think she suspects I just don't like her cooking." He gave her an appraising look. "And you? You scarcely look a day older than when last I saw you. . . . What? Ten years ago?"

Gamine pursed her lips and shook her head. "Something like that." She threaded her arm through his and steered him further into the house, through the milling crowd. "Come, we've just got time to get cups of wine before the performance begins."

Huang let himself be led across the floor to a table at the side of the hall, where small porcelain cups had been carefully arranged before delicate carafes of rice wine. Gamine picked up two, handed him one, and they clinked their cups together before taking sips.

"So how is your family, Huang? Are your parents well?"

Huang gave a slight shrug. "Father is alive, but in his dotage, I'm afraid. He remembers little these days, and often thinks he's a boy again and that I am his father. Mother handles it well enough. To be honest, I think she's a little relieved. He was never happy that I had sold off all the business's assets after poor health forced him to retire. At least now we don't have to hear endless lectures about how an employee-owned mining collective is no kind of proper business. Nor complaints about the years I let them believe I was dead. I think Mother harbors suspicions about where I was all that time but keeps them to herself."

Gamine nodded in sympathy, a ghost of a smile tugging the corners of her mouth. She took a sip of wine. "To be honest, I was surprised that you were able to accept the invitation. I'd have thought you would be in the north, busy overseeing the mine."

Huang shook his head. "I leave that to Ruan most often these days. He's found his true calling as a foreman, it seems. The miners and loaders all love him in their off-hours, in the taverns, but when they're on shift, they find him terrifying. So he can motivate with love and with fear alike." He sipped his wine. "Anyway, I'm needed here in the city to see to the finances, and to make sure any of us actually see a profit from our work and investments."

"And to harass the authorities, I understand." Gamine raised a bemused eyebrow. "With considerable success, I might add."

"Well . . ." Huang blushed, averting his eyes. "It doesn't hurt that my brother holds a high position in the cabinet of the new governor-general."

"False modesty doesn't suit you, Huang," Gamine said with a grin, playfully punching his shoulder. "You've managed to get all manner of safety and salary protection legislation approved, and I doubt there's a miner, farmer, or laborer in all the north who doesn't know who they have to thank for it." She became more serious for a moment. "And you shouldn't think that I don't know how often you've interceded on my behalf with your brother, too. I thank you, and the city's poor thank you."

Huang opened his mouth, awkwardly searching for the appropriate response. "I didn't think you knew . . ."

He was saved when Gamine's attention was diverted by a new arrival at the entrance to the hall. Gamine painted an appropriately professional expression on her face and gave a curt wave at the old woman now being helped down the steps, and then turned back to Huang with a sly grin.

"Know who that is?" When Huang shook his head, she explained. "Madam Chauviteau-Zong."

Huang's eyes widened, and he turned to get a better look.

"Remember my plans for vengeance?" Gamine's grin broadened. "Now I revenge myself on her every month, at least, shaming her into donating large sums of money to the House of the Eternal Blue Sky. I've got all her peers on the rolls of our regular contributors, and now Chauviteau-Zong is terrified that she'll lose her social standing if she doesn't contribute, as well." Her gaze followed the ancient woman as she was helped into the hall by her servants. "She doesn't recognize me, of course." Gamine sighed. "I wonder how many children went in and out of the gates of the Chauviteau-Zong estate over the years, how many times she and her friends played their little game." Her eyes focused on the middle distance. "And I wonder what became of the others."

Then Gamine snapped from her reverie and turned back to Huang.

"Oh, it's been some years now, but I remember reading about the death of your friend. . . . Well, not friend, I suppose, but still . . ." She trailed off.

Huang nodded. "Friend is as good a name for him as any, I suppose. It's all a long time ago now." Kenniston An had died in a skirmish with Parley gang members not long after Governor-General Ouyang had been sent back to Earth in disgrace, when the Bannermen had been dispatched to act in concert with city guardsmen. But Kenniston had not died in vain, as the operation had netted Thompson Mary of the Diggers, along with the leaders of several other rival gangs. "A very long time."

Gamine reached out and squeezed Huang's shoulder. "Oh, look," she said, pointing to the rear of the hall. "The performance is about to begin."

The Red Crawler Opera Company had taken the stage, and Mama Noh stepped forward and recited the preamble. The opera was a relatively new one, never before performed in Fanchuan, but already a roaring success at the Imperial Fuchuan Opera House in the east.

"Did you make this selection?" Huang asked in a whisper while the performance began.

Gamine smiled but shook her head. "It was Mama Noh's idea. She found it . . . amusing, I suppose."

Huang looked somewhat embarrassed and took a deep sip of his wine.

"Don't worry," Gamine said, laying her hand over his. "No one knows. Besides . . ." She smiled. "As you say, it was all a very long time ago."

Huang chuckled and nodded.

Then the two fell silent, and along with the rest of the hall lost themselves in the performance. It was the story of a boy and a girl who had come together at a time when their people needed them most, and led an uprising that toppled a foul dictator and changed a world. Then the boy and girl had disappeared as mysteriously as they had first appeared, and were never heard from again.

It was all a fiction, of course, based on hearsay and rumor, but it had the ring of truth to it, and that was enough. It promised to be the most popular opera of the day. In time, perhaps, art would outlive history, and fiction would supplant fact. Perhaps, one day, audiences would never guess that the two people who gave their names to the piece had actually lived. Would never guess that there had ever been two such people, *Iron Jaw and Hummingbird*.

AUTHOR'S NOTE

I'M THE KIND OF PERSON WHO WON'T BUY A DVD IF THE only special features are trailers for other movies, and who always feels a little cheated when the last words in a book are *The End*. I always like a little extra material to dig into after I finish a story, a peek behind the scenes.

With that in mind, I offer the following notes.

ON THE CELESTIAL EMPIRE

The world in which *Iron Jaw and Hummingbird* takes place is one in which I've set many stories and novels. Called the Celestial Empire, it is an alternate history in which China rose to world domination in the fifteenth century.

Iron Jaw and Hummingbird begins in what our calendar calls the year 2515 in the twenty-sixth century, and which the calendars of the Celestial Empire alternatively refer to as the year 5152, the fifty-second year of the Tianbian Emperor, or the 254th Fire Star year.

ON FIRE STAR GEOGRAPHY

The red planet Fire Star is, of course, Mars. Five centuries before Gamine and Huang were born, the spaceships of the Dragon Throne first touched down on its red sands. (The Aztecs were already there, but that's another story entirely.) The spaceships brought colonists, who with a process known as terraforming began the slow transformation of the red planet into a habitable world.

All the places to which Gamine's and Huang's journeys take them can be found on any map of Mars, like the one available at www.google.com/mars. The Tianfei Valley is the Valles Marineris, Bao Shan is Olympus Mons, the Three Sovereigns mountain range is the Tharsis Montes, the Forking Paths is the Noctis Labyrinthus, the Great Yu Canyon is Echus Chasma, and so on.

ON UNITS OF MEASURE

Some of the units of measure employed on Fire Star are roughly equivalent to those used on Earth today. For instance, a day on Mars—the time it takes for the planet to make a complete rotation and for the sun to return to the same point in the sky—is about half an hour longer than a day on Earth. Whenever reference is made to a "day" in this novel, then, it could as easily be a day on Earth or on Mars. The same is true of hours, weeks, and months.

Seasons and years, on the other hand, are a little more complicated. A year, in general terms, is defined as the time needed for a planet to make a complete rotation around the sun. On Earth, this is a little more than 365 days. Mars, however, is farther away from the sun, and takes more than 668 Martian days to make a complete rotation. As a result, the Martian year is almost twice as long as an Earth year (it's 1.881 Earth years long, to be precise). And the seasons are correspondingly longer as well, with spring lasting for some 194 days on Mars, as opposed to 93 days of spring on Earth.

In the interest of avoiding confusion, dates and ages in *Iron Jaw and Hummingbird* have been converted from Martian years to Earth years. It just seemed too confusing to say that Huang Fei was nine and a half years old when his parents sent him off to join the Green Standard Army, but that those nine and a half years were equivalent to eighteen years on another planet entirely.

(Anyone bothered by this can always convert them back. Simply divide the number of years in question by 1.881, and the resulting sum will be the number of Martian years.)

ON INFLUENCES AND INSPIRATIONS

The story of Gamine and Huang is inspired in large part by the historical Boxer Rebellion, an uprising that took place in China at the turn of the twentieth century. Names like "the Society of

Righteous Harmony" and "the Harmonious Fists" are shamelessly stolen from the pages of history, as is the idea of bandits and religious ecstatics colliding to start a revolution.

Likewise, the story of Gamine and Temujin on the Grand Trunk is an homage to (or stolen from, depending on how charitable one is) Rudyard Kipling's *Kim*. I had the great good fortune to finish work on this book while staying at Kipling's house in Vermont, Naulakha, where the author lived for four years in the 1890s. It was while living there that Kipling started work on *Kim* (and there that he wrote *The Jungle Book* for which, because of Disney's adaptations of the Mowgli stories, he is probably best known today). It seemed somehow fitting that I should end work on Gamine's story in the same house. And I got to sleep in Kipling's room and use his toilet. How cool is *that*?

Chris Roberson
Austin, Texas

CHRIS ROBERSON's novels include *Here, There & Everywhere*; *The Voyage of Night Shining White*; *Paragaea: A Planetary Romance*; *X-Men: The Return; Set the Seas on Fire*; *The Dragon's Nine Sons*; and the forthcoming *End of the Century* and *Three Unbroken*. His short stories have appeared in such magazines as *Asimov's, Interzone, Postscripts*, and *Subterranean*, and in anthologies such as *Firebirds Soaring, Live Without a Net, FutureShocks*, and *Forbidden Planets*. Along with his business partner and spouse, Allison Baker, he is the publisher of MonkeyBrain Books, an independent publishing house specializing in genre fiction and nonfiction genre studies, and he is the editor of the anthology *Adventure, Vol. 1*. He has been a finalist for the World Fantasy Award three times—once each for writing, publishing, and editing—twice a finalist for the John W. Campbell Award for Best New Writer, and twice for the Sidewise Award for Best Alternate History Short Form (winning in 2004 with his story "O One").

Chris and Allison live in Austin, Texas, with their daughter, Georgia. Chris is online at www.chrisroberson.net.